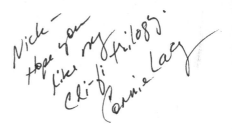

Nick —
Hope you like my tri-fi trilogy.
Connie Lacy

THE SHADE RING

The Shade Ring Trilogy Book 1

Connie Lacy

April 2015

~ ~ ~

Atlanta, GA

ISBN-13: 978-1511816915
ISBN-10: 1511816910

Sign up for occasional updates: www.ConnieLacy.com

Contact the author

Email: connielacy@connielacy.com

Website: www.ConnieLacy.com

Facebook: www.Facebook.com/ConnieLacyBooks

For Doug, who encouraged me to write.

~~~

Also by Connie Lacy

Albedo Effect, Book 2 of The Shade Ring Trilogy
VisionSight: a Novel
The Time Telephone

Chapter 1

Her stomach lurched as they climbed higher. Neave didn't normally suffer from motion sickness but flying in a helicopter on a windy day was a whole new experience.

Maybe part of it was her body punishing her. She'd allowed herself to be bullied into this expedition by the family dictator. Just like when she was a kid and he plopped her into the Atlanta Science Academy so she could spend every waking hour mixing chemicals, dissecting cats or looking through a microscope, not once did he ask what she wanted. Of course, there was also the guilt trip her father used on her, saying the world needed more scientists to figure out how to slow the melting. And that guilt weighed heavily on her.

But graduation had triggered a yearning for independence and she dreamed of shedding her science skin, especially since she couldn't imagine how she could make a difference when so many others had failed. So while she licked her wounds and considered her options, she would play along. Still, she dreaded spending even one miserable day at the nasty shore in the stifling heat.

She was already uncomfortable, crammed into the small passenger compartment with Nat seated close beside her. Dr. Osley, her father's chief rival for Climate Secretary, sat directly across from her but refused to make eye contact.

Terrance Osley was a slender, balding, black man who insisted on wearing glasses instead of implants, giving him a studious, old-fashioned appearance. He was known for his quick intelligence, his bluntness and his impatience with those who had smaller brains. He also opposed the shade ring Neave's father was pushing. No doubt Osley viewed her as the enemy.

Nat's leg brushed against hers as the chopper bounced along, like they were riding in a jeep on a rutted dirt road. He'd been trying to get her to go out with him for months. Nat had Bollywood good looks and was about to get his PhD, but he was her father's assistant. And although she wasn't sure why, that bothered her.

She scooted closer to the window and decided to break the ice with Osley. Maybe that would cool Nat's restless legs.

"Dr. Osley, are you looking for anything in particular on the coast?" She had to speak up to be heard over the double rotors roaring in opposite directions above them.

"Just going down for a look-see," he said, immediately turning his attention to Nat. "Mr. Patel, did you specify you wanted the smallest helicopter in the fleet? Where the hell am I supposed to put my samples?"

"You can bring back any samples you like," Nat said, nodding at the stack of containers on the seat next to the professor. "We'll manage."

"And how old is this heap anyway?" Osley asked, poking his finger through a tear in the upholstery.

"The one we were supposed to get was rescheduled at the last minute."

"Did you tell them Terrance Osley was one of your passengers?" Osley barked.

Neave actually felt sorry for Nat as he rubbed the back of

his neck. Just then, the copter took a sudden dip and she barely got a barf bag in place before losing her lunch.

The beach was even worse than she expected. Her iCom read 113 degrees as the group walked the short distance from the dorm to the shore for a quick foray before sunset. Despite being sheathed in a pale green climate suit, she felt like she'd been basted with butter and popped into a four hundred degree oven.

The reek of rotting jellyfish was overwhelming. Their plate-sized, gelatinous carcasses dotted the sand like pepperoni on a day-old pizza, along with dead crabs, clumps of seaweed, bits of concrete, rotten wood, broken metal railings, shards of glass and other remnants of a once thriving city. She'd seen movies and images of people swimming in the ocean but they were like fairy tales to her.

Holding her sun hat on her head, she turned south into the hot ocean breeze. She trailed behind the others, threading her way carefully through the ugly obstacle course and keeping a safe distance from the water. She wasn't sure what they were looking for but whatever it was, she didn't want to find it.

A hundred yards down the shore she could see what was left of downtown Charleston. The historic section of the city was mostly submerged, the waves splashing against battered walls, broken windows and a swaying church steeple. The rickety buildings the water hadn't yet reached sat empty, awaiting the same fate.

At one time more than two hundred thousand people had lived here but the city was abandoned as sea level rose, like many others, including New York, New Orleans and all of Florida's coastal cities. A booming industry sprouted as they tried to hold the water back with all sorts of high tech dams, dikes and water diversion projects. When those expensive efforts failed, the insurance industry refused to underwrite coastal areas anymore and the cities were abandoned to the waves and the wrecking ball.

Seeing it in person made her father's guilt trip very real. "I just want to impress upon you the seriousness of our environmental predicament." Those were his words, not fifteen minutes after commencement exercises were over. And she had yanked the mortarboard off of her head and raised her voice to him for the first time in her life. "Everyone on the planet knows the oceans have risen fifteen feet, Father! We all know how many cities are under water. But there are thousands of scientists around the world working on it!" And that's when he delivered his threat. "If you quit now and don't get your PhD, you will never see another penny from me or your mother. And I will make sure your decision follows you the rest of your life." So much for celebrating graduation.

As the sun sank below the horizon she noticed a small white crab dart across the sand in front of her like a delicate ballerina. She refastened her billowing hair into a ponytail and tucked it under her hat, turning her attention to two huge demolition machines attacking piles of rubble just out of reach of the incoming tide. The machines were bright yellow with great robot arms moving back and forth, taking bites of concrete and brick and depositing the remains of buildings into enormous dump trucks, like mother birds feeding their young.

Mesmerized by the sight, she didn't notice the others had returned to the cool of the dormitory. She strolled closer so she could see the deserted streets descending into the waves, as though the people who used to live here might've driven their cars down to the bottom of the sea in search of Atlantis.

The air cooled a bit as the light began to fade and the sound of the waves somehow made her muscles relax as she gazed north, away from the city. When she squinted her eyes, the shoreline was rather beautiful – the breakers following each other in an endless procession onto the beach. But, of course, those waves were continually scraping grains of sand into the sea, along with people's homes and businesses, like the ocean was a giant creature, clawing its way onto the continent, bit by bit. She shivered at the thought.

And that's when she felt something brush against her leg, followed immediately by sharp pain. She screamed as she looked down and saw the over-sized pincer of a gigantic crab attached to her ankle. It was orange and blue and stood knee high – the biggest crab she'd ever seen.

She screeched and kicked but the claw was firmly attached and cutting through the cloth of her climate suit and, more importantly, her skin. She looked around frantically for something to use as a weapon only to discover another huge crab was scurrying towards her from the dune. She kicked harder and shrieked louder as she hopped backwards in desperation. And then she was in the surf, water splashing her face, as though the ocean had joined in the attack. She'd never been in seawater and was stunned by its warmth and strength. It was like a large wet mouth trying to swallow her. She was losing her balance along with her equilibrium and thrashed helplessly in the rough water, salty spray stinging her eyes. She wanted to cry but instinct told her to hold her breath. Just as she was about to go under, something grabbed her from behind, wrapping itself tightly around her waist. She snatched and clawed, trying to pry the tentacle or whatever it was from her body, only to discover it was a large hand.

"Hold still!"

It was a man's voice in her ear. But she was on the verge

of hysteria and her arms and legs continued to flail and she couldn't stop screaming.

"Don't move!" he shouted.

So she closed her eyes, gritted her teeth and tried to breathe. She was sure her foot was about to be severed but the pressure suddenly disappeared and when she opened her eyes, she was standing on wet sand, the tide pulling back, preparing for another strike. The crab was frozen directly in front of her.

"Let's go!" the man cried, pulling her by the arm towards the dune as another wave chased them onto dry sand.

She was sniffling and hiccupping as she tried to catch her breath.

"Come on," he said, guiding her through the debris and the tall grass towards the dorm building. "The crabs come out at sunset."

He used his stun stick twice more before they reached the safety of the guest quarters. When they made it through the door, she closed her eyes and leaned against the wall. She was shivering and hugging herself, trying to calm down. Her hair had come loose and was plastered to her shoulders, her hat was gone – probably floating out to sea – and her climate suit was soaked and heavy on her body.

"You all right?"

His voice was like a comforting balm.

She wiped her eyes and nose with the backs of her hands, which were shaking she noticed, and took a deep breath before opening her eyes. What she saw was a tall man staring down at her with a mixture of concern and, she thought, a hint of amusement. He was one of the guys on the demolition crew and had the look of a manual laborer – tan face, unkempt brown hair, and a lean, muscular build. But he also had blue eyes, which were rare these days. And he looked vaguely familiar, like a former classmate or someone she'd seen in a play.

"I think you need a chair." He gestured towards a nearby door with one hand and touched her arm with the other as though to steady her.

"I'm fine," she said, pulling away.

But as she took a step, her right leg cramped, causing her to wince in pain. Her Good Samaritan caught her under the arms and reached down as though to pick her up.

"I don't need your help!" she snapped.

"Okay."

He stood close beside her as she limped into the kitchen and collapsed in a chair at a big, rectangular table. Then he bent down on one knee, peeled the torn green cloth away and examined her ankle.

"Skin's broken, but it's not deep. Just wash it good and put some of this on it," he said, getting up to retrieve a tube of ointment from a first aid kit on the wall. He tossed her the tube and a small towel, which she used to blot her face and hair.

She guessed he might be older than her, but not by much. He was wearing jeans tucked into black safety boots and a white, long-sleeved sun shirt. He was as wet as she was.

"Cuppa coffee?" he asked.

"God, no," she blurted. "I don't suppose you have some wine."

She focused on breathing, trying to get more oxygen to her leg to ease the charley horse. In short order he returned with a biofoam cup half filled with red wine.

"The name's Will." He smiled down at her, a dimple appearing on his right cheek.

"Neave," she said.

She was about to thank him for rescuing her when his co-workers burst in, boisterous and stinking of the beach and their own sweat – a short guy with an infectious grin who Neave guessed was Mexican American and a tall black woman with ultra short hair who laughed and rolled her eyes.

"Ah, the damsel in distress and the knight in shining armor!" she said. "I'm relieved to see you both survived the attack of the mutant crabs."

Her voice was husky and she whooped when she laughed, smirking at the others as she wiped her face with a pink rag. They helped themselves to cold beers from a large cooler. Neave forced a weak smile and fortified herself with the wine.

"Come on, Jaz, don't give her a hard time," Will said, sliding the wine bottle back in the fridge.

"Me? Never! I was just worried the young scientist might've been injured by one of those horrible monster-wonsters."

"Yeah, man, we were very impressed." The short guy said. "Don't tell me – your real name is Zorro!"

Will laughed along with them.

"Let me introduce you guys to Neave," he said, pausing so she could supply her last name.

She considered keeping her mouth shut but figured it would be awkward.

"Neave 'not-a-damsel-in-distress' Alvarez," she said.

Which prompted snickers from his two friends. And Will looked at her in surprise, as most people did, since she looked nothing like an Alvarez. Her cousin Lena always wanted to know how she inherited nada from her father and everything from her mother, including her auburn hair and green eyes. And she was sure everyone else wondered the same thing.

They were just more polite.

"Jaz – chief smart ass," Will said, gesturing at his co-workers, "and Macho Martinez."

Then he excused himself and left her sipping her wine as the others scrounged for food and discussed the planned implosion of a large building. She drained her cup, tossed it in the recycling bin and left her new acquaintances to their dinner, pocketing the tube of ointment. She'd taken only a few steps down the hall when she heard Jaz, in her snarkiest tone, hurl the word "scientist" like it was the punch line to a joke, prompting a belly laugh from Macho.

Chapter 2

Just after dawn the next morning, Neave reluctantly joined Nat, Kwan and Lena as they ventured north of the crumbling city to collect water samples along the shore. Kwan was entertaining them with his cussing in Korean routine, although everyone suspected he couldn't actually speak the language. He was a head shorter than Nat, buff, with spiky black hair and mischievous dark eyes.

Lena had on her usual uniform – skimpy halter top and mini-shorts to show off her assets to the greatest advantage. A floppy sun hat and her ever-present e-cig completed the look. She'd worn the same basic outfit when she piloted the helicopter the day before. It boggled the mind to think she was at the controls with Kwan as her co-pilot on their flight from Atlanta.

Wearing chest waders to protect them, the men stepped into the surf, filling containers to analyze the water for pollution, acidification, methane levels and microscopic life forms. Neave and Lena labeled and stored them in a sample wagon they dragged across the sand until the sun became unbearably hot.

As they finally headed back to the dorm Nat clicked his iCom.

"You guys wanna see the latest shade ring animation?" he

asked.

The others gathered around, peering at the tiny screen. But Neave had already seen it and walked ahead of them, adjusting her hat. It was an artist's rendering of what scientists said the Earth would look like with a solar shade ring in place. Interesting, she thought, how romantic they made it look – like Saturn and its rings – only these rings would be made of millions of space umbrellas designed to reflect the sun's rays back into space.

"Very cool," said Kwan. "Get it? Cool?"

"But Dr. Yong says…" Neave started.

"We don't care what that Chinese clone has to say." It was Nat's deep voice behind her. "We all know Dr. Osley brought him to the university as part of his anti-shade ring campaign."

She couldn't decide what irritated her more – that he shushed her or that he used the word clone like it meant vermin.

"Dr. Yong's research shows even if we launched a shade ring tonight it could be decades before any possible ocean cooling might occur," she said. "And there's no guarantee it would work."

"*His* research?" Nat said dismissively.

"Published in a dozen scientific e-zines," she snapped.

"Dr. Yong Li! Even his name is funny," said Lena. "I wonder if he's got old Dr. Zhang's personality."

"What I wonder," said Kwan, "is whether he's got old Dr. Zhang's wang."

And they cackled at their own cleverness, causing Neave to pick up her pace.

"Which reminds me," said Kwan, "you guys hear the one about the clone who had sex with Siamese twins? This is so brutally good…"

Neave put her hands to her ears and hurried ahead of them to the dorm, thankful the waves muffled their voices.

After misting off in the tiniest shower she'd ever squeezed into – her elbows bumping the shower walls – she hid out in her room. She sipped a wine chiller from her private stash and took a nap to give her strength because their work day wasn't over yet. They were headed for a night trawl on the high seas.

~~~

"Is there room for all of us?" Dr. Osley sniped as they boarded the *Lady Evita*.

"Plus a dozen more," Nat replied, sounding upbeat.

The *Lady Evita* was not as grand as her name implied. It was a rental boat any group could hire for short cruises in coastal waters. Dirty white with her name on the side, it was sixty feet long with basic computer and lab equipment tucked into a cramped cabin. It was nothing like the research ship Neave had sailed the summer she was seventeen. The *R/V Jameson* was three hundred feet long and had a submersible launch on the back. Osley had, no doubt, sailed on similar vessels.

He was dressed in a broad-brimmed sun hat, a white sunshield shirt, and long pants tucked into protective boots. Nat was wearing a short wetsuit, which Neave found amusing. She wasn't sure what the purpose of a wetsuit was if it didn't cover the entire body.

"Good to see you again," a shirtless crewman greeted Nat as they boarded. "I think we've got just what you're looking for tonight."

"Thanks, Mike."

Mike, amazingly enough, was the ship's captain. He was what Lena called a gorgeous hunk. He had brown skin, brown eyes and might be all of 25. Which was not particularly reassuring.

Puffing on her e-cig, which smelled like a margarita at the moment, Lena gave him a serious once over. She ran her hand through her short, wavy, black hair and turned away from him so he could see the neon messages scrolling across her backside: "Fish or cut bait" and "Cheeky chica." It was obvious she wanted the young captain to notice. And he did.

When they pulled away from the marina and headed towards open water it was past eight o'clock. Thankfully, the ocean was calm. Neave tried to keep her imagination in check – she didn't want to visualize any scenarios involving stormy seas as she stood on the tiny top deck, letting the warm breeze whip her hair out behind her. The sun was about to dip below the western horizon, with crimson clouds rippling across the sky. For some reason, they reminded her of an animal's ribs and she had the momentary sensation of being inside the body of a living thing.

The plan was to use a light lure to sample organisms in floating sargassum. Low tech, but an efficient way to see what creatures currently inhabited these waters. About thirty minutes out, they passed a sargassum pad and she heard Captain Mike tell Nat it wasn't the one he'd requested. Which made her wonder whether one sargassum pad wasn't as good as another. They continued zipping across the waves another fifteen minutes, by which time it was full dark. LED lights came on all over the boat so they could see what they were doing, but it made the ocean seem that much darker and more sinister.

The boat finally slowed and Mike brought the vessel alongside the sargassum, shining two spotlights on the huge, brown mesh floating on the water's surface.

"God, how big is it?" Neave asked.

"About the size of a soccer field," said Nat.

He unloaded two long-handled dip nets. Then he and Kwan deployed a large aquatic light over the side.

"The light attracts the sea creatures," he explained. "We float along the edge of the pad, pull up small sections of sargassum and dump them into those tubs," he said, pointing to two rectangular plasteel tubs on the aft deck.

"And eat very fresh sushi," said Kwan, "assuming they don't eat us first." And he flashed a smart-ass grin at Neave.

"Ha! And another ha!" she replied. They'd been razzing her mercilessly all day about her run-in with the crab.

Nat lowered a net over the side and lifted a small section of sargassum from the water.

"God," Lena whispered, taking a drag on her e-cig, "what an ass."

"My sentiment exactly," Neave replied.

"You can't tell me that body doesn't hubba your bubba."

It was true, Nat could've been a model on a photo shoot in his black and green wetsuit. And there was no denying he had the strong, slender build Neave admired. Then she understood why he was wearing it. He wanted her to see his body.

"And why the hell are you dressed like that?" Lena whispered, giving Neave a disapproving look. "Jean shorts down to your knees and a boring white T-shirt? Hay-soos, hermana, you need to show a little T and A."

"You show enough for both of us."

Lena was her cousin and her friend but they had precious little in common. And Neave was tired of her nagging. Lena had been telling her for months she was an idiot for refusing to have sex – that everyone had sex. "That's what those contraceptive shots are for that you've been taking since you were twelve," she always said. But Neave wanted to be in love first. Passionately in love. She didn't care how old-fashioned it sounded, and she knew it sounded plenty old-fashioned. She remembered the Science of Love unit in Human Biology and was positive she'd never experienced a surge of dopamine and norepinephrine. She wondered if Lena might have inherited enough hormones for both of them.

"Make way!" Nat shouted as he swung the long pole over the deck.

They jumped back, barely avoiding the dripping water cascading from the net. With a swift turn of the handle, he emptied the contents into one of the tubs and they all gathered around to peer inside. Two bright LED lights above them lit the mass of brown algae. Dr. Osley donned goggles and protective gloves. Neave watched over his shoulder and could now see the berry-like structures. They were gas-filled pneumatocysts, or bladders, that acted as floats for the sargassum colony.

Lena eagerly grabbed the other net and Kwan took charge of returning the sargassum to the water from the tubs using a short-handled net. Neave was assigned camera duty, for which she was grateful. Dr. Osley seemed only too happy to go back and forth between the tubs, tapping the algae on the side of the tub to shake out the more tenacious creatures. He was excited when he discovered a long-spined porcupine fish about the size of a golf ball, holding it in his gloved hand for Neave to record the images. Once he'd sifted through the sargassum and they had pictures and video, Kwan lifted the mass of algae and specimens from the tub and dumped them overboard, except for those Osley wanted to take back as samples.

Neave was beginning to enjoy the process, listening to Osley as he named each creature, occasionally referring to an online database if he wasn't sure.

"Good God!" he cried.

Neave zoomed in on the tub he was peering into.

"Lionfish," he said. "Make sure you don't touch it. Those spines have venom in them."

Neave recorded the beautiful red and white striped fish, about eight inches long with spines along its back and fan-like fins on the sides.

"Just one of the reasons there are so few fish worth catching in these waters anymore," Osley said. "Lionfish eat 'em up. And this is a small one."

She backed off to get a wider shot and that's when Kwan suddenly shouted at everyone.

"Look out!" he cried.

She looked up just in time to see one of the long-handled dip nets land on Dr. Osley. It struck his head and shoulder, then bounced onto the deck.

"You okay?" Kwan asked, rushing over.

Still seated on his low stool, Osley squinted at Kwan and then yanked off his right glove, holding his hand up to look at it.

"I've been stung," he said.

"Jellyfish," said Kwan, kneeling beside him. "Get some vinegar!" he shouted.

Lena disappeared into the cabin and reappeared immediately with a bottle from the first aid kit. She poured vinegar liberally over Osley's wrist and hand. Kwan yanked his shirt off, balled it up and used it as a rag to wipe a nearly invisible tentacle.

"My neck!" Dr. Osley cried.

Kwan moved behind him, ripping Osley's shirt off. Lena poured the vinegar as Kwan used the shirt to pry a tentacle from the professor's upper back. She splashed more vinegar over both stings and she and Kwan searched for more tentacles. By this time, Dr. Osley's eyes were shut tight.

"Watch your step," Neave said.

Two more tentacles were visible on the deck along with a small, light blue gelatinous blob with a couple of tentacles still attached.

"Shit, I hope I'm wrong," said Kwan, "but I think this might be a box jellyfish."

"Can't be," said Nat, moving in for a closer look.

Neave noticed Osley leaning precariously to the left. She grabbed his shoulders and called for help. Kwan and Nat hoisted him up and slung his arms over their shoulders to haul him inside.

"What I wanna know, Nat," said Kwan, as they struggled to carry the professor, "is how you managed to drop the fucking net on him."

"That's a stupid question," said Nat. "It slipped out of my hands."

"Can you die from being stung by a box jelly?" Lena asked.

"Yup," said Kwan. "They're mean sons-a-bitches."

"But if this really is a box jellyfish," said Nat, "it's a long way from home. Dr. Alvarez will be very interested in this bit of news."

"That Osley was stung by a box jelly?" Neave asked.

"Hell, yeah. It means Chironex fleckeri is spreading far beyond its natural territory," he said.

"I'll ask the captain if he's got any antivenin," she said, turning towards the bridge.

"I'll go," said Nat. "You help with Osley."

He hurried off after laying Osley on a padded bench. Kwan immediately got on his iCom to talk with a doctor in Atlanta while Neave opened the first aid kit and rummaged through the contents.

Nat returned, saying there was no antivenin. He said if they'd been on a science vessel in the tropics, antivenin would've been part of the first aid kit. But not off the coast of South Carolina.

Neave gave Osley an antihistamine and a pain reliever as the doctor ordered. And then they were underway, heading back to shore at top speed.

~~~

When she entered his room that night, Osley looked like he'd been laid out by an undertaker – covered by a white sheet, hands clasped loosely on his chest. But Neave tried to banish the morbid thought from her mind as she set a tray on his nightstand and placed her hand on his forehead. He felt warm.

"I'm not dying," he whispered, without opening his eyes, "as much as your father might appreciate the gesture."

She handed him a cup of water and two pills, which he swallowed without comment, immediately closing his eyes again. She stood for a moment, considering whether she should stay but he waved his hand in dismissal.

Just outside the door, she found Will leaning against the wall, dressed in khaki shorts and a faded blue tee, smelling faintly of shampoo. She was still in the clothes she'd worn on the boat and knew how she must look – and smell.

"How's the professor?" he said.

"The doctor says he'll be all right but that he was lucky only a couple of small tentacles landed on him."

"Glad to hear it."

"Will," she said, "I never got a chance to thank you properly for coming to my rescue. Although I've since been told repeatedly, emphatically, and with a good deal of sarcasm, that I was in no real danger and that I would've known that if I'd come to the expedition briefing."

"Au contraire. I think you *were* in danger. In danger of having a heart attack." There was a chuckle lurking behind his smile. "Livened up my day, actually."

She found herself smiling back, though her ears were burning. She hoped the blush wasn't too noticeable. He was attractive, though not in a movie star way, and that dimple she'd noticed on his right cheek had no twin on the left. His most striking feature was his animated eyes, which she now realized she was staring into. She looked down, but not before noticing they were the color of the sky in late afternoon and were fringed with full, dark lashes.

"I should've paid more attention in Marine Biology," she said, flustered. "But science isn't..." and she shrugged, not wanting to go into all of that. "Anyway, thanks, even if those crabs weren't going to drag me into their lair for a private dinner."

"So, the cruise didn't go well," he said.

She sighed.

"Kind of hard to figure how anyone could dump a dangerous jellyfish on someone's head," he said. "And I hear the boat didn't even have antivenin."

"We didn't know box jellies were this far north."

"They've been here a while. The crew should've known that, even if you guys didn't. And, besides, don't scientists always take safety precautions when they're doing research?"

His expression was still friendly but there was a mocking tone, especially when he said "scientists."

"Anyway," he said, shaking his head, "I hope the professor feels better in the morning."

She mumbled "thanks" and hurried to her room, where she

tried to remember all those boring safety rules in classes she'd taken. Like how you should wear protective gear when collecting samples. But Dr. Osley was the one wearing boots, long pants and a protective shirt and he was the one who got stung! Who was Will to point the finger of blame?

Later, as she lay in bed, she kept replaying the accident over in her mind. She realized there was one simple precaution that would've prevented it. They should've made sure the nets were never lifted above anyone on the deck. So Will was right to be sarcastic. How do you dump a deadly jellyfish on someone's head? You let people stand below the nets. More troubling still, he said box jellies had been here a while and the boat should've had antivenin. Which didn't help her fall asleep.

Chapter 3

Their last day at the coast included a morning excursion along the Cooper River to see how far inland salinization had occurred. It was just Neave, Lena and Kwan this time. Nat claimed he had other work to do.

She found it disturbing walking through abandoned neighborhoods along the river's edge. It was like a ghost town where some disease had killed all the people. Even though her hair was in a topknot under a sun hat and she was wearing her pale blue climate suit, the heat sapped her energy. And despite slathering themselves with repellent, they were plagued by gnats, mosquitoes and horse flies. They were supposed to be back at the dorm by eleven but it was nearly one o'clock when they came dragging through the door as the temperature reached 118 degrees.

After two sweltering days of schlepping equipment, entering scientific minutiae, enduring the unpleasant boat trip and eating cardboard, she was more than ready to return to civilization.

Kwan and Lena headed to their rooms for a shower but she was weak and decided to swing by the kitchen first for something to eat. Just as she approached the door she heard angry voices and stopped in her tracks. It was Nat and Dr. Osley.

"I've never been on any field expedition," Osley said, his voice booming, "where we didn't have the appropriate transportation with enough cargo space for specimens. Not once." He'd obviously recovered from his encounter with the box jelly.

"I'm just as frustrated as..." Nat said.

"And I've never been on an expedition where my life was jeopardized because of someone's carelessness, for Christ's sake. Even Alvarez's other lackey – the one who overdosed – even he wasn't as sloppy as you are."

"I'm no one's lackey," Nat said, his tone turning angry.

"And like I told Robert, if you two think you're pulling the wool over my eyes about that goddam shade ring, you're dead wrong! I know exactly why you're so keen on it. And I'm going to make it perfectly clear when I meet with the President next week."

"Dr. Osley," Nat said, taking a conciliatory tone.

"And why would you bring someone like Lena Ruiz along on this expedition? I don't even know why she's a student at the university."

"I..."

"She came to my room the first night we were here! Tried to seduce me. Me, of all people!"

"I'll talk..."

"I want to fly home this afternoon, Mr. Patel, *with* all of my samples. Do you understand me?"

"Yes, I...."

Osley burst through the door and sailed past Neave, muttering under his breath. She hurried after him, pulling her hat off as she trotted to keep up.

"Dr. Osley?"

He only picked up his pace. When they reached the computer room where the samples were stored he turned abruptly to face her.

"Why are you following me, Miss Alvarez?"

She nearly ran into him in the doorway.

"I couldn't help overhearing your conversation with..." she said.

"Spying!" he spat, turning his back on her as he began stacking storage containers.

"I'd be very interested to hear why you think my father and Nat support a shade ring."

He peered over his shoulder, squinting at her for a second, then turned away.

"You'd make a good actress, Miss Alvarez. All innocence and sincerity. Now, you can run along and report back to Mr. Patel that I don't talk to undercover agents."

"I don't report to Nat."

"Fine, fine. And he's not your father's errand boy. Whatever. Just leave me alone."

"But, Dr. Osley..."

"Miss Alvarez," he said, giving her a hard look, "you need to make like a jellyfish and float away."

She hadn't had many dealings with him, which made her thankful now. Funny, she thought, he was just as maddening as her father. But while her father was smooth as a Desert Rose with its thick, shiny green leaves and pretty pink blooms, Dr. Osley was more like the Prickly Pear cactus. There were pitfalls with both – every part of the Desert Rose was toxic, while the cactus was dangerous because of its impossible to remove spines. But at least with the cactus you knew to keep away. Rosa, her parents' long-time housekeeper and cook, grew both plants in their back yard and always told

Neave they were proof you shouldn't judge a book by its cover. Rosa was actually her father's cousin but the sole family resemblance was their black hair. She had intelligent brown eyes, a pretty, round face and a caring heart. It was Rosa who provided the only warmth of Neave's childhood.

As she headed to her room for a shower, she thought about Rosa's admonitions as she was growing up. Rosa had a mystical quality about her. As she was leaving her parents' home after her father lowered the boom on graduation night, Neave stopped by Rosa's cheerful yellow and white kitchen for some affection and sympathy.

"Has my father always been so domineering?" she asked.

Sitting in the booth below framed pictures Neave had painted as a child, Rosa didn't answer. Instead, she pushed a plate of homemade fudge across the table. They sat together eating the candy and making little moans of pleasure. When she finally spoke, it was a story Neave had heard before.

"You know, your mother thinks your name is Irish for 'radiance.' You heard the story often enough about the Neave in Irish mythology who was the daughter of a sea god. Of course the Irish don't know how to spell, so your parents fixed the spelling. Anyway, your father agreed to that name because it's also Spanish for 'snow' or 'snowy' – Nieve," she said, pronouncing it in the Spanish way – nee-*eh*-vay. "And, as we all know, even if we didn't grow up in el norte, snow can be soft like una capa de nieve – a snowflake – or hard like una bola de nieve – a snowball." She nodded her head, her eyes full of meaning.

It was Rosa's way of telling her she should grow a spine and stand up to her father.

By four-thirty, Nat, Lena and Osley were gone and the dormitory was a quieter place. Nat had asked Neave and Kwan to stay behind an extra day to make room in the helicopter for all of Osley's samples. Neave was furious but Nat said he would make it up to her. She was also starving since their provisions were gone. So she was relieved when Will messaged her that they should join his group for supper.

They convened at the big kitchen table for spaghetti, which he claimed he'd prepared. While she found it hard to believe a young man could actually cook, it smelled heavenly and tasted even better. She had to use all her willpower to resist begging for seconds. She did let him refill her wine glass with Chianti though, so she was thoroughly relaxed by the time they pushed away from the table.

She volunteered for cleanup to repay him but Will insisted on staying to help. Casting about for a topic of conversation that would avoid any mention of their ill-fated boat trip, she asked him how he passed the time at such an isolated job site.

"I read a lot."

"Like, what do you read?"

He set a stack of plates on the counter and retrieved a book from atop the fridge, holding it up so she could see the title. It was an old-fashioned, bound book.

"*A History of Dance?*" she said, reaching for it. She couldn't hide her astonishment. "This is a very old book, published in 1993. Where on earth did you get it?"

"Well, when my company does these teardowns we get the contents of the buildings," he explained. "And you'd be amazed at the stuff people leave behind."

"Your company?"

"Yeah, you know, Galloway Demolition and Recycling?"

She realized her mouth was open and closed it.

"You don't look old enough to have your own company."

"I started young."

25

"How young?"

"Started recycling when I was thirteen. Demolition when I was sixteen. It's *the* industry in Florida, you know."

Florida had shrunk dramatically from its glory days, losing the once booming southern tip of the state, along with a lot of coastline on the east and west as the ocean continued to rise. She'd never been there – never wanted to – after hearing it was filled with scavengers diving for booty in sunken cities.

"You own your own business and you're reading a history of dance."

"I read a lot."

She chuckled, amazed at how far off the mark she'd been. Don't judge a book by its cover, indeed. Which was not exactly the message she'd gotten from her mother and father.

When they joined the others in the common room he re-filled her wine glass before she could object, then poured himself another.

"So how's the sissy book, compadre?" asked Macho.

"Your problem," Will replied, "is that you have absolutely no culture."

"Hey, man, I have culture! Plenty of culture. I play Virtual Mariachi Band four or five times a week."

"When was the last time you read a book?" Will asked.

"Uh…February, I think. Yeah, it was February."

"Yeah, the February you turned ten?"

Everyone guffawed on cue.

"What 'sissy' book are you reading, anyway?" Kwan asked.

"*A History of Dance.*"

"Dance! Now that's a good idea," said Macho, jumping up and transmitting some music from his iCom to the speakers. "Authentic Mexican hat dance," he cried, and began dancing around the room.

Jaz joined in as Kwan pushed the black vinyl couch out of the way. Suddenly, it was the Comical Dance Hour with everyone taking turns selecting music and teaching the others how to do the Mocha Slide, the Tsunami and others. Macho ran into the kitchen, breaking out a twelve pack of beer.

The scene reminded Neave of her best friend J'nai's twelfth birthday party when a bunch of girls had laughed themselves silly, dancing like maniacs. It was okay to be messy and crazy at J'nai's house. The exact opposite of her own home where Neave never once had a party. She had long ago concluded her own parents didn't like mess, noise or children. Why, she wondered, did they have a child at all?

When everyone sat down to rest, Will pulled his iCom out.

"My turn," he said, a grin on his face. "I'm gonna teach you guys how to do the waltz."

"Bor...ing!" Jaz said, rolling her eyes.

"You're wrong," he said. "And there's a fascinating story behind it."

"No doubt," she said.

"It started out as a country dance," he continued. "Something the lower classes did. Scandalized the upper crust."

"Come on, man," said Macho. "The waltz? Really?"

"The lords and ladies were used to dances where they marched around in patterns and bowed to each other, just barely touching hands now and then," Will explained. "But with the waltz, the man grabs the woman by the waist and pulls her very close. It was described as scandalous, passionate, indecent."

He raised his eyebrows.

"And what kind of music did they do all this scandalous, passionate dancing to?" Kwan asked.

Instead of answering, Will touched his iCom, transmitting an audio file to the sound system.

"This is one of the most famous waltzes of all time," he said.

Groans and sighs erupted from the group but Neave was intrigued. The music started slowly, quietly, gently – gradually building to the recognizable, romantic strains of *The Blue Danube Waltz*. She remembered it from a music appreciation class and smiled, letting her head sway back and forth.

"Scandalous!" she whispered.

"Okay, who wants to waltz?" Will asked, holding his arms out wide.

"You're not serious," said Jaz. "That music's gonna put me to sleep."

"What happened to the dance fever?" he asked.

"How about a game, guys?" Macho suggested, gesturing with his head towards the kitchen.

They got up and wandered out except for Will and Neave. He looked directly at her then, his eyebrows lifted high.

"I don't suppose you know how to waltz?"

"Oh, my parents would never have allowed me to do such an indecent, scandalous dance," she said, giving him what she realized was a flirtatious grin.

He held out his hand and pulled her up from her chair, his eyes on hers.

"Milady," he said, making a courtly bow.

She had drunk enough Chianti by then that she had no qualms about accepting his invitation, although dressed in white shorts and a green top, she could never have passed for an eighteenth century lady of either high or low birth.

He led her to the center of the room and put his right hand

on her waist, holding out his left hand. She stepped closer and placed her hand in his, letting the other one rest on his shoulder, hoping her dance training might come back to her.

"Now, it's one-two-three, one-two-three," he said. "Just follow me."

They started slowly, though it was difficult at first, and she stepped on his toes if he changed direction in the slightest. But after a few moments of twirling carefully around the room, she began to get the hang of it.

This close, she could see how blue his eyes were, with a dark halo around the edge of the iris – the limbal ring. She couldn't remember the last time she'd seen blue eyes. But then one eyebrow came down.

"Something's missing," he said. "Don't move. I'll be right back."

He released her and jogged from the room. She continued twirling without him, practicing her steps – one-two-three, one-two-three – until he returned a moment later with a white bed sheet.

"You can't do the waltz unless the lady is wearing a long dress," he said. "It just doesn't feel right."

And he flapped the sheet open and directed her to tuck one corner into the waistband of her shorts. He circled her, draping the fabric around her until he was satisfied. He stepped back at last and clapped his hands as though he'd performed a feat of magic.

He restarted the music, then planted his hand on her waist again and held her firmly. A smile sprouted on her face as they careened around the room, one-two-three, one-two-three. Her skirt trailed behind her and she imagined they were actually doing the waltz at a ball in nineteenth century Vienna. She would be wearing an elegant long green dress, with a voluminous skirt – the bodice cut low to show her cleavage to greatest advantage. Her hair would be piled in lovely ringlets. He would cut a dashing figure in close-fitting breeches and stockings with a fancy brocade coat. With his trim physique he would certainly look enticing in those form-fitting pants. She giggled at the thought.

"Why, Miss Alvarez, I do believe you're drunk."

"Why, Mr. Galloway, I do believe you're correct."

He pulled her closer as they whirled about the room so that she had to look up into his face. His dimple appeared on his right cheek as he smiled a perfectly charming smile. God, she felt as though she'd been magnetized. She couldn't take her eyes off him. And while the sheet didn't flow like expensive silk, it did make a billowing skirt that trailed behind her as they spun round and round until she became quite dizzy. Finally, the music came to a crescendo before ending abruptly. He immediately stepped back, still holding her hand in his, and bowed his head jauntily. She responded with her best approximation of a curtsy, concentrating hard so she wouldn't lose her balance and fall over.

She was breathless and flushed and there was something about the look in his eyes that made her feel like she actually did look elegant.

"Well," she said, "I understand now why the waltz might've been seen as too…"

"Sensual," he said.

And he suddenly stepped closer, bending his head towards hers, hesitating a second as though to give her time to object, which she didn't, and kissed her. It was no tentative first kiss. She closed her eyes and returned it, holding nothing back, her hands on his shoulders. His lips were soft and warm and he smelled so deliciously male. But then it was over too soon and he withdrew, looking uncertain.

"Sorry," he said. "I don't know what came over me."

"I guess it was that indecent dance," she said, giggling nervously as she ran her hand through her hair.

"And maybe a little too much vino," he said, laughing. "Alcohol is indeed a great provoker."

She wanted more than anything to touch his cheek. It was obvious he'd shaved after his work day and she found herself wondering whether that's when he always shaved or whether he might've done so on her account. Which made her feel silly. And she realized she was staring at him.

"So... where did you learn to do the waltz?" she asked, pulling one corner of the sheet from her shorts.

"My mother. She loves to dance. Taught all of us kids these old dances." His wistful smile made it obvious the memory brought him pleasure. "The waltz, the polka, the Lindy Hop and the slide – those were her favorites. It was loud and messy."

He helped unwind her long skirt, spinning her around as he held the end of the sheet until she plopped dizzily into a chair, skirtless and laughing.

"Sounds like loads of fun," she said.

"Yeah, and it helped us forget we didn't have all the gizmos and gadgets we saw advertised on the web."

Which made her jealous – she, who had grown up with more gizmos and gadgets than she knew what to do with and a house filled with order and silence.

Then he stepped back and tucked the folded sheet under his arm.

"I have some work to do before I turn in," he said. "Thanks very much for the waltz."

And he picked up the Chianti and the wine glasses and

mumbled something she didn't understand as he left the room.

Why, she wondered, had he kissed her and then backed off completely? Maybe she was a bad kisser. Maybe he had a girlfriend. Or maybe he just didn't want to appear to take advantage of her. But maybe if she'd taken the second step after he'd taken the first step? Maybe she was so inexperienced, that she didn't know how to take the second step. Or maybe she was just a wimp.

The strains of *The Blue Danube Waltz* floated through her head as she lay in bed that night. She could feel again the softness of his lips and the heat of his hand on her waist and wondered if the churning in her stomach might be the result of dopamine and norepinephrine coursing through her body. Eventually, she drifted off to a dreamland filled with music, flowing skirts and a voice like burgundy velvet.

It felt like she'd just fallen asleep when she was roused by tapping on her door. The clock said 5:03. She pulled on her robe and reached for the doorknob.

Kwan nearly fell into the room.

"Dr. Osley's dead," he said.

Chapter 4

Kwan paced the floor while Neave sat slumped over the kitchen table. She'd thrown on a pair of jeans and a faded blue top. Her fingers were wrapped around a cup of coffee as she stared out the window towards the ocean. Dawn was breaking as though nothing were amiss.

"Nat said the fucking door just gave way," Kwan said.

"Why wasn't he buckled in?"

"He thinks maybe Osley unbuckled so he could reposition his specimen cases. They'd had a little turbulence. And then, the chopper, you know, it tilted to the right and – boom! – he was gone!"

He grunted under his breath.

"God," Neave said, "don't those doors have safety locks?"

"You'd think," Kwan said, popping his knuckles as he continued walking to and fro. "This is crazy weird – way, way, way too crazy weird. How the hell does the chairman of the Climatology Department at Georgia Geosciences University fall out of a helicopter?"

"Good question." It was Jaz, sleepy-eyed, but already dressed for work in boots, jeans and a long-sleeve sun shirt. "I heard about the professor," she croaked, pouring herself a cup of coffee. "Helluva way to go."

"No kidding," said Macho as he and Will wandered in. "I

never heard of someone falling out of a helicopter. I mean, you'd have to really work at it to fall out of a helicopter. You ever hear of anyone falling out of a chopper, jefazo?"

Will shook his head, waiting his turn for coffee. He nodded at Neave when she glanced his way, a nod and a look that seemed to say how much he'd enjoyed their time together the night before – and maybe the kiss – while at the same time acknowledging the morning's shocking news.

"You guys seen any coverage yet?" Jaz asked, setting a box of blueberry muffins on the table.

Kwan shook his head in reply.

"Well, let's find a report," she mumbled, as though they were dimwits, turning on the wallscreen and clicking her iCom just in time to catch a newscast. There was a wild scene at a water park – shaky video of people running and grabbing kids in a pool.

"Nah," she mumbled, clicking on another news site with a stunning headline: "Scientist dies in fall from chopper, nearly killing children at water park."

"What the hell?" said Kwan as Jaz clicked on the link.

An anchorwoman with furrowed brows stared into the camera.

"One of the nation's most prominent scientists died a horrific death late yesterday when he plunged thousands of feet from a helicopter ferrying him from the South Carolina coast to Atlanta. And it nearly became a much bigger tragedy as the body of Dr. Terrance Osley landed in a shallow children's pool at the Jackpot Casino Waterpark near Covington. We have team coverage, starting with Dave Florez, live from the scene on this morning after. Dave?"

"Maria, it was pandemonium here yesterday," he said, motioning towards a large yellow water slide behind him, "that left the children, their parents, and bystanders here at the Casino Waterpark shaking and crying. We have video shot by the mom whose kids were playing in the toddler pool at the time, and came within a heartbeat of being killed. And we warn you, the video is rather intense. It starts as Amina Blackmon pans up from filming her kids splashing in the water to the sunny sky above, after hearing a sound that she thinks might've been a distant scream."

The reporter stared into the camera for a second until the amateur video began. At first there was a quick shot of two brown-skinned children smiling into the camera as they toddled about in the shallow pool, both with orange life vests on. Then the camera jerked skyward where it was yanked this way and that until it focused on a small dark object plummeting out of the sky. All at once, screaming could be heard and jumbled voices yelling "get the kids, get the kids, get the kids!" The video then showed a woman and a man lunge into the shallow pool where the kids were playing. They grabbed the children roughly and yanked them towards the edge of the pool just as the object hit the water. There was a loud splash and thud, like the sound of a huge belly flop, and water splashed in all directions. Shouting and crying could be heard as children and their parents reacted in horror. The woman shooting the video could be heard repeating over and over: "Oh my God, Oh my God, Oh my God!" The camera focused on what was clearly a man's body, face down in the water, a dark stain spreading out from his head. And that's when the video came to an abrupt halt and a professional shot appeared of the reporter facing a woman and a man sitting side by side on a couch, holding two little girls.

"It was the most terrifying moment of my life," the woman said to the reporter. "I don't know why I kept shooting. I don't know. I heard something above me, kind of like a voice, and I aimed my iCom that way, you know... looking for... looking for... and, my God, it happened so fast. I didn't know what it was at first, but then I could see arms and legs. It was a body. A body falling out of the clear blue sky! Like a horror movie, you know? And then I realized it was gonna land on my babies."

She hugged the little girl on her lap closer and looked at the man next to her.

"Holy shit!" Kwan said.

"Thank God you heard the voice," the father said, kissing his daughter on her head. "Because if you hadn't..." but he just closed his eyes and shook his head. "I'm never gonna gamble again. I think it's a message from God."

"Christ," Macho whispered.

Then there was another shot of the reporter standing in front of the waterpark.

"The water park has been closed and management says they're not sure when it'll reopen. They've got cleaning and maybe some repairs to do and an inspection to be performed. And the Muscogee Indian Tribe, which owns the waterpark and casino, is talking with attorneys about possibly suing the pilot and maybe Georgia Geosciences University, which owns the helicopter. And now, for the other part of this story, let's throw it to Yusef Omondi at the Augusta Police Department. Yusef?"

"As you mentioned, Dave, the body that fell from the sky was that of Dr. Terrance Osley, a top candidate for U.S. Climate Secretary and the head of the Climatology Department at Georgia Geosciences University. The body has been taken to the GBI crime lab in Atlanta. Osley had been on a scientific expedition to the coast – doing research at sunken

Charleston – and was flying back to Atlanta in a university helicopter piloted by grad student Catalena Ruiz."

Video of a shaken Lena and Nat was shown as they were escorted by police. And then a shot of the copter was shown with its right side door missing.

"Miss Ruiz is being questioned by police and the National Transportation Safety Board, which is also investigating the safety history of the aircraft. Sources tell us the door came off in flight and that Osley fell out by accident. His death comes as President Cohen was narrowing her list of possible nominees for Climate Secretary. And sources tell us Osley was considered one of the top two candidates." As the reporter spoke, recent footage of Osley speaking at a scientific conference was shown. And then Neave's father was onscreen. The graphic identified him as Dr. Robert Alvarez, Director of the American Climate Institute. Neave noticed his black hair was perfectly styled, his mustache neatly combed and his grey eyes appropriately somber.

"It's a real tragedy," Alvarez said. "Terrance Osley was a friend and a colleague who made important contributions to our understanding of global melting and rising seas."

The camera focused on the reporter again.

"With his death," the reporter said, "political analysts now predict President Cohen will nominate Robert Alvarez for the job. Terrance Osley was the most prominent American scientist to publicly criticize the proposed launch of a solar shade ring into space around the earth's equator as a way of cooling the oceans. Dr. Alvarez continues to support such an effort as essential to preventing a continued rise in sea level. Alvarez would not comment on the prospects for the shade ring or his possible appointment, saying it would be inappropriate at this time."

"Damn, I can't believe they interviewed your dad," Kwan said, taking a muffin.

Jaz clicked off the report and the screen went dark.

"That's your padre?" said Macho, scraping a chair as he sat down across from Neave. "Your father's the shade ring king?"

Disapproval hung in the air like the stench of a squirrel that died from the heat and rotted in a gutter.

Kwan made a slight grunting noise that expressed his remorse for opening his big mouth.

"Yes," Neave said, feeling trapped. She didn't like to broadcast that information. Her father's notoriety sometimes put her in an uncomfortable position. People assumed she supported his views and his politics, when, in reality, she didn't know whether the shade ring was a good idea or not. Then there was the other reaction people sometimes had – thinking she expected special treatment because of who her father was. And she preferred to be judged on her own merits, whatever those might be. So she did her best not to even mention her last name if she didn't have to.

Of course, she often wondered why people held her responsible for who her father was. But she guessed it was human nature to judge people that way. And now, she figured if they hadn't already done so, her new friends would categorize her as a spoiled rich kid with connections in high places. And she had to admit they would be correct. She'd been brought up in the lap of luxury, even if her parents had been too busy to spend any time with her. She'd gotten into the best schools because of money and connections. And here she was on a scientific field expedition led by the esteemed, late Dr. Terrance Osley, making a fool of herself on the beach because she didn't know diddley about crustaceans.

"I'm so glad those children weren't hurt," she said.

"You're the daughter of Robert Alvarez and Molly Sullivan?" Will asked, his coffee mug halfway to his lips, as though he hadn't heard her speak.

She nodded.

There was a brief exchange of glances between him and Jaz. Neave decided this was a good time to vamoose. She stood up but he blocked her path to the recycling bin.

"Your mother's a cloner," he said, looking down at her. It was a statement, not a question.

"She's a geneticist," Neave said, stepping around him, wondering how he knew who her mother was. Lots of people knew about her father. He was famous, but not her mother.

"A geneticist *and* a cloner," he said. The warmth in his eyes from a moment before was long gone.

"I don't know where you get your misinformation, but that's exactly what it is," she said, stepping around him and tossing her cup in the bin as she headed for the door. Kwan sighed as he trailed behind her.

She bounded up the stairs to her room, slammed the door behind her and started packing her things. "God," she whispered, yanking her clothes and shoes from the wardrobe and throwing them in her bag. "Falling out of a helicopter – Jesus!" she mumbled. "Into a toddler pool at a water park, for Christ's sake! What if those kids had been killed!" She swept her toiletries into her bathroom tote and tossed it carelessly on the bed. "What the hell happened?" she said aloud. She was so pissed off she couldn't be still and paced back and forth in her tiny room. "Dr. Osley is dead and all he can think about is who my parents are! What is the matter with him?"

And before she knew it, she was charging downstairs, re-tracing her steps to the kitchen.

Will, Jaz and Macho were seated at the table, eating breakfast. They didn't notice her in the doorway, her hands balled into fists beside her.

"What's the price tag gonna be for that shade ring anyway?" Jaz asked.

"An arm and a leg," said Will.

"Correction," said Macho. "Trillions of arms and trillions of legs. But, who knows, man, maybe the Chinese government can reduce their population by launching poor Chinese people into space. You know, providing biodegradable objects for the space ring."

"You're sick!" said Jaz. "Mucho sick."

"I try," he said.

"What I wanna know," said Will, "is who's gonna get the contract for a space ring."

"Only a contractor would think of that," said Jaz.

Neave cleared her throat and they all turned. She took two steps into the kitchen and stopped, glaring at Will.

"We'll be gone in an hour," she said, a hard edge to her voice. "And as for you, Mister Look Down Your Nose at Someone Because of Who Her Parents Are Galloway, have I asked you – any of you, for that matter – who the hell *your* parents are? What they do? What they think? How they vote? How much money they make, or don't make? Hell, no! You wanna know why? Because I don't give a damn! I either like you or don't like you based on who *you* are, not who your mommy or daddy is. Like anyone can choose their parents, anyway! Jesus!"

"I'm..." Will said, looking somewhat chastened.

But Neave wasn't through.

"Besides," she said, glowering at him, "you're wrong – dead wrong."

"Well…" he said.

"And dumping all that judgmental garbage on me right after we hear about Dr. Osley. I don't think it fazed you at all! He's dead! And those little kids were nearly killed!"

He sighed and opened his mouth to speak, but she wasn't done.

"You, sir," she said, raising her voice another notch, "are an asshole – with a capital A!" She whirled around to leave, but then stopped and turned to face him again. "Make that all caps!"

Chapter 5

"What would make a copter suddenly tilt to the right?" Neave asked.

She was sitting beside Kwan as the Peach Flyer zoomed through the sunbaked countryside at 200 miles an hour. The bullet train was smoother, quieter and much more pleasant than a helicopter. Especially now.

"Wind? Pilots are always talking about wind. Headwinds, tailwinds, crosswinds."

"I don't think there was much wind. Maybe the load was too heavy. Did he have a lot of specimens?"

"His specimens couldn't have weighed as much as we do if we'd been on the chopper. Maybe if he fell on the door and the door was, you know, damaged or something and it popped open, you know. Maybe that might've caused an inexperienced pilot to lose control."

He'd touched on the issue no one wanted to talk about: why Lena, with so few pilot hours under her belt, was at the controls of a university helicopter ferrying a V.I.P. on a long flight.

Neave gazed out the window for a moment but the landscape was whizzing by so fast it made her dizzy. It was like riding an elevator that was moving horizontally instead of vertically. She was tired of trying to figure out how Osley fell to his death. Nothing made any sense. She pulled her iCom out and clicked on a link to an Atlanta news site. The picture was transmitted to the T-view screen in front of her as her ear buds caught a reporter's voice.

"...missing door was located today," the reporter explained, as video was shown of a battered hunk of plasteel lying on a residential street. "Authorities say it's a miracle a car or a child wasn't hit when it dropped out of the sky. Investigators will closely examine the hinges as they search for the cause..."

Then footage was shown again of Lena and Nat as they were escorted from the police station to a waiting patrol car as the reporter continued talking.

"The door was found by residents in the Dos Santos subdivision, on the outskirts of Covington. It's not known yet why the copter returned to Augusta rather than making an emergency landing at the nearby Covington Airport."

They were nearly to Atlanta, Neave thought, scrunching her eyebrows.

"Yeah, they were," Kwan said.

She didn't realize she'd spoken.

"Shh!" she said, listening to the report.

"...some question," the reporter continued, "about whether the young woman at the controls had her pilot's license. We're told she's a student at Georgia Geosciences University. That's another question authorities will be investigating in the coming days. Megan?"

And the picture of the reporter shrank as another camera focused on the news anchor. Neave clicked off then and closed her eyes for a second.

"Of course, she has her license," she said. "But why would they turn around and fly back to Augusta?"

Which would've revived the discussion yet again if they hadn't begun decelerating for a brief layover at the Augusta train depot. Kwan hopped off to stretch his legs while Neave clicked her iCom again just in time to see the tail end of a video of her father as he walked into a building in New Washington behind two Asian looking men in dark suits.

She turned it off again and sighed. She wished she could erase the last twenty-four hours. If only she could click her iCom and order a re-do. Dr. Osley would still be alive and she wouldn't have waltzed with Will Galloway only to have him treat her like a disease vector. She shook her head and took several deep breaths, hoping to get oxygen to her brain.

It also bothered her that every time she turned around her father was on the news. And how had he become so enamored of all things Chinese? She remembered his trip to Beijing when she was ten. She'd asked if they could all go and make it a vacation. She liked the idea of walking the Great Wall of China and seeing the Terra Cotta Soldiers. But he said it was a business trip and he didn't have time. She remembered him shaking his head and jutting his chin. Even her ten year old self realized how silly it was to suggest a family vacation. It was an idea rooted in fantasy that if they tried harder they could be like a family in some long ago movie – a family that might walk the Great Wall together, taking pictures to post for friends back home. A family that would sit at the dinner table and smile and talk about what happened that day. Pure fantasy. Her father took his trips and vacations solo. And so did her mother. They had separate bedroom suites and led separate lives. That was the first time she wondered why they were married.

The smell of bananas brought her back to the present. Kwan had returned, carrying biofoam bowls filled with chunks of bananas and oranges. The mixture of smells made her mouth water. He handed her a bioplastic fork and took his seat beside her, digging into his own bowl.

"I ran into a Chinese friend of mine at the fruit stand," he said.

"Chinese?"

"Okay, not Chinese. He's actually about one fourth Filipino. Maybe a little Middle Eastern. Anyway, his wife's a cop. And she told him a high-powered lawyer showed up to help Lena and Nat jump through the legal hoops last night."

~~~

She felt heavy as she walked the few blocks to the University Cantina, weighed down by more than just the blazing sun. She usually avoided going out when it was 118 degrees, but she had to talk with Lena face to face. She wrapped her silvery cooling cloak around her but it wasn't helping much. Her head hurt and there was an uneasy feeling in her stomach, like she'd swallowed a rock.

As she walked, she was struck again by the transformation of the city. She'd seen images of Atlanta from a hundred years before when verdant lawns and lush shrubbery nestled beneath a canopy of green. But the towering pines, oaks and magnolias that once lined the streets had been replaced with scattered cottonwoods and mesquite. And now it was the cactus capital of the south.

When she arrived, Lena was waiting at the cantina entrance. She looked like she was sleepwalking – hair flattened on one side, dark circles under her eyes, no lipstick, dragging on her e-cig. There was also the unmistakable odor of stale sweat.

"You okay?" Neave asked, on the verge of giving her a hug. But Lena headed off towards the Geology School like she was in a hurry.

"Super. Caffeine helps," she said, taking another drag on her e-cig. Lena preferred to inhale her caffeine when it was scorching hot.

"I'm serious, Lena. You wanna talk?"

"Is that why you asked to meet up? So you could play psychologist?"

Which took Neave by surprise. She assumed Lena would be glad to see her and might even want to confide in her. She hadn't expected to find her so angry. But she couldn't help feeling it might help Lena to talk with somebody. And Neave wanted to know what happened.

She would have to tread carefully though. Their friendship had always suffered from Lena's resentment. She'd only made oblique references, but it was obvious she felt Neave had no clue how hard life could be. Lena was Rosa's niece – the niece she rescued from a mother who turned to prostitution when she couldn't keep a job. Neave's father had pulled some strings to get Lena into the university. So they never discussed Lena's childhood. Neave knew she appreciated the chance to escape that life, but she also knew Lena didn't want to feel like a charity case.

They walked through a courtyard landscaped with gravel – a big expanse of white pebbles with long, curving lines of pink and tan stones. In the middle, three desert willows in full bloom filled the air with their sweet scent.

"What do you think happened?" Neave finally said, as gently as possible.

"The fucking door fell off! That's what I *think* happened," Lena blurted, stopping and glaring at Neave.

"But…"

"What're you driving at?"

"Lena, I'm just trying to…."

"Look, we all want to know the answer to that question." She gave Neave a cold stare. "The N.T.S.B. is investigating as we speak."

They resumed walking in an uncomfortable silence. When they reached the central arroyo, Lena stopped.

"Listen, I've got stuff to do. So…"

"Lena…"

"I don't know! Comprende?" she snapped, waving her e-cig in Neave's face.

Neave sighed as she watched her storm off. Usually, Lena's stride was easygoing, playful, sexy. Not now. Her steps were fast and angry and Neave wished she hadn't upset her. She knew Lena must be struggling. But she just couldn't wait months for federal investigators to do their thing.

~~~

She was sipping a mocha and finishing a banana, trying to ditch her headache and the queasiness in her stomach, when Nat sat down across from her.

"That's the first time you've ever called me," he said, leaning heavily on the table.

"Well, I know the timing's not great, but…"

"But you wanna know what happened."

So he gave her his version of events, which boiled down to everything was fine – he and Lena were chatting in the cockpit about nothing in particular – when they hit some minor turbulence.

"And then the chopper started shaking and we dipped to the right. Lena got things back under control and I turned around to see if Dr. Osley was okay but I couldn't see him. He was gone and the door was missing." He shook his head slowly and stared into space. "It was terrifying."

His demeanor was unusually quiet, his shoulders drooping slightly. Very unlike him.

"But, I wonder why..."

He sighed.

"Lena said we hit a rough pocket. I don't know – maybe she wasn't ready for it. I don't know." He shrugged and shook his head again. "I should've hired an experienced pilot. But Lena begged me and I was trying to save money."

"And the door?"

"Yeah, the door. If the door hadn't come off, Osley would be complaining today about the lousy pilot and maybe nursing a bumped head or a bruised shoulder or something. I guess he'd be complaining about me not getting a professional pilot or a decent helicopter to fly in. And he'd be right," he said, his voice dropping to a whisper.

He lowered his head so she couldn't see his face. When he finally raised it again, he looked grief-stricken and she nearly reached across the table to touch his hand, but stopped herself.

"I guess the investigators will figure out why the door came off," he said.

"So the door came off first?"

"I don't know. And I don't know if we'll ever know."

When she stood to leave, he didn't try to walk her home or ask her out or anything. Which was also very unlike him.

~~~

The funeral was a large affair, held at Sacred Heart Catholic Church – Osley's church. Abstract stained glass windows flooded the sanctuary with color that washed over white pews and wine-colored cushions.

Osley's battered body had been reduced to an urn full of ashes. The blue urn sat next to a large bouquet of white lilies on a pedestal at the front.

The focal point of the church, though, was a stunning painting, quite large, of the Virgin Mary and baby Jesus that hung above the pulpit. Mary looked like a contemporary Israeli woman with short black hair and a white dress. It was her eyes, though, that drew Neave's attention. They looked down on her baby with such intensity that Neave became emotional gazing up at it. How did the artist imbue a painting with so much love? There was more love in that painting than Neave had felt in her entire life. She never remembered seeing that look in her mother's eyes. And certainly never in her father's.

There was some movement at the front as the priest, dressed in long white vestments and a purple stole, made his way to the altar. Then she saw her father and Nat approaching Dr. Osley's widow, who was dressed in black and surrounded by family members on the front row.

Adela Mercado was a justice on the Georgia Supreme Court. Her family was Amerindian and Spanish from Bolivia. Her once black hair was short and liberally streaked with grey.

Dr. Alvarez leaned close and spoke to her briefly. But Neave noticed Judge Mercado did not look up. In fact, she didn't appear to respond in any way. Then Dr. Alvarez nodded his head and moved away, Nat in tow.

The service included a eulogy by the president of the university, Dr. Sreeparna Bhattacharyya. Dressed in a traditional sari with a black scarf covering her hair, she praised Dr. Osley's efforts to push government and business to get serious about transitioning to clean technologies. Neave had the distinct impression she was taking Osley's side against her father, though she never mentioned the shade ring.

While she and Kwan saved a seat, Lena never showed.

Chapter 6

Two weeks later nobody was surprised when President Cohen announced her nomination for Climate Secretary – Robert Alvarez. Images of the two of them shaking hands and smiling were shown on all the news broadcasts. But this cabinet position was always the subject of much debate and disagreement. So, as part of her lobbying effort to get Dr. Alvarez approved in the Senate, the President invited him to a state dinner entertaining the President of Mexico. All the pivotal votes in the Senate were also invited.

Which is how Neave came to be frowning into a full-length mirror, aghast at how her breasts were bulging from the bodice of a designer evening gown. The material was a light honeydew color and was so thin she could see her nipples through the fabric.

"No way," she said, reaching for the zipper in back.

"Neave, you look stunning," her mother said from where she sat on an overstuffed white sofa behind her.

They were in a private dressing room at Machada's Atlanta boutique.

"The dress brings out the green in your eyes," her mother added. "We can get you some adhesive bra cups."

"You mean pasties?"

Her mother shook her head. Always formal in manner and

appearance, Dr. Molly Sullivan was wearing white slacks with a green and white jacket, which accentuated her eyes. Neave and her mother shared their auburn hair and fair skin but her mother's eyes were a vivid green while Neave's were green with brown flecks. Her mother had obviously been a great beauty and still looked considerably younger than her sixty-four years. She was Neave's height – five, seven – with a trim figure. There was more than a little silver in her short hair but she refused to hide the grey, insisting it was suitable for a scientist.

"It's a state dinner, Mother, not Oscar night. And I'm not a model trying to get a contract to pose nude in an e-zine."

There was a loud knock on the dressing room door.

Neave hid behind an Oriental screen as her father burst into the room, not waiting for an answer.

"Where's the beautiful daughter of Robert Alvarez?"

His voice was loud and artificially cheery.

"She's..." her mother started.

"Let me see you in one of those fancy evening gowns!" he called out, his voice overwhelming the fitting room.

Dr. Alvarez was only an inch taller than his daughter and a bit stocky. His Mexican American father had given him his build and his thick, black hair but his mother, who he loved to describe as a "Heinz 57 American," had passed along the hazel eyes. His demeanor was that of a man used to being in control.

"I've just started trying them on," she replied.

"I'm waiting!" he bellowed, sitting down on the far end of the couch from his wife and stroking his greying mustache.

"She and I..." her mother said.

"Neave!" he snapped.

"Robert," Dr. Sullivan said, "she's..."

"I want to see you in one of those expensive dresses, cariño!" he called. "Your mother may be a competent scientist, but she's no judge of fashion. It takes a person with some originality and creativity to choose the perfect dress for an occasion as important as this one."

She imagined her mother folding her arms across her chest and gazing nowhere in particular. That's what she always did when her husband put her down. She never defended herself. Maybe that was one reason Neave wanted to find someone to fall passionately in love with. She didn't want to end up in the kind of marriage her parents had, devoid of warmth.

She pulled the dress down over her hips, draping it over a chair, then grabbed another one and slipped it on, the fabric swishing loudly.

"Hop to!" her father roared.

"This is women's work, Father," she said, just loud enough for him to hear, wondering why he'd come. "We can handle it."

She hoped he would leave without a fuss but that was not to be. He jumped up, crossed the room in a few quick steps and picked up the Oriental screen and lifted it aside. Neave turned in surprise, holding the bodice of the dress over her breasts. Her mother hurried to zip up the back.

He looked her up and down, harrumphing and clicking his tongue.

"Let's be clear," he said. "I expect excellence."

Then he stalked from the room, slamming the door behind him.

"I'm not going," she said, reaching behind her to unzip the dress.

"Neave, dear..."

"Why do you stand for it, Mother?"

52

"I don't let such things bother me."

She stared at her mother, who busied herself choosing another dress from the rack.

"It's not worth getting upset about," Dr. Sullivan continued, giving a little shrug. "Your father didn't have compassionate behavior modeled for him as a child." She removed the hanger from a mint green chiffon gown and handed it to Neave. "We'll do our duty and accompany your father to the White House," her mother said, returning to her perch on the couch. "Now, let's see how that one looks on you."

"How can you be so..."

"Dear, you know your father is trying to make the best impression he possibly can."

"Right."

"And he really wants Nat to be there."

"Of course."

"And it would be best if Nat had a beautiful date for the evening."

"Nat could have any date he wants. And I mean *any* date."

"He wants you," her mother replied. "And your father believes he'll make a much stronger impression if he has his wife and daughter with him – the family man, you know."

Which made Neave roll her eyes as she stepped into the chiffon.

If Osley hadn't died, it's possible she might've been able to muster a tiny bit of pride in her father's nomination. But it was like the Olympic athlete who wins the gold medal when his strongest competitor's country pulls out of the Olympics in protest. You have the medal, but an asterisk appears forever beside your name.

When she looked in the mirror, there was a sour expression on her face which didn't go well with the green chiffon at all.

"It'll be a lovely evening," Dr. Sullivan said encouragingly.

"You'll get a chance to see the new White House too."

Neave turned to examine the side view.

"So my job is to be an ornament on Nat's arm."

"Your job is to be charming and non-controversial."

"Then forget these low-cut dresses."

She made a big show of rummaging through the gowns, looking for an acceptable neckline as she snuck a look at her mother, suddenly wondering about Will's accusation.

"Is that what you specialize in, Mother? Being charming and non-controversial?"

Dr. Sullivan joined her at the dress rack, sighing in reply.

"Mother, have you ever been involved in cloning?"

Dr. Sullivan pulled a Kelly green gown from the rack and studied the bodice.

"Dear, you know I've been working on cloning a heart."

"I mean human cloning."

"I oppose cloning of humans, dear. You know that, don't you?"

Neave took the dress from her mother.

"Someone I met on the coast accused you of being a cloner," she said, noticing then that all the dresses were green. Of course – to match her eyes. She held the gown against her body and turned towards her mother.

"Well, your new acquaintance has made faulty assumptions based on inaccurate references to my work in some unscientific journal," Dr. Sullivan replied. "You know what kind of research I do. We're very close to perfecting our technique for human heart regeneration, which would be a major milestone. It would eliminate the need for heart transplants if we could regrow damaged heart muscle in situ. The implications would be enormous."

Which only made Neave wonder how her mother could be so passionate about her professional life and so passive about her personal life.

Chapter 7

After arriving in New Washington, Neave spent the afternoon getting her nails and hair done. The stylist was so delighted to see some long locks, she wanted to create a fountain of braids on the back of her head. But Neave asked for something less showy. So it was pulled back in a lovely chignon, with several strands of her auburn hair framing her face.

Back in her hotel room, she'd just finished adding a touch of pale green eye shadow, auburn mascara and frosted coral lip gloss when there was a knock at her door. It was exactly 5:15.

Dr. Sullivan looked regal in a deep green raw silk gown with three quarter sleeves and pearls. Her hair was fluffed up higher than usual on top and swept back on the sides. And she had allowed a cosmetologist to apply her makeup for the evening. The combined effect was to make her look younger and prettier. And her eyes were as green as Irish clover.

Neave oohed and aahed, which seemed to please her mother, whose cheeks reddened at the attention.

Of course, Dr. Sullivan was there, not so much to help, as to make sure Neave didn't get cold feet and disappear. Which was a smart move because it had definitely crossed her mind. Being Nat's official date for a White House dinner in order to impress the Washington elite was not her idea of a fun time. There was also the problem of how Nat would take her acquiescence. As encouragement, no doubt. Still, here she was, slipping into a designer gown.

"Let me help you," her mother said as Neave pulled the dress up over her hips.

She stood behind Neave and zipped it up, looking over her shoulder into the full-length mirror.

"Tres chic."

That was her mother's accurate assessment of the dress Neave had chosen. It was pale silvery green silk that hugged her body and flared at the hem, but only showed a little cleavage. Dr. Sullivan draped the emerald pendant necklace they'd chosen around her daughter's neck. When she added the matching earrings and stepped into her silver heels, Neave had to admit she did look like an ornament for an ambitious man.

"With the addition of your beautiful smile, your ensemble will be complete," her mother said.

When they joined Dr. Alvarez and Nat in her parents' suite, the men were standing in front of a large view screen admiring the newest version of the shade ring animation. They'd been polishing it to prepare for Dr. Alvarez's Senate confirmation hearings.

Dressed in tuxedos, the men turned as the ladies entered, gazing with obvious appreciation. The expression on Nat's face took Neave back to her best friend's tenth birthday party when J'nai's mom and dad carried in a pile of presents wrapped in sparkling paper and ribbons. J'nai's eyes had grown big as she bounced with anticipation. And that's how Nat looked now, which made Neave feel more than a little uncomfortable.

"Lovely times two," Dr. Alvarez purred, nodding in approval.

Interestingly, while she'd been worried about looking like an ornament for a man, Nat came pretty close to looking like an ornament for an ambitious woman. He could've passed for a handsome prince in his white vest, black bowtie and expensive black tuxedo. She was sure she'd be the envy of every woman there, perhaps even the President herself, who was known to appreciate the company of a good-looking man.

Nat handed Neave and her mother flutes of champagne and they all drank a toast.

"To the next Climate Secretary," Nat said, raising his glass.

They downed the champagne quickly before heading out. Nat held out his arm and she took it as they left the room.

"Dios mio!" her father said. "The perfect couple."

Nat looked down at Neave and gave her a disarming smile so that she found herself responding in kind.

"You look absolutely breathtaking," he whispered.

"Likewise, I'm sure."

Which caused him to laugh amiably.

Her parents said the White House wasn't the same since it was moved to New Washington to escape the rising waters of the Chesapeake which had swelled the Potomac River. The surging water damaged the levees that protected old Washington. They tried bigger levees and movable dams but no amount of federal dollars could hold back the rising tide. So, after considerable gnashing of teeth, the historic section of the nation's capital was relocated to a rural area of Virginia where property owners were bought out for a pretty penny and the original layout of the capitol city was reproduced. The monuments that couldn't be moved were built anew, copying the originals as closely as possible.

But to Neave, the president's home was charming. From all the pictures and web video she'd seen, she thought they'd done an admirable job of transporting the building piece by piece and reconstructing it. The best talents in the world had been brought in to painstakingly recreate the setting of the White House grounds as well. The Lincoln Memorial and Washington Monument, along with the reflecting pool, were just as grand in their new home.

The evening began with the grand entrance of President Cohen in deep blue satin, accompanied by Mexican President Alberto Guzman. His wife entered behind them on the arm of Vice President Booker. Dr. Alvarez seemed at ease as he spoke to President Cohen and President Guzman in the receiving line, introducing Dr. Sullivan, Neave and Nat. Neave noticed President Cohen's eyes light up when she looked up into Nat's face, and it was not a maternal gaze. But there was an uncomfortable moment when the Mexican president switched to Spanish for Dr. Alvarez's benefit. Her father shrugged his shoulders genially and said "no hablo."

Neave dutifully remained at Nat's side as the four of them made the rounds, chatting with influential senators and dignitaries from other countries, including the new Chinese ambassador, Fu Jiechi. Neave noticed her father gave Fu an especially warm greeting, trying out some Chinese expressions to the ambassador's delight.

Then it was on to the State Dining Room, resplendent in white and gold, with white candles and floral centerpieces of peach and coral roses and lilies. Thirteen large, round tables were covered with cream damask floor-length tablecloths and set with the Silverman china, complete with a White House design on the plates. Neave was sure this was no accident. The nation's first Jewish president was being honored by its second Jewish president.

Neave and Nat were seated at a table with a couple of important senators. The president's press secretary, Barry King, represented the Cohen administration at the table. He was a tall, handsome black man in his thirties who took the chair on Neave's left and kept brushing against her arm throughout dinner. His job was to help Nat spin the shade ring plan, but it quickly became obvious Nat didn't need any help.

Once the pleasantries were out of the way, the conversation veered immediately to the shade ring. Senator Lopez of California was keen on delving into specifics with Nat, who was only too happy to indulge him with details of the nanotechnology that would be used in creating shade ring mirrors and how they would be launched from a number of locations to speed deployment.

"But I saw a speech recently by Dr. Terrance Osley at a scientific conference, given only a few weeks before he died, saying the shade ring was not the answer," Lopez said, as the spring pea soup was served.

"I saw it too," said Senator Jefferson, the powerful Pennsylvanian who would chair the confirmation hearings. She was an attractive middle-aged black woman in a deep burgundy evening dress sitting on Neave's right. "And I have yet to hear Dr. Alvarez answer."

"Now, Latasha," Senator Lopez said, chuckling, "why don't we hold our questions for the hearings? Let's not grill these two young people."

"I'm not grilling them, Victor," she replied. "And I think these two young people might be in a good position to know quite a lot about Dr. Alvarez's proposal. This is his daughter, for heaven's sake." And then she turned to Nat. "And I believe you're his right hand man, aren't you, Mr. Patel?"

Nat smiled, nodding his head at the waiter who was at that moment filling his wine glass with an expensive Chardonnay.

"Well, I do assist Dr. Alvarez in many ways. And I'm more than happy to discuss the latest research on ocean warming. In fact, Neave and I just returned from a scientific expedition to the South Carolina coast where we found a species of jellyfish that has, until now, been confined to the tropics. It was the first sighting of Chironex fleckeri that far north, which means warming is definitely continuing. And if we don't do something soon to cool the oceans, there will be many more cities in need of evacuation."

Neave thought he made their little field trip sound a lot more impressive than it actually was.

Senator Jefferson lowered her chin as though she were going into battle.

"Have you listened to Dr. Osley's arguments, Mr. Patel?" But she didn't pause long enough for him to get a word in edgewise. "Because if you have, you know that finding a tropical jellyfish along the South Carolina coast is no argument at all to support the expense of launching a bunch of space umbrellas. In fact, finding that jellyfish might be an argument for getting the lead out – pardon my French – when it comes to changing over to green energy."

Nat smiled and nodded.

"I couldn't agree more, Senator," he said. "But how do you force struggling economies to make the jump to non-polluting technologies? Millions of people would lose their jobs in existing industries, even if their countries could afford to make the necessary upgrades. The shade ring would help cool the oceans while we give those countries and those industries time to make the transition."

"But the expense!" Senator Jefferson said.

"The expense would be huge," Nat conceded. "But think of all the jobs the shade ring would create. And we wouldn't be footing the bill by ourselves. Our proposal calls for U.S. allies to share the financial burden."

Neave couldn't help but admire Nat's cool under fire. For every objection raised, he had an answer.

After dinner was over and the formal toasts concluded, the president's press secretary jumped up and pulled Neave's chair out for her.

"I have to tell you, Ms. Alvarez," he said, "your gown is the most elegant dress in the room tonight."

"Why, thank you, Mr. King."

"Of course, you'd look beautiful regardless of what you were wearing."

"You're too kind," she said, immediately moving towards Nat, who was schmoozing with a senator from Texas. Nat placed his hand lightly on her back as if re-establishing his territory.

"Mr. King," he said, nodding at the press secretary as he guided Neave to the East Room for the evening's entertainment – a concert by Murphy Jeffs and her jazz trio. Several feet in front of them, they watched as her mother and father were greeted by Senator Jefferson.

"Ah, Dr. Sullivan, Dr. Alvarez," the senator said, reaching to shake her father's hand. "I had the pleasure of sharing a table with your beautiful daughter and your right hand man. He's quite a debater."

"Nat Patel is very..." Dr. Alvarez began.

"Oh, and your daughter – she looks so much like you!" Senator Jefferson interrupted, looking at Dr. Sullivan. "And what a fabulous dress! How do two scientists afford a

Machada? Not that I would know anything about matters of high fashion, but two different people mentioned that you and your daughter are both wearing designer gowns. Do those swanky designers loan them to you like they do to President Cohen?"

Dr. Sullivan smiled and nodded at her husband, who laughed heartily as they moved through the door into the East Room.

~~~

When the evening was finally over, all Neave wanted to do was go to bed and frown all night to rest her cheeks from the hours of obligatory smiling. During the limo trip back to the hotel her father and Nat were busy comparing notes on how many senators they'd managed to talk with and how many they'd shown the shade ring animation to. Not to mention chatting up the president herself.

Neave and her mother walked into the lobby ahead of the men. The Hunan Hotel was decorated with Chinese wall hangings, bamboo and calligraphy. She was sure it was no accident they were staying at a Chinese hotel.

"Even Senator Jefferson was eating out of your hand before it was over," Nat said, chuckling like a little boy telling a dirty joke to his buddy.

"Yeah, and she's one tough cookie too," Dr. Alvarez said, grinning proudly.

It was like they were high on drugs. Neave had never seen Nat so animated. He and her father had forgotten the women entirely.

When the elevator doors opened, an Asian man emerged and nodded politely to them.

"Ni hao, ni hao," Dr. Alvarez said, a warm smile on his face.

"Do you know him?" Neave asked once the elevator doors

closed.

"No. I just try to use my Chinese whenever I have the opportunity. It's good for my brain synapses," he said, tapping his head.

Ironic, she thought, that he could speak Chinese with perfect strangers but couldn't converse at all with the president of Mexico, who assumed an Alvarez would be fluent in Spanish. Her father only knew a handful of words and phrases from the Mexican side of his family. It had been the only rough spot of the evening, though.

~~~

"You were wonderful tonight," Nat said, as he escorted her to her room. "Beautiful, intelligent, sophisticated. I owe you."

"Glad I was able to serve my purpose," she said, pressing her forefinger on the keypad.

"I've got a special thank-you treat for tomorrow night."

"Nat, you don't have to…"

"Two tickets to *Mandarin Daughter*. The original Broadway cast!"

"How…" she blurted, but stopped.

She'd been dying to see the new musical. It had gotten rave reviews. Everyone in the theater world was buzzing about it. But how did he know?

"I'll come by your room around five-thirty," he said. "We can have dinner, then take in the show."

Once inside, she tried to rationalize going with him. He did owe her for being his date to the White House dinner and for staying an extra day at the beach, which had turned into such a nightmare. So, she decided it was only fitting that he repay the debt. Of course, she couldn't deny she was thrilled at the prospect of seeing the play that many predicted was a shoo-in for Best Musical.

Chapter 8

She settled on dressy black capris and a silver evening top she found in a boutique near the hotel. Just right for dinner at an upscale Indian restaurant Nat found where bright Indian tapestries decorated the walls, soft sitar music played in the background and waiters bustled about in black slacks and long white Indian shirts. Compared with them, Nat looked very American – and very handsome – in a pale aqua dress shirt and grey sport coat.

It was kind of an Indian Tapas bar where they ordered several small plates of what Nat explained was Punjabi-style food. He recommended Alu Tikki – some crispy potato patties with curry, chutney and onions – and a flat Indian cornbread topped with an eggplant and tomato spread that Neave really liked, along with some other vegetarian dishes.

The delightful smell of warm curry filled the dining room. And Nat's selection of a sparkling rosé was a nice touch. Neave could feel herself relaxing as they tried various dishes and he explained each one. Talking about the food led to talking about his family.

"I seem to recall you have a sister," she ventured.

"My parents are very proud of my sister. She's quite the rising star. CEO of a pharmaceutical company. Makes a ton of money, of course."

"Must be nice to have a sister."

He laughed.

"She's thirteen years older than me," he explained, "and mostly a symbol my parents have shoved in my face to make it clear what they expect from their children. She got a PhD, I've gotta get a PhD. She's rich, I've gotta be rich. She's got a job at a big drug company, I've gotta have some kind of fancy job they can brag about to family and friends."

He shrugged and emptied his glass.

"The prominent Patels," he said, dripping with sarcasm.

She remembered her father telling her, in what she assumed was an attempt to impress her with Nat's pedigree, that Nat's mother was CEO of Bank Mumbai USA and his father was a professor of chemical engineering at Caltech. But she decided to comment on how good the wine was, hoping to change the subject. Which prompted Nat to order two more glasses.

"I heard Senator Coleman," he said, "or was it Senator Liu? One of them said that since Rachel Cohen was elected president, there aren't any White House galas or parties on Friday night anymore."

"Mm, the Sabbath."

"Right. I mean, I don't think anyone minds, but it's been a bit of a surprise."

"Well, it's not like she hid the fact that she's Jewish," she said.

"True, but I think she downplayed it during the campaign. I read that she has an advisor who coaches her on how to appear observant but not overly observant."

"Is that a problem?"

"Not for me. I'm as open as you can get about religion."

And then she understood what the conversation was really

about. His religion. Her religion. Not the president's religion.

"I'm Hindu, officially," he said, "but, you know, Hindus accept pretty much any religion – Jewish, Catholic, Protestant, whatever."

He dipped his flatbread into the sauce and took a bite.

She almost said, 'like mine, you mean?' but managed to hold her tongue. Her father's family came from the Mexican Catholic tradition. Her mother was nominally Irish Protestant. But the reality was that she hadn't been brought up with a religious tradition at all. Unless you counted science as a religion. Her only visits to church were for funerals and weddings. But Nat probably didn't know that.

"By the way," she said, changing the subject again, "I was curious about the speech Senator Jefferson referred to last night, so I did a search."

"What speech?"

"A speech Dr. Osley gave at the Global Climate Conference in Norway this spring."

Nat's jaw tightened.

"I found it on the web. Are you familiar with the research Osley…"

"You know, research is a lot like scripture – you can find research to support just about any position if you look hard enough."

"That's exactly what Osley said about supporters of the shade ring."

Nat shifted in his chair and wiped his mouth.

"In fact," she continued, "Osley said it was all this talk and speculation about a shade ring that prompted governments around the world to back away from banning coal-burning plants and gasoline-powered cars. They must think they can keep delaying clean energy forever. And he said there's actually been an uptick in…"

"Bullshit!" he said, bringing his fist down on the table, causing her to jump. "There's been an uptick in bullshit."

He glared at her but she pressed on, refusing to be cowed.

"And," she continued, "Osley raised an interesting point: who stands to benefit financially from deploying a shade ring?"

"Dammit, Neave, who're you gonna believe – Terrance Osley, a man with an agenda if there ever was one, or your own father?"

He was almost hissing at her.

"Like my father doesn't have an agenda?"

He sighed heavily, then smiled.

"You're right. I guess we all have an agenda. But, honestly, if you'd take the time to read over your father's position paper on the shade ring I think you'd see he's right. In fact, your father gave a speech at that same climate conference. Did you watch his speech?"

She shook her head.

"Well, you should. See what you think after you've heard his side of it."

He glanced at his iCom and waved at the waiter, then looked again at her.

"You're even more beautiful when you're riled up."

Ironic, she thought, since he's the one who'd gotten riled.

~~~

The Reagan Theatre had been designed to resemble a Broadway playhouse from the 1930's with Tuscan gold stucco walls and patron boxes along the sides of the balcony. Luxurious teal drapes hung from the arched proscenium.

They had the best seats in the house – third row, dead center. She was on the verge of asking who he'd bribed to get them, then decided instead to pretend she wasn't overly impressed. But the play itself was amazing. *Mandarin Daughter* was about a young Chinese American woman trying to deal with a mother who was governor of California who had White House ambitions. The daughter had to sort through the attentions of all kinds of suitors more interested in gaining access to the governor than they were in a relationship with the daughter. And there was the other theme – the governor didn't speak a word of Chinese and knew very little about her cultural history, but used her ethnicity to political advantage. Lilly, the Mandarin daughter, was expected to use her Chinese name – Liling – and to wear the sexy, form-fitting Cheongsam dress at public events to help her mother achieve media darling status.

The acting, singing and dancing all lived up to the hype. Of course, the plot was of particular interest, which is one reason Neave wanted to see it. She was so enthralled, she almost forgot who she was sitting with and why.

Afterwards, over a luscious chocolate dessert and wine at a nearby cafe, she couldn't help but gush.

"Sarah what's-her-name was so believable as Lilly," she said. "And the mother – wow! Great stage actresses and what full, rich voices!"

Nat nodded as he savored the red wine, a twinkle in his eye.

"And the choreography! That scene with the reporters and their eye cameras! Amazing!" she continued, the music still playing in her head.

"I'd actually like to download that song – what was it called? *Chinese is as Chinese does.* And God, the other song: *How many knees does a ni hao have?* Hilarious."

She laughed and drained her glass.

She was still floating on air when they arrived at the door of her hotel room to find a bottle of red wine chilling in a silver ice bucket along with two wine glasses.

"Ah, just what the doctor ordered," Nat said, picking up the tray from the floor and giving her a mischievous grin.

Her brain told her she didn't need any more wine, but she felt young and free and full of music and, for once, she threw caution to the wind and invited him in. After three glasses of an expensive Cabernet and more conversation about the play, she was totally chilled out.

"I didn't know you were a theater buff," she said. "Have you seen other Broadway plays?"

"Never had the time or money."

"Do you see plays in Atlanta?" she asked, pushing her shoes off.

"Now and then," he said, leaning over to refill her glass. "But not recently. Working on my doctorate, you know. Very time consuming."

"What's your favorite of the plays you've seen?"

"Oh, I can't remember the name of it – a new drama I saw last year. A little abstract, though."

"Oh, maybe I saw it. Which theater?"

He paused before responding.

"El Teatro in Lawrenceville."

"I've never been there. I'll have to try it sometime."

She finished her wine, set the glass on the table, yawned and stood up.

"Well, that was fun, Nat. Really fun. Thanks for taking me. Best musical I've ever seen!"

"I want to thank you," he said, rising from his chair. "Being with you this evening was a dream come true."

He followed her as she strolled to the door.

"I think you know," he said, stepping very close behind her, "that I'm in love with you."

"Nat..."

As she turned around to face him, he put his hands on her waist. She looked up into his eyes, then quickly tucked her chin down, trying to think of what to say. Because the truth of the matter was, even though she was more than a little tipsy, and even though they'd had a fun evening that she'd enjoyed more than anything she'd done in a long, long time, she didn't want to kiss him. And it made her feel guilty.

Why couldn't she give him a chance, she thought. So when he leaned down and placed his mouth on hers, she didn't pull away. There was nothing wrong with his kiss, she thought, except that she felt like she was outside herself watching. There were no surging hormones. She waited politely until he was done.

"I want you, Neave," he whispered into her hair.

"Nat, I can't."

He ignored her, kissing her neck and caressing her back. She pushed away but he held tight and it was only too obvious that he was very turned on.

"Neave."

He leaned down to kiss her again, but she turned her face. So he kissed her neck, holding her firmly with one arm, while the other hand moved down her back until he was caressing her butt. She grabbed his hand.

"Nat, I think we need to call it a night."

"God, you feel so good," he said, his hand moving to her breast.

"Stop!" she said, pushing his hand away.

He looked down at her, a wildness in his eyes. But then he sighed and his shoulders drooped as he loosened his grip.

"We had a great time, didn't we?"

"Yes, we did," she said, backing away and smoothing her top, trying to keep her voice under control. "The play was wonderful."

"Great seats too," he said.

"They were."

"Delicious dinner. Excellent wine."

"Yes. And I kissed you good-night," she said.

He walked slowly to the door, opened it and turned to her.

"I'm sorry, Neave. I guess I went too fast. Forgive me?"

She nodded quickly, closing her eyes, hoping he would leave.

When the door closed, she turned the security lock, and hugged herself as she collapsed on the couch. There was either something wrong with her, she thought, or something wrong with him. She wasn't sure which. But she just couldn't have sex with him. Even if he *had* spent a wad on her. Maybe she could reimburse him for half the cost. She could find out how much those tickets cost and the dinner and the wine. That way she wouldn't feel so obligated. From one moment to the next she veered from feeling like the whole thing was her fault, to being sure he'd manipulated her. She thought he'd trapped her by surprising her with the invitation in the first place, then taken her out for the kind of date she'd been dying to have. But then he'd acted as if she owed him her body in payment.

Of course, she realized she'd accepted his invitation. Then she'd acted like she was having a fantastic time – and she was. She'd invited him into her room with a bottle of wine that he'd ordered especially for the occasion. She'd played along, giving him the expectation she would continue to play along with *all* of his plans, from start to finish.

She picked up the wine glasses and heaved them against the wall. They splintered into tiny pieces, the shards falling to the floor, red wine splattering the creamy white paint and dripping down the wall to the carpet. She padded about the room, wiping her hands together as though they were dirty. Finally, she pulled off her clothes, tossing them carelessly in a trail behind her and headed for the shower.

The flow of water was gratifyingly strong in this five star hotel – more water than she was used to, in fact. She closed her eyes and let it pound her back and neck, then washed until she was satisfied the scent of his woody cologne was completely erased from her skin and hair.

Chapter 9

Neave and her mother flew back to Atlanta the next day, leaving the men behind to do more politicking. By the time she arrived at her apartment, there were three voice messages and two text messages on her iCom from Nat, asking her to have dinner with him when he got back. She hit "delete."

There was also a message from the university telling her if she didn't register for classes, she'd be dropped from the graduate program. She daydreamed about ignoring that one too, but then she'd have to find a job. Doing what? Teaching, maybe. But teaching what? Science? That didn't excite her. And live where? She'd have to find some roommates and a cheap apartment. She wasn't ready to make the break, considering she didn't have a plan or money. And there was also a nagging uncertainty that maybe she *should* join the fight against rising oceans.

When she checked the Geosciences page she discovered Dr. Yong Li was speaking that evening. Now that Dr. Osley was gone, she really wanted to hear what his young protégé had to say.

~~~

Attendance was sparse. Small groups of students were scattered about the auditorium. Neave sat in the second row so she could see his face.

His English was pretty good, although he spoke with an accent. And he looked very Chinese – black hair, styled in a long buzz. He wore black slacks, a long-sleeved white shirt and black tie, making him look more like a waiter than a scientist, and a far cry from American professors in their shorts and polo shirts.

He described recent warming trends and measurements, how the tipping point occurred with the collapse of the West Antarctic ice sheet and rapid melting in East Antarctica – the usual stuff. But she listened more closely to his description of the reluctant movement in many countries towards wind, solar, ocean and nano power. Coal mines were still operating in China, India and a long list of other countries – even the United States. Because so many developed countries abandoned gasoline in the twenty-first century, the price of gas had taken a nosedive, luring millions of people in third world countries to continue producing, buying and driving gas-powered vehicles. Yong seemed wise beyond his years when he talked about how industries and governments were foolhardy for not changing their polluting ways.

When he looked up from his script, she thought his eyes looked sad.

"Much news has been created about launching a shade ring into space to cool ocean waters. But if computer models are correct, it could be modest cooling and it would be slowly. Funding such a ring also depletes money to eliminate pollution and reduce world population. The transition to clean technology costs much but it would reduce anthropomorphic warming. A shade ring is expensive bandage to let pollution continue."

When the lecture was over several students made their way to the front, including Neave. She waited patiently as he answered questions. Finally, he headed towards the side exit. She dashed after him, catching up as he reached the door.

"Dr. Yong?"

He turned towards her and nodded politely.

"I'm sorry about Dr. Osley," she said.

"Thank you." He nodded again, very formal.

"I was on the expedition with him to the coast," she said. Which caused his left eyebrow to rise.

"You were on the helicopter as the accident occurred?"

"No."

"You are a student at the university?"

"Yes," she said. "My name is Neave. Neave Alvarez."

She noticed his jaw tighten, though his expression carefully remained the same.

"Yes, my father is Robert Alvarez," she said. "But I'm not on the shade ring team."

He bowed his head slightly and stepped back.

"It has been a pleasure to meet you," he said. "Good-bye."

He nodded again and walked out the door.

"Dr. Yong!"

"My shuttle bus approaches soon."

"Can I walk with you?"

He hesitated, then nodded, setting a brisk pace as they walked through a pool of light from a street lamp. It was a hot night and there was not even a hint of a breeze so she wrapped her cooling cloak around her.

"Were you close to Dr. Osley?" she asked.

"Please say what you want to discuss, Miss Alvarez."

Before she could reply, a campus shuttle appeared. She followed as he hurried towards the street.

"So sorry. I must board," he said.

She kept pace behind him, determined not to let him get

76

away. When the driverless shuttle stopped, she climbed on as well and slid in beside him in the first seat. Some students were talking in the back of the small bus and paid them no attention. He laced his fingers in his lap and stared straight ahead.

"Miss Alvarez…"

"Please call me Neave."

He gave a small sigh and lowered his head.

"I do not believe you and I have much to discuss about."

"I know you probably think I'm a spy or something, but I'm not. And I really need to talk with you. Please."

He pursed his lips.

"You see," she continued, her voice almost a whisper, "I think Dr. Osley believed my father had some ulterior motive for pushing the shade ring. And if that's true, I'd like to know."

"Perhaps you may ask your father."

It was her turn to sigh.

"Did Dr. Osley ever say anything to you?" she asked.

The shuttle pulled to a stop and two young men got off, glancing at Neave and Yong as they passed by. Then the door closed and the bus lurched forward again.

"It is possible you will receive negative fame sitting beside the Chinese clone," Yong said. "People hypothesize that clones are evil because they have no soul. I have been targeted by a tomato and a rock."

She gasped.

"That was in China," he explained. "Americans only shoot tomatoes and rocks with their eyes."

"Nice to know Americans are more civilized," she said.

But he immediately retreated back into his formal, reserved mode.

"Do you have any idea why my father would push the

shade ring if, as you say, it's not a real solution?" she asked.

"Perhaps you may ask your..."

"My father would never tell me."

He looked directly at her.

"That is regrettable," he said.

"Dammit, Dr. Yong, I'm trying to figure out if this is anything more than a professional difference of opinion."

He gazed towards the front of the bus.

"And I think you're stonewalling," she said.

"I have no stones."

"Don't play dumb with me!" She was practically shouting.

All conversation at the back of the bus ceased.

A moment later, she was jogging along the sidewalk, her cloak billowing out as she tried to catch up with him.

"I'm sorry. I didn't mean to yell at you," she said.

He kept walking, moving fast, so that Neave had to double time it. Sweat was pouring. He turned onto Professors Row where many of the school's administrators and senior professors lived. The adobe homes looked like a neighborhood in Santa Fe. It was a style that had become popular in Atlanta decades before as a way to beat the heat.

"Please, Dr. Yong."

He stopped suddenly and turned towards her. Though his face was mostly in shadow with a streetlight behind him, she could see the tense line of his body. And when he spoke, his voice was firm, almost angry.

"I must go now. Please, good-bye."

He nodded and walked away.

She watched him until he reached the corner, where he turned right and disappeared behind the houses.

She wrapped her cooling cloak around her as she headed for Peachtree Street, glancing up at the pair of rotating skyscrapers towering above her, ribbons of blue light changing to purple and then to a deep red, accentuating their fluid, ever-changing contours. At that moment, they reminded her of daggers twisting into the earth.

~~~

Dinner at Pamplona's was supposedly her mother's idea. It was renowned for its South American and Spanish cuisine. Neave tried to beg off since she'd just spent enough time with her parents in New Washington to last her the rest of the year, but her parents insisted. Pamplona's was on the top floor of The Sevilla, the revolving skyscraper a block north of its twin, The Cordoba, where she had an apartment on the thirty-third floor.

When she opened her walk-in closet, the gown she'd worn to the White House was hanging front and center in a clear garment bag. She remembered all the compliments and the looks she'd gotten. How much had her parents paid for it, she wondered. The cost had seemed irrelevant when she was trying on dresses. Her parents were, in effect, forcing her to wear it, so it was their problem. But now she was curious.

It only took a few seconds to find the Machada website and a picture of her dress. To say she was stunned would be a gross understatement. The price tag was $35,000. Mindboggling. Why would her mother and father want her to wear an outrageously expensive designer dress? And what about her mother's gown? She found the J.J. Diaz website and discovered her mother's outfit had cost $20,000. Is that what the New Washington elite did? Spend wads of money on clothes to attend White House functions like French courtiers during the reign of Louis the Fourteenth?

She had balked at being Nat's date, but maybe she should've balked at being used as an accessory to her father's political ambitions, like the diamond stud earring he wore in his left ear when he left for his solo vacations. How much money did the earring cost? How much did the vacations cost?

How much did her apartment cost? She was embarrassed to admit she'd left it all to her parents who took care of her finances and kept money in her account. There was a glimmer of understanding now about Lena's occasional sarcastic comments. Neave had never had to worry about money. Her account was always funded. She bought whatever she wanted. And apparently, so did her parents.

The irritation was like a spring sandstorm when grains of sand got in your ears, your nose and between your teeth.

Instead of choosing something sophisticated, she rummaged through her drawers until she found what she was looking for: the blue T-shirt with a picture of Niagara Falls that made the water look like it was actually moving. She'd bought it on a lark while visiting the falls with her Geological Studies Summer Camp group when she was fifteen. And she found the short denim skirt her friend J'nai had given her when she was thirteen. They were both tight and tacky. She added red flip flops and the ladybug earrings Rosa had given her when she was eight. No cooling cloak tonight. A little sweat would complete the look.

Chapter 10

She knew she'd achieved her goal when she saw disapproval in her mother and father's eyes as she approached the table. Nat was seated with them and he jumped up to hold her chair.

The men wore fashionable silk shirts. Nat's was deep blue, her father's was grey. Her mother had on a full-length, three quarter sleeve dress in several shades of green. Not a designer dress, but expensive enough.

The dining room had a Spanish feel to it, although she had to admit she'd never been to Spain. So it was probably what Americans expected a Spanish restaurant to look like. Lovely faux stone arches, touches of ornate wrought iron, cream-colored fake stucco walls and thick, royal blue carpet with a geometric crimson pattern. The walls were decorated with reproductions of Picasso, Goya and el Greco – in elaborate golden frames. Of course, the outside wall was all glass to allow an unimpeded view of the skyline as the building rotated. A bit like getting your world view by heading to Denver to visit Disneyworld, she thought.

"You didn't tell me Nat was coming," she said, aiming for a light, breezy tone as she took her seat on Nat's left.

"We thought we'd surprise you," her father said conspiratorially, looking from Neave to Nat to his wife.

Her mother's smile was not a Duchenne smile – there was certainly no smile in her eyes, which looked more nervous than anything.

"Doesn't Stone Mountain look lovely this evening," Dr. Sullivan said, pointing toward the window.

And it was true. The setting sun cast an orange glow over the giant granite boulder in the distance. Neave had climbed it twice on winter outings with school groups and several times with Rosa. As a child she always imagined she was a pioneer walking up that mountain. It was like she was in the middle of the wilderness hiking up the back side of the mountain, until she got to the rock covered with wads of bubblegum and graffiti – Tamara loves Peabo, Graciela ama Luke.

"Beautiful," said Nat, but he was looking at Neave, not the mountain.

"I registered for my classes today," she announced.

"Excellent, sweetheart," her father said.

"I also signed up for a class in genetics. Thought it might broaden my horizons a bit, maybe help me understand your work, Mother."

She thought her mother would be pleased but that's not what her expression suggested.

"I've taken a couple of genetics classes myself," said Nat. "We've already got the capability to track people down using a sample of their DNA. Pick up a piece of trash along the road, test it for traces of DNA, and find the littering culprit and send him to jail. Wonder how long it'll be till we can find people by satellite, using their DNA."

He beamed like he was proud of himself.

"God, that's so 'big brother,'" said Neave. "Of course, big brother's already here. They don't need your DNA to keep track of you. Every time you use your iCom to pay for your morning coffee or rent a scooter, they've got a real-time trail of where you are and what you're doing. Ditto, every time you send a message or talk on the phone."

"Or," said Nat, "buy tickets to a Broadway musical."

She looked up, expecting his eyes to be on her but found instead that he was pumping his eyebrows in a boastful sort of way at her father who nodded approvingly, a hint of a grin around his mouth.

"It's enough to make you want to use cash," Dr. Alvarez said, chuckling. He rubbed one finger over his mustache as though he were combing it into place.

Neave was impatient for the purpose of the dinner to be revealed. Her parents didn't just invite her out for no particular reason. But the dinner passed with a lot of small talk.

"How are the frogs?" Dr. Alvarez inquired of Nat with a good deal of animation.

"They're almost full-grown," Nat said.

"Frogs?" her mother asked.

"Oh, I brought Nat some frogs from a save-the-frogs project in Colombia on my South American trip a few weeks ago," said Dr. Alvarez. "As you know, many kinds of frogs have become extinct over the last century. So these frogs are rare, indeed. They're actually poison dart frogs."

"I set up this fantastic terrarium," said Nat. "They're a stunning golden color. I'd love to show you sometime."

And he looked straight at Neave.

They had what the menu described as Valencian Paella – a seafood and rice dish seasoned with saffron. And when the waiter offered dessert she was surprised her father agreed enthusiastically, ordering slices of chocolate almond cake for everyone and a bottle of Cava champagne, which made her think he might announce he'd finagled the support of some important senator to put a lock on his Senate confirmation. She might be a little naïve, but she knew that Cava was fine stuff.

Dr. Alvarez turned to Nat who grinned in reply, pulling something from his pocket. The hairs prickled on the back of her neck as she eyed the little burgundy box he set on the table beside her glass. Her mother cemented another fake smile on her face as her father held his champagne glass by the stem, rolling it one way and then the other, the corners of his mouth twitching.

Nat turned to her then and swallowed before speaking.

"This is for you."

He slid the box towards her and laced his fingers together on the table, glancing from her to Dr. Alvarez and then back again.

She took a deep breath and looked at each one of them in turn, wondering if her parents really thought she might be in love with Nat. It's possible he'd led them to believe that. And being the kind of parents who didn't naturally communicate with their own child, they wouldn't have thought to ask her about it, as ridiculous as that sounded.

Her father cleared his throat and swirled his champagne. Her mother sat stock still.

Nat reached over and slid the box closer so that it sat right next to her chocolate cake.

She shouldn't have come. She should've followed her instincts. She wished she were anywhere but here. Her life felt wrong. These people felt wrong. She felt like a pawn in a chess game whose fate was unimportant as long as it served the king.

Nat couldn't wait any longer, reaching over and opening

the box himself, revealing a sparkling diamond ring.

"To the perfect couple," her father said, holding his glass aloft.

Nat lifted his glass as well.

"We're not the perfect couple!" Neave cried. "We're not even the imperfect couple. You wanna know why? Because we're not a couple!"

She pushed her chair back and stood up, shaking her head from side to side.

"This is so surreal," she said, and then walked briskly towards the elevator, ignoring Nat as he called her name.

As luck would have it, two couples had just emerged from the elevator and she slipped through the doors as they closed again. Nat had waited a few seconds, staring at his mentor, before dashing after her, but he wasn't quick enough and she made her escape. It was an express elevator and took only a moment to descend to the lobby.

Of course, her iCom was buzzing before she reached the corner. She turned it off so she could have some peace. Why Nat would surprise her with an engagement ring while having dinner with her parents was beyond comprehension. It was like he'd been watching too many twentieth century movies, only she didn't think he ever watched movies. So it had to be her father. Engagement rings were so passé. Neave didn't know any young women who wore diamond rings. They wore other kinds of rings, but not diamonds and not engagement rings. Nat must've been led to believe she would be impressed. She couldn't think of any other explanation.

But there was also the question of why on earth he would presume to ask her to marry him in the first place. They had dated one time and that was only by entrapment. And he knew it.

This jumble of thoughts was still bouncing around inside her head as she kicked her flip flops off in her bedroom, dropping her purse on her bed. But before she could yank her tacky outfit off, she was startled to hear her front door open.

"Neave, it's me, sweetheart."

Her father had never used his code to enter her apartment. She'd given it to her parents when she first moved in after she left home. It was an effort to make them feel comfortable about her living on her own when she started college. How stupid of her not to have changed the code!

But it wasn't Dr. Alvarez she found gazing out her living room window at the skyline. It was Nat.

"What are you doing here? And where's Father?"

"He let me in. Hope you don't mind."

"I do mind."

Her only question at the moment was who to be more angry with – Nat or her father.

"I've gotta talk to you, Neave."

"Talking might've been a good idea *before* you bought a diamond ring!"

She hurried to the door and opened it, gesturing with her head for him to leave.

"You're right. I'm socially inept," he said, refusing to budge. "I should've realized your father's a little behind the times, I guess. He thought it would be a romantic gesture, you know. But you have to admit you're an old-fashioned girl."

Neave grunted under her breath in exasperation.

"Lena told me you've never..."

"Just go, please."

"Five minutes. Give me five minutes."

So she crossed her arms and waited, leaving the door wide open.

"Okay, here's the deal," he said, pausing to clear his throat. "Your father's right – we *are* a perfect match."

"That's proof you don't know me at all and you sure as hell shouldn't be asking me to marry you!" she said, jabbing the air with her finger.

"What's proof?"

"Why do you keep bringing up my father? I don't want to hear what my father thinks! My father has nothing to do with..."

"Well, I know, but..."

"But nothing! That's all you ever talk about!"

And then it came to her – the look on his face at dinner, that look of admiration and affection on his face. It wasn't for her. It was for her father. And when they were at the White House and afterwards, it wasn't her he was trying to impress. It was her father.

"Jesus, Nat. It's you and the eminent Robert Alvarez who are the perfect match."

She pointed angrily at the open door. Mrs. Salinas, who lived down the hall, walked by on her way to the elevator, staring at them as she passed.

"Can we close the door for one minute, please?" he said.

"No need. You're leaving."

But, instead of walking out, he slammed the door and stepped close, his jaw clenched, his eyes on fire.

"You're being irrational, Neave," he said, grabbing her arms.

"Let me go."

His grip tightened.

"You're going to listen to me."

"You're hurting me!"

"You need to stop pushing me away. I've been very patient.

I thought an engagement ring was what you wanted. You know – commitment first, having sex second. So I'm prepared to tie the knot. God, your skin feels so…," he said, caressing her arms.

He covered her mouth with his, pulling her tightly against him. His tongue was thrashing in her mouth, so that she tasted onions and garlic. She felt his hard-on too and pushed his shoulders in a futile effort to get him off of her. Finally, he pulled his mouth from hers.

"Let me go this instant!" she screamed in his ear. "I'm sure my father didn't suggest you rape me!"

He released her then, the veins in his neck bulging, his hands balled into fists.

"I want you so bad. Can't you understand that?"

"I said no! Can't you understand *that*? Now, if you don't go, I'll call security."

He stared at her for a second as though he might actually force himself on her, then wiped his hand across his mouth and stalked out the door.

Chapter 11

A bouquet of flowers arrived an hour later with a card that said "Please forgive me." It was a stunning Japanese Ikebana arrangement that must've cost a week's salary. Neave gave it away to Mrs. Salinas.

And then her mother called, leaving a voice message that she and her father were on their way over. Which was more than Neave could bear so she threw on her navy climate suit and skedaddled.

She snuck out the back way and headed north on Crescent till she dead-ended on 14th Street. She turned right and crossed Peachtree, realizing she was in the heart of the theater district when her eyes were drawn to The Piedmont Playhouse marquee.

High Water was playing. She'd seen a review that included glowing praise for the lead actress – Neave's childhood friend, J'nai Walker, whose image was on the view screen out front. It was past show time but, on impulse, she entered the front door and asked if she could still see the show. They had seats available and let her in during a scene change.

She was deeply impressed. J'nai was a consummate actress – perfect in this Tennessee Williamesque play about a dysfunctional family. When she cried in the last scene, Neave cried with her. And when the curtain came down she stood and applauded.

Afterwards, she slipped backstage. Waiting by the dressing rooms, she studied images of past performances that flashed across a view screen. It amazed her how different J'nai looked in each of the shows. She looked young. She looked old. She looked beautiful. She looked ugly. She looked big. She looked small. She'd done what she set out to do. She'd become an actress.

Neave's heart still ached when she thought about how their friendship had come to a screeching halt when J'nai transferred to the Atlanta School of the Arts when they were thirteen. Her father told her at breakfast one morning she could no longer be friends with J'nai. He said she needed to focus on her science studies. Her mother had raised her eyebrow but said nothing. How many times had Neave seen that eyebrow raised? Her mother had raised that eyebrow when her father insisted Neave quit dance classes when she started at the Science Academy, saying she would have no time for dance. She'd raised that eyebrow when her father made her skip Iceberg's only Atlanta concert when she was sixteen, insisting she join him for a lecture on the increasing rate of permafrost melting. But the eyebrow was the only thing Dr. Sullivan ever raised to her husband.

When J'nai came out and saw her waiting, she hugged Neave close, squealing happily.

"Neave! Oh my God!"

"J'nai, you were awesome!"

She stood back and gave Neave the once over.

"You look fabulous, hermana," she said. "How've you been?"

"Great. Super. And you – you're a real actress! I cried in the last scene, you were so good."

"Thanks, thanks."

And then J'nai looked around as though she was searching for someone else.

"Are you alone?" she said.

"Yeah, just me."

Neave started to tell her she was just walking by, escaping from her parents, but decided not to go into all of that. "I just had to come and see your play!" She giggled like she was thirteen again. "You have time for a drink or maybe some coffee?"

"Actually, I've got a date," J'nai said, glancing at her iCom. "But I've still got a few minutes."

She invited her into the dressing room, sitting in front of the makeup table and motioning for Neave to sit in a chair across from her. The room was small and cluttered, with costumes tossed willy-nilly on an old sofa.

"Oh, J'nai, it's so exciting to see you on stage."

"Well, I'm earning peanuts, but I'm getting some good parts and having a blast. I'm going to NY2 next week. I've got an audition for a Broadway play. Actually, it's for an understudy, but still, it's Broadway. Wish me luck."

She dazzled Neave with her smile. She'd blossomed into a beautiful young woman with flawless brown skin and sparkling, brown eyes that made Neave realize how happy her old friend was. She wore her hair in an ultra-short Afro that somehow made beautiful black women look even more striking.

"How can they not choose you!" Neave gushed.

"Yeah, right! So, where's your fiancé? I thought I'd get to meet him."

"My fiancé?"

"Matt, right? He seemed so nice on the phone."

"On the phone?"

"Didn't he tell you? He called me a few weeks ago, out of the blue, and said your dad had given him my name. He wanted some ideas for a really special surprise gift for you. Said your dad told him you and I were best friends when we were younger and he thought I might have some idea of something you'd always dreamed of doing. Which I thought was so neat, you know – so romantic. So I told him you used to dream of performing on Broadway, that you were an aspiring actress back then. And I told him unless you'd changed a lot, you might be totally thrilled if he took you to see *Mandarin Daughter*. And he thanked me and said he looked forward to meeting me in person. And when you showed up tonight, I figured he was with you."

If J'nai had really been looking closely at her old friend, she would've noticed her stiffen, but she was glancing at the door, waiting for her boyfriend.

"So when are you guys getting married?" she asked.

Neave sighed and looked at her hands clasped in her lap.

"Well..."

"And how was the show? I haven't seen it yet, but I'm dying to."

"The best musical I've ever seen."

"I knew it! I knew it! I can't wait!"

She looked at Neave and took a deep breath.

"So, you're a scientist now?" she asked.

Neave sighed without meaning to.

"Not yet."

"If you don't mind my saying so, I never thought you were very excited about it. And you still don't seem like you're exactly thrilled."

"Well, you know..."

"That's one good thing about having working class parents," J'nai said. "They're happy as long as you graduate and start paying your own rent."

They both laughed, but it was bittersweet for Neave. J'nai was right. The Walkers had no expectations for her except that she do something she liked and do it well enough to support herself. What a gift.

If she'd been angry before, she was livid now. Any guilt she'd felt about possibly leading Nat on had evaporated. He didn't give a damn about theater. It was a ruse to make her think they had something in common. And he lied to her old friend, pumping her for information. As she walked along Peachtree she wiped sweat from her face, despite her cooling suit. She was walking too fast and tried to slow down. But she wanted to yell at someone – at Nat, her father, maybe even her mother. She wanted to tell them all to butt out of her life, that she didn't have any intention of ever marrying Nat Patel. If he wanted to be close to her father, fine! But there would be no marriage between the Patel and Alvarez families. She tapped her iCom, on the verge of sending him a nasty message, but thought better of it.

She was too angry to go home where she knew she'd burn a hole in the living room rug pacing back and forth. And she didn't want anyone to find her. So she just walked, not really caring where she went. By accident or subconscious design – she wasn't sure which – she ended up on Professors Row where she'd parted company with Yong Li the night before. The street was empty and quiet, except for the chorus of insects serenading her. She strolled slowly, gazing at the tidy homes. On the corner, there was a wooden bench under a sun awning. She allowed herself to sit, fatigue weighing her down.

Shaded from the light of the antique streetlamp, she finally

93

relaxed, breathing deeply. After several minutes, a little creature darted across the street. Then a bird called and another answered. She'd been sitting still long enough that they'd forgotten she was there.

She kept thinking about J'nai – about her success, her happiness, her ambition. Which caused her to slump further on the bench.

The sound of a vehicle approaching interrupted her reverie. The small car turned onto the street from behind her and pulled into the driveway of the second house on the left. She watched as a man and a woman emerged. A front porch light came on as they headed up the walkway to the door. It was Yong Li and Judge Mercado – Dr. Osley's widow.

She was on her feet and trotting towards them before she had time to figure out what she would say. She reached the front walkway just as the judge touched the keypad to unlock the door. Yong turned around, alarmed.

"Miss Alvarez," he said.

"Dr. Yong, Judge Mercado."

Osley's wife nodded, but didn't speak. She was dressed in a well-tailored black pantsuit and white blouse and wore a regal expression, her head tilted back so that she looked down her nose at Neave.

"Miss…" Yong began, but Neave cut him off, addressing herself to Judge Mercado.

"I'm Neave Alvarez, daughter of Robert Alvarez. I'm so terribly sorry about your husband. I was on the expedition to the coast with him, but I wasn't on the helicopter when…" She paused for a second to regain her composure, but then hurried on, trying to avoid the expected brush-off. "I heard him say while we were there that he knew the real reason my father wants a shade ring. And I'm trying to find out what he meant."

Even in the dim porch light, the pleading, earnest tone in her voice was also visible on her face.

"Judge Mercado has worked many hours," Yong said, stepping forward slightly as if to block her path.

"It's all right, Li," the judge said. "I can spare a few minutes. Let's go inside where it's cooler."

The living room was a well-appointed jumble of rich brown wood tones and bright colors – a commingling of African and South American art. Several African drums sat on the floor, two colorful Bolivian rugs hung on one wall and there was a striking painting of a very dark African woman and a baby, both swathed in flowing white, on another wall.

The judge sat in a brown leather arm chair next to a lamp that cast a warm glow over the room. She motioned for Neave to sit on the sofa.

"So," Judge Mercado said, steepling her hands in front of her as though she were hearing a court case. "Tell me why you were sitting outside my house at midnight."

Neave sighed and pushed her hair behind her ear, feeling rather like she'd been accused of a crime.

"I..." she said, then closed her eyes tight for a moment. "I have an uneasy feeling," she finally said.

"About?"

"Well, I know scientists lobby hard to fund their programs. They have to if they believe in their research. And, of course, their own jobs are at stake. I understand that. And I know competing for funding can make for some pretty strong rivalries. I would guess your husband had to fight for funding sometimes."

She looked from Judge Mercado to Yong but their expressions were unreadable.

"But I'm beginning to wonder if my father might have...

95

whether my father's motivation…" She shook her head slightly, searching for the right words. "Did your husband ever…"

"Miss Alvarez, I assume this is important to you, otherwise you wouldn't be here. But I really don't have any information to share with you. Terrance did tell me he felt duped into going on that expedition. He said your father's assistant encouraged him. I know he suspected your father was doing more than pushing his pet program. But he didn't share specifics with me that I can recall."

She stood then as though the audience she'd granted Neave was over. Yong rose too and started towards the door. Neave got to her feet and crossed the room to Judge Mercado, holding out her hand.

"Thank you for your time. I'm very sorry about your husband."

She accepted Neave's hand. The judge's eyes were so dark, they looked almost black in the living room light. They were intelligent, kind eyes, Neave thought. She imagined Adela Mercado was a fair jurist.

"Miss Alvarez, do you think my husband's death was not an accident?"

"It had to be an accident," Neave said. "Lena would never have… I mean, it had to be an accident."

There was an unspoken "but" that hung in the air like an alarm pheromone secreted by ants to warn the colony of danger. Neave tried to unknot her brows, but they'd been furrowed for so long now, she figured they stayed that way even when she slept.

The judge moved to the table and retrieved her iCom from her purse. Without a word, she slid her finger over the screen and held it out in front of her.

It was a message Dr. Osley had left his wife while he was in the helicopter. He was speaking loudly over the roar of the engine in the background.

"Hi honey. I'll be home in time for supper. I'll be glad to get out of this pile of junk I'm..."

Then there was a loud sound.

"Dammit!"

And then the message was over.

Neave stared at the iCom, stunned at hearing Dr. Osley's voice again, recorded right before his death.

"I shared this with the investigators but it's not overly revealing," the judge said. "And now, I must bid you goodnight."

Neave nodded and followed Yong onto the front porch.

"I am sorry, Miss Alvarez," he said, closing the door behind them.

But his eyes seemed to say more, she thought. They were warm and apologetic, as though he really wished he could help her.

"I wish you would call me Neave."

Which made him smile. It was the first one she'd seen on his face. She had begun to wonder whether the anterior cingulate and basal ganglia regions of a clone's brain were the same as other people's, since those were the regions that created true smiles. And whether clones could have a sense of humor or warmth.

"I also invite you to use my personal name – Li."

"Miss Alvarez!" It was Judge Mercado standing in the doorway. "You might do some research about Chang NanoTec. I did hear Terrance make reference to it once in connection with your father." She tightened her lips, turned and disappeared into the house.

Chapter 12

She dragged herself out of bed the next morning after troubled sleep, which was the norm lately. She padded into the kitchen in her rumpled pajamas, fixed herself a cup of coffee, lightened it, sweetened it and took it with her to the desk in the living room, where she plopped down and clicked her iCom to check for messages. She was sipping her coffee and nearly dropped her cup when she saw "TSUNAMI" in all caps in the subject line of a news update. She immediately went to a news web and transmitted the broadcast to her view screen.

She recognized the name of the volcano right away. She'd studied Cumbre Vieja in her Volcanology class. Scientists had been predicting for decades that the volcano in the Canary Islands off the northwest coast of Africa could erupt, sending a huge chunk of the western face plunging into the ocean. There'd been rumblings for years. And now it appeared the worst-case scenario had come true. When the landslide slammed into the ocean, it caused tsunamis that fanned out in all directions. She had to blink her eyes repeatedly to see the screen as she clicked on the news site for details.

To the east, a mega tsunami was already bearing down on the African coast. To the west, a tsunami was racing across the Atlantic at the speed of a jetliner. It would strike U.S. soil in a matter of hours.

She clicked on the U.S. Climatology website. They reported the first wave about to crash ashore at Morocco was over a hundred feet high. She covered her mouth with her hand. She didn't know if her heart actually skipped a beat, but there was an odd sensation in her chest. She'd read about such monster waves but the images of tsunamis she'd seen had been of smaller waves – thirty to fifty feet. Of course, those waves were huge, but the towering tsunami about to slam into Morocco would inundate land for miles and miles inland. And unlike much of the U.S. coast, which was now largely abandoned, the Moroccan coast was home to millions, including residents of Casablanca. A frenzied evacuation was underway but there would, no doubt, be substantial loss of life.

An update on the Web Network said the tsunami heading west across the Atlantic would only be a fraction of the size of the Moroccan wave – about forty feet by the time it reached the coast of Georgia and the Carolinas.

"Oh my God," she whispered.

She thought of Will. He was probably doing a demolition job on a submerged city. He would know all about it, of course. He would already be evacuating, probably moving his equipment to higher ground, assuming he knew. Which, of course, he would. Everyone knew about it by now, didn't they?

She scanned her iCom, found the code for Galloway Demolition and called his number, but got a recording saying his communications were down temporarily due to damage from Hurricane Kelly. She felt weak as she left a voice message. She felt weaker still after texting him and getting no reply.

In frustration she slammed her fist on the table, knocking her cup of coffee over. The hot liquid spilled across the laser keyboard on the white desk, so that half the letters were brown.

"Dammit!"

What if he didn't know, she thought, getting a wet cloth from the kitchen and wiping the desk. Surely, he knew. She was getting bent out of shape for nothing. And why should she freak out? He had friends, relatives, co-workers – lots of people to look out for him.

She called Lena, who gave her Macho's iCom code. If he was with Will, he couldn't get calls either, but she tried anyway and was relieved momentarily when she got an answer. He said Will had started a new job at Savannah. But Macho said he didn't want to work at Savannah, that it was too dangerous, so he was working a construction job in Atlanta and didn't know who was working with Will. Her heart sank.

"Why's Savannah too dangerous?"

"Well, it's the lay of the land," he said. "The old downtown area is kind of like a little peninsula, you know, surrounded on three sides. So I told him 'sorry, man.'"

He kept saying Will would know what was happening. No reason to worry. But what if he didn't know and everyone just assumed he did?

There had been three tsunamis she could remember during her lifetime. One along the Pacific Northwest coast, one that struck Chile and one in Japan. They had become more commonplace as temperatures rose. The recent tsunamis had caused relatively few deaths and officials bragged about how well the tsunami warning system worked. But, of course, that system relied on communication. And if

Will's communications were down and he was working on the coast... she closed her eyes and rubbed her temples.

She spent twenty minutes calling FEMA and the state emergency management office. They both said every effort was being made to contact anyone along the coast, but since the coast had been evacuated, they didn't seem to think there was any real emergency. She explained about the demolition company working at Savannah. But they tried to reassure her that anyone working along the coast would be keeping up with weather reports and would have plenty of advance notice. It was during her conversation with a Georgia official that she lost her temper.

"People's lives are at stake!" she shouted. "You've got to find them!"

Which just made the woman on the other end use an even more patronizing tone so that Neave hung up, completely exasperated.

She paced frantically around the living room. She couldn't just leave his fate up to luck and a bunch of complacent bureaucrats! If she had to, she would fly to the coast herself.

~~~

Nat was solicitude incarnate when she found him in the lobby of the Climatology building. It was nearly noon and hot as hell outside. Her blue climate suit wasn't doing its job very well so she wiped perspiration from her upper lip and fanned herself with her hands as he led the way to an elevator. They got off on the fourth floor and she followed him into an empty classroom.

"What're we here for?" she asked.

"To talk."

He sat on the instructor's desk at the front of the room and folded his arms across his chest.

"Nat…"

"I know, I know, you're in a hurry. No time to lose."

She sighed and waited.

"Why should I help you get a heli-scooter? You treat me like I'm a twentieth century untouchable."

She looked down at the floor and sighed again.

"This is one helluva hair-brained idea that you, and you alone, should save their lives. What if you crash into the ocean? What if you can't find them? What if…"

"Please, Nat."

He screwed his mouth up as he stared at her, then closed his eyes and shook his head slightly. Finally, he stood and crossed the room to look out the window.

"You're not asking your parents to sign for you because they'll say no. So you come crawling to me because you know I have the insurance and…"

"I can't just let them die."

"I'm sure they've already evacuated."

"We don't know that."

He turned towards her then.

"I already feel responsible for letting Lena fly the chopper to Charleston. Now you're asking me to let another inexperienced…"

"It's not a helicopter. It's just a heli-scooter and I've had plenty of experience."

"And there's another issue," he said, walking towards her, "I heard rumors about Mr. Galloway, so I did some research – trying to figure out whether it was worth risking your neck to save his ass. And I discovered something you need to know. William S. Galloway is listed as a board member of Clone-Aid. You've heard of Clone-Aid, right?"

He closed the distance between them and looked down

into her face.

"Clone-Aid," he said, "is a group that monitors cloning. They keep tabs on scientists and 'out' them if they clone humans. And they help clones find jobs and advocate for clone rights. Interesting, huh?"

Which might explain Will's behavior at Charleston, she thought.

"And then I checked further," he went on. "And guess what. You're gonna love this: all the board members of Clone-Aid are fucking clones!"

He stabbed the air for emphasis.

"I don't believe that," she said. "You're making that up."

She remembered how Will's eyes looked when they were twirling around the room, doing the waltz. No way he was a clone. No way.

"Don't believe me?" he said. "Dig around for yourself."

She sat down in a desk, suddenly feeling weak.

"And, who knows," he said, "maybe his workers are clones too."

There was a crowing quality to his voice as though he'd won a bet about some obscure scientific fact.

She crossed her hands in her lap and lowered her head. Her eyes were unfocused and her brain was in neutral, not thinking, not feeling, just existing for a moment. Could it be true? Was it possible?

She'd always thought of clones as copies. Flawed copies. And although she had defended Yong Li to her friends, she'd done so more on principle than on personal conviction about his value as a human being. It was easy to be principled in the abstract.

"You still want to risk your life to save a bunch of clones?" he said.

His tone now was sneering, condescending. Which pissed her off and woke her from her momentary stupor.

"Clones or not, they're people," she said.

"Not *real* people."

She stood up to face him.

"They're as real as you and me," she said. "And I can't take the chance that they might be washed away. So I'm asking you to sign for a heli-scooter. But if you won't, I'll find another way."

She looked at her iCom, knowing full well that Nat was her last hope, short of stealing one. And although she'd never stolen anything in her life, there was always a first time.

"Okay, what if I agree to help you?" he said. "What's in it for me? I mean, I've already helped you out – let's see – how many times is it now? Not that I'm counting, of course. I got you a spot on the coastal field expedition when the trip was already full. I took you to see that Broadway show, which cost me a bundle and got precious little thanks in return. Now this. For which I could get into serious trouble. So, I want to make sure you understand that if I do this humongous favor for you, then you'll owe *me* a favor. A very sizable favor."

His look was a little unnerving.

She opened her mouth, but nothing came out. She tried to recall Will's face, his eyes, the sound of his voice. Was there anything about him that should've tipped her off? She always imagined clones would be obvious – that there would be something different about them, something less human about them. When she'd heard Yong Li speak at the university, she'd known ahead of time. And she was keenly aware that he sounded like his clone antecedent whose voice she'd heard on the web in her climatology classes. They didn't look identical, but she'd only seen Dr. Zhang as an old man and Yong Li as a young man. But she had thought during his presentation he seemed distant and unemotional. Clonish, she thought. Her impression was that he had the mind and body of Dr. Zhang, but not his soul. That he might, in fact, be soulless, like everyone said. But she'd finally seen a glimmer of friendliness the night before when he asked her to call him Li.

But what about Will? When he'd given her that cold look after he found out who her parents were, it was definitely an emotional scowl – hot with anger. And she'd seen the glint in his eye when he was dancing with her. It was far from a detached, unemotional look. And when he'd kissed her – well, she knew he was very human indeed.

Still, she was stunned. She found it hard to believe she could fall for a clone. The rational and emotional parts of her brain were operating on different planes. Of course, he was a real man, no matter how he was conceived.

And that might explain why he had such a visceral reaction when he learned who her mother was. If he thought she was a cloner, he might view her as the enemy. Which was illogical, in a way, since it would take a cloner to create a clone. God, she couldn't think!

But she could definitely feel the terror in her gut that the only man who'd ever vibrated her molecules might be killed by a tsunami. She remembered the tingle she'd felt when his hand rested on her waist as he guided her around the floor. She remembered the kiss.

"You owe me, Neave," Nat said. "And make no mistake – I plan to collect on that debt."

Chapter 13

She was sitting in the cockpit of a heli-scooter, eyeing a wind sock hanging limp in front of her, thank goodness. Her flight plan was entered in the onboard computer. Her destination was listed as Statesboro, Georgia.

She put on her headphones, flipped the switch and powered up. When she got the okay, she throttled up and veered immediately towards the southeast, settling into her designated altitude of five hundred feet. Her iCom started buzzing before she was even in the air, but she wasn't about to answer. She knew it was Nat. She just hoped he would keep his mouth shut, at least for a while.

It was at that moment that a gust of wind took her by surprise. The scooter dipped and she tightened her grip on the handlebars. So much for the limp windsock. Despite her climate suit and the cooling bubble, she could feel beads of sweat on her upper lip and a trickle of perspiration between her breasts. Occasional wind gusts buffeted the scooter as she whizzed over the rust-colored landscape, which scared her more than she wanted to admit.

The bumpy ride, coupled with a mental picture of Will being swept away, made her queasy. Nothing she did could banish the image of him sitting in the cab of one of his big yellow deconstructors as the tsunami thundered ashore. She'd seen images of past tsunamis and the destruction they left behind. She pictured how he and the others would be washed inland, then sucked back out to sea, to drown or be killed by debris. For a moment, she thought she was going to throw up. She wished she could take a sip of water but was afraid to let go of the handlebars, even for a second, afraid the wind would take control. She focused on the horizon, which finally helped ease the nausea, if not the terror.

"It's a good thing I'm driving," she said to herself.

She figured it would be worse if someone else were piloting the heli-scooter, like Lena, who insisted on flying to the coast for their ill-fated science expedition, eager to accrue flying time. But Neave didn't want to think about Dr. Osley's death right now. It made the danger of this wild ride much too real. And she needed all the courage she could muster. She had no choice, no matter how scared she was. There was no doubt in her mind, or in her heart, that she had to try. Even if she'd only imagined Will cared for her that night, she couldn't leave his survival up to chance. If she did nothing and he died, she'd never be able to live with herself. It was as simple as that.

Still, she realized she was uneasy about him being a clone. Clones had been so abstract to her before. Could she really have feelings for a clone? She was ashamed that this bothered her, but it did. She liked to think she was not a bigot, but she'd grown up hearing the word "clone" used as a slur and maybe it sank in on a sub-conscious level.

Once she passed Statesboro she used her iCom to track her position as she headed to Savannah. A large part of the city was already submerged and had undergone demolition off and on as the sea rose. Macho had given her more specifics on where Will's job site was, but the closer she got, the more nervous she became.

She didn't know how many people were at the site and it finally dawned on her that this heli-scooter wasn't exactly a good choice for a rescue. It had a 500 pound limit and since she weighed 120, that meant she could carry another 380 pounds. But, of course, it was only a two-seater.

"God..." she whispered.

What if she couldn't see him when she got there? What if he was driving his truck? What if the wave arrived before she did? She squeezed her eyes shut for a second to clear her vision. There were too many questions she didn't have answers to.

She jumped when a voice came over the headset.

"Atlanta to Heli Six."

"Six here," she responded.

"Ms. Alvarez, you have exceeded your destination."

"Uh..."

"Because of the coastal emergency, you're ordered to turn back."

"Understood."

But she flew on.

The calm voice came through her headphones again a few moments later: "Atlanta to Heli Six."

She could see a river below her and knew she was getting close. She zoomed the map screen so she could see the features more clearly.

"Atlanta to Heli Six. Come in, please."

She yanked the headphones off and let them fall to the floor.

Finally, in the distance she could see the ocean, causing her to shiver.

She gradually reduced her altitude to two hundred feet so the trees zoomed past just below her, making her dizzy if she looked down for more than a second. So she kept her eyes straight ahead, looking for the downtown area. Within moments, she spotted the buildings of Savannah, surrounded by water as the ocean and the Savannah River came together so you couldn't tell where one started and the other ended.

The water appeared normal when she glanced towards the ocean, but her heart was pounding nevertheless. Her head was pounding too and her hands ached from holding tight to the handlebars.

Her eyes burned from straining to pick out deconstructors in the ruined cityscape. And then she noticed something that made her skin crawl. The water was receding along the edge of the city, like it does just before a new wave comes in. But this drop in water level was much greater. Panic welled up inside her chest as she looked out to sea. In the distance she thought she saw the giant wave. But she wasn't sure, it was hard to tell as tears welled up in her eyes. She blinked hard several times. She had to stay focused. She had to use her eyes, dammit!

She kept scanning as she zigzagged over the buildings. The water drew down further. She didn't want to look but had to. And when she glanced at the ocean, there was no mistaking it this time. She could see the wave off in the distance, out at sea – a wall of water. It was impossible to gauge how high it was, not having any point of reference.

Her muscles knotted up.

"Where the hell are you?"

What if she couldn't find him? What if he wasn't even here? What if he'd been warned and had evacuated? Maybe he was safe in a hotel room in Macon right now. Maybe she was scared witless for nothing.

The water continued to draw back, leaving more submerged streets and buildings exposed. She glanced instinctively towards the ocean. When she did, the hairs rose all over her body and her hands jerked on the controls, causing her to dip slightly. It was a terrifying sight – a giant wave bearing down on the coast. It suddenly occurred to her that she, herself, was in danger.

And that's when she saw it – a big yellow deconstructor sitting next to an abandoned hotel.

"Will!" she cried.

She throttled up a notch, picking up speed. She could feel the wave looming large on the horizon and knew she was running out of time. She throttled back when she was close enough to see that it was indeed one of Will's machines. And in that instant she questioned her sanity. If he was in the cab, how would she rescue him in this heli-scooter? There was no time to land and let him climb inside.

The tsunami was now visible as a giant swell that must've towered forty feet or more above the shore. She slowed as she approached the deconstruction site, staring hard at the cab atop the machine.

"Oh my God," she whispered.

There was a man inside it. The building and the machine stood about the length of a soccer field from the water. She used the emergency horn, which issued an ear-splitting shriek like that of a fire truck. The man stood up inside the cab and she hit the horn again. She was close enough to see him turn towards her and though she couldn't see his face, she knew it was him.

In another minute, the wall of water would be upon him. Time had run out. He took off his headphones and stepped from the cab, and when he did, he realized something was amiss. As she slowed for her final approach she could see him look towards the ocean. Then he turned towards her, though, of course, he couldn't know who it was. She was inside a dark tinted plastic bubble. But he did realize she was his only possible ticket to safety. He glanced from the heli-scooter to the ocean as she hovered closer and closer. The wave was perhaps sixty seconds from finishing the demolition job he'd begun as he scrambled on top of the cab and stood waiting for her to lower the heli-scooter within reach. He would have to grab the landing skids. That's all there would be time for. But she had to lower the craft slowly so she didn't hit him.

She'd only piloted solo about a dozen times. She'd certainly never done any precision flying before and there was the very real possibility she would knock him over, just in time for the wave to sweep him away. She was trying not to cry as she lowered the copter foot by foot.

She glanced at the ocean and realized the wave would hit within seconds. There was no more time for finesse. She would have to climb fast and high as soon as he grabbed hold and just pray he could hold on. And so she looked down below her and lowered the scooter as he raised his hands to grab the bar. She looked up again in time to see that the wave was so tall now, it was higher than the heli-scooter. She gasped as he leaped for the bar. The heli-scooter wobbled as his weight made the aircraft sink. She throttled up hard and fast.

The wave was chasing them as she strained at the controls, trying to lift the copter higher as she picked up speed. She was afraid to look down for fear she would see him fall to his death. She gained altitude as she pulled up on the handlebars while at the same time squeezing the accelerator. She could feel the monstrous wave behind her and braced herself to be swallowed up.

"Hold on, hold on!" she shouted.

Fifty five, sixty feet. She looked below her and saw water. God, it looked like his feet were covered by water! She strained upwards, her whole body pulling, trying to lift them higher. She was zooming when she reached an altitude of seventy feet. That should be high enough. But she kept climbing. She glanced below her and could still see water, but she could see his feet now.

She looked up again just in time to avoid slamming into the top branches of a pine tree.

"Agh!" she yelped, swerving to the right.

She slowed down a bit but maintained altitude. He just had to hold on. The water was still flowing inland beneath them. And she knew there could be second and third waves. When the last tsunami struck the U.S., the second wave had been the biggest.

Finally, the ground began to rise slightly as they left the downtown area behind. The water was flowing more slowly beneath them. But it was still moving inland. They were still in danger. Or, more specifically, Will was still in danger. If she didn't set down soon, he would tire and fall. She slowed down and reduced her altitude to twenty feet. The air scooter wobbled as though someone was jumping up and down on it. She had to find a place to set down, at least long enough for him to get inside.

A few hundred feet ahead she saw a small hill. It would have to do.

"Hang on!" she yelled, knowing he couldn't hear her above the roar of the rotors.

She slowed and then lowered the scooter until she was about ten feet from the ground. She was going to lower it a little more when the aircraft wobbled. She looked down and saw him drop to the ground. She throttled up, rising back into the air, then found a spot on the far side of the hill and set it down. The rotors were still turning as she jumped from the scooter, keeping her head low. She clambered up the grassy hill to find him lying flat on his back, eyes closed, his shirt in shreds.

"Will!" she cried, kneeling beside him.

He opened his eyes and stared at her, a dazed, confused look on his face.

"Neave?"

"Come on!" she blurted.

He groaned and sat up slowly.

"We've gotta get out of here," she said, helping him stand.

She took his hand in hers as they started down the hill, only to be stopped by water rushing around both sides. Dark, filthy water swamped the heli-scooter, turning it on its side, sending the still-spinning blades crashing into the ground. They covered their heads, retraced their steps up the hill and stood side by side, watching the water rise around them. Floating debris, including a chair, pieces of wood and concrete, made it look like a pyroclastic flow from a volcano.

"No, no, no!" she cried, trembling.

He wrapped his arms around her and she closed her eyes for a moment, leaning into him, listening as the water surged and hissed around them. When she opened them, the hill had turned into a tiny island only a couple of feet across. They were stranded.

Watching the water inch higher made her angry. She'd reached him. She'd saved him. They were together. Now the water was going to sweep them away?

"God, I'm sorry, Will. I set the scooter down too soon."

As dirty seawater covered their shoes they spread their feet to steady themselves and held tight to each other. She tried to think of something meaningful to say but there was too much to say and not enough time, so she just held on.

Chapter 14

"I think it's receding." Will's mouth was on her ear, his voice low.

Sure enough, she could feel the water level recede a tiny bit on her ankles. In another moment, it dipped below their feet and started slowly retreating on all sides of the mound.

"As soon as it's gone down enough, we've gotta make tracks," he said.

So they watched and waited until finally, the water was only a few inches deep on the inland side of the hill. Making their way past the wrecked heli-scooter was hard work now that the ground was mucked up with jellyfish, seaweed and the remains of human habitation. Chunks of concrete jutted from the soil at odd angles, along with shards of glass, metal rods, pieces of furniture, car parts, rocks, seashells and fish carcasses. They struggled towards higher ground, looking behind them constantly for another wave. At last, they'd put enough distance between them and the ocean that they could slow their pace.

"Was there anyone with you?" she finally asked, dreading the answer.

"I was working solo."

The knot in her stomach finally unraveled and she took a ragged breath, collapsing onto the cracked earth. Great sobs shook her. In an instant, he pulled her to her feet and put his arm around her waist, urging her onward.

"The ants will eat us alive if we don't keep moving," he said.

He was right, of course. The ground was crawling with them. So she ordered herself to save the tears for later.

They had no water with them and soon the heat drained them of any desire to speak. Just putting one foot in front of the other was challenge enough. The sun beat down on their heads and her climate suit had long since stopped working, though it was keeping her skin from burning in the harsh glare of the sun.

He said they weren't far from a cave he used for storage where they could rest and get water. But it didn't take long in 120 degree heat for her to tire, so when they came upon a small pine tree, she leaned against it for a moment in the sparse shade.

"Only a little farther," he said, his voice rasping from fatigue.

Some forty-five minutes later they reached a mound of large rocks with a hidden entrance behind some scrub bushes. She followed him into the cave, more exhausted than she'd ever been in her life.

Goose bumps rose on her sweaty skin as they descended into a cool passageway. A thin line of blue paintlight along the floor was the only source of light. Finally, they entered a large chamber, also dimly lit by blue stripes on the floor. It was filled with objects she couldn't make out. He crossed to the opposite wall and turned a switch that started a power generator. With the quiet hum came soft light from antique lamps scattered about the cave. They were standing in the midst of what amounted to a small warehouse. Furniture was crammed together along with shelves of books and other household objects. To the right was a large shed that must've been assembled inside the cave.

He held the door for her. Inside, it was a room just large enough for a bed, a small table and two chairs, a kitchen counter with a tiny stove and sink, and a bathroom that took up one corner of the room. The air was dry, unlike the dampness of the cave.

He poured them tall glasses of water from a jug, which they quickly drained. He refilled the glasses and set them on the small table and they collapsed in the chairs and drank the second glass more slowly.

She breathed deeply, trying to ease her pounding headache. And then, without warning, a violent sob escaped and she was crying and holding her hands over her face. All the tension, all the fear, all the emotions came pouring out. He pulled his chair beside hers and draped his arm around her shoulders and let her cry.

At length, he suggested she take a shower.

"It's rain water but it'll make you feel better," he said.

And he was right. Once she peeled her filthy climate suit off and showered, she felt like a human being again. She slathered herself with the soothing lotion on the counter, brushed her hair with a brush by the sink and cleaned her teeth with toothpaste and her finger. Having nothing else to put on, she slipped into the blue cotton robe hanging on a hook.

When she came out, she found him munching on crackers and peanut butter, despite a dirt-streaked face, a frayed shirt and the overwhelming stench of stale sweat mixed with the odor of dead fish.

"Your turn," she said.

He pushed the pack of crackers and jar of peanut butter across the table along with a knife.

"I'll swap you," he said, and disappeared into the bathroom.

She fixed herself a few crackers and ventured out into the cave, eating as she meandered through the cavern, surveying the varied inventory. Each item had a tag on it with a code. There were old computers, desks, kitchen and dining room chairs, tables, dressers and chests, coolers, lamps, bicycles, and quite a few boxes with labels like 'paintings,' and 'mystery novels.'

After a few minutes, she heard the door open and his footsteps behind her.

"Mystery novels?" she said, her back towards him.

"Yeah, I read 'em first and then sell 'em."

"You like mysteries?" she said, turning around.

He was a few feet away, a glass of wine in each hand. But it was his bare chest that drew her attention. Not because of its perfection, though there was that – it was the angry scratches that ran from his right shoulder, across his chest, nearly to his waist.

"You're hurt," she cried.

He turned around so she could see his back, which was scratched as well.

"Oh, Will!"

"It was that tree we flew through," he said, chuckling. "I thought you were trying to lose me there for a second."

She winced.

"God, I'm sorry. I was looking down, trying to see if you were okay and when I looked up..."

"Don't worry. We made it. Thanks to you."

His eyes were glistening. And the humming of the generator seemed to have gotten louder, or maybe it was her blood surging through her veins. Just looking at him made her want to wrap her arms around him. He was a real man, clone or not. She swallowed hard just thinking about how close she'd come to losing him.

"I seem to recall you like wine," he said, handing her a glass.

"Mm," she said, taking a sip.

"How'd you find me?" he asked. "And…why…"

He trailed off, as though he didn't know exactly what to say. But his gaze was intense. The question was much more than just how she found him and they both knew it. What he really meant was why she came, why she risked her life to save his.

"Well, it's a long story," she said, looking around the cave. She wasn't ready to reveal what she knew about him. She also wasn't ready to reveal how much she cared, because there was the distinct possibility that he didn't feel the same way. So she changed the subject. "What do you do with all this stuff?" she asked, nodding at the eclectic inventory.

"Sell it. I'm actually in business with my mom. She's got an e-biz that sells all kinds of things. I help provide the merchandise. She minds the store."

"She must really be something, your mother."

He nodded enthusiastically.

"I was wondering if you could put some antibiotic cream on my back. I managed the front," he said looking down at his chest.

~~~

He handed her the tube and turned his back to her, standing by the kitchen table. She squeezed some cream onto her fingers and was about to begin when he took a sudden breath.

"I'm not sure I can stand it," he said.

119

"Don't be a baby. I'll be gentle."

Her eyes were level with his shoulder blades and she could see quite clearly that his skin was rippled with gooseflesh. It was a handsome back that tapered to the waist. When she touched him, he shivered.

"Sorry," she whispered as she smeared the ointment ever so lightly across the long scratches that spread diagonally from his shoulder, across his back.

"I knew I couldn't stand it," he said, turning around and taking the tube from her. He set it on the table, all the while looking into her eyes.

He put his hands on her waist and pulled her to him, leaning down to kiss her. Her hands came to rest on his shoulders as she opened her mouth to him. He kissed her long and deeply and her head was swimming when he finally pulled back. He kissed her cheek and neck as he caressed her. And then his mouth was on hers again and every atom in her body wanted every atom in his body. Badly. She caressed his arms, not wanting to hurt his back.

"Neave," he whispered, his lips brushing her ear. "I want to make love to you."

She answered by rubbing her palms lightly across his chest, reveling in the feel and smell of him. There was the scent of mild soap and something very male. Then he untied the belt on her robe and pushed it from her shoulders, letting it fall to the floor. His warm hands stroked her skin. Her breathing slowed as he brought his hands to her breasts, pressing his thumbs softly into her nipples and kissing her lips again. Then he took her hand and led her to the bed. He slipped his pants off as he sat down, drawing her close so that she stood between his legs. He kissed her breasts, first one, then the other, and rubbed his face over them before pulling her down with him.

She opened herself completely and lost herself in the spaces where their bodies met. The sweetness of his lips, the saltiness of his skin, the passion in his eyes. Then as he pressed more deeply into her, there was a look of surprise on his face. She rubbed her hands over his body, thrilling at the feel of him, so solid beneath her fingers. A dizziness overcame her as blood pounded in her ears.

He moaned as he finished, collapsing slowly upon her for a moment, his heart thudding against hers. Then he rolled onto his back, pulling her on top of him.

"God, this is my lucky day," he said, his mouth on her ear. "A beautiful woman saves my life and then lets me have my way with her."

She could hear the smile in his voice and she smiled back and nibbled his earlobe.

"Okay, what made you come?" he said, running his fingers through her hair.

"Your sexual prowess, of course."

He laughed quietly and then rolled onto his side, laying her on the bed beside him. They lay face to face, his hand stroking her hair.

"Tell me," he said.

"I tried to reach you, to warn you, but your communications were out," she said, shrugging. She hoped he would be satisfied.

"So you risked your life to rescue me. I guess you've paid me in full for saving you from the crabs."

The way he was looking at her made her feel like he was making love to her with his eyes, which shifted from azure to cerulean, depending on the light.

She smiled to herself. It turned out she did indeed have

dopamine and norepinephrine after all, because something sure as hell was surging through her body.

She awoke the next morning to the delicious aroma of bacon cooking. Will was at the tiny stove, his back to her.

Grabbing the robe off the floor, she hurried into the bathroom to shower and make herself presentable. When she emerged, wrapped in his oversized robe, breakfast was waiting, steam rising from a bowl of eggs and two cups of coffee. He crossed to her in three steps and hugged her warmly, kissing her forehead and then her lips.

"Hungry?" he asked.

"Starving."

They sat down together and he gestured for her to go first.

"Take out and eat," he said, smiling.

She looked at him quizzically.

"Old family expression, probably from the nineteenth century," he said. "Haven't the slightest idea what it means."

"This is unbelievable," she said, surveying the spread. There were scrambled eggs, bacon strips, biscuits, jelly, orange juice and coffee.

"Well, it's just dehydrated eggs, frozen biscuits and pre-cooked bacon. I wouldn't call that real cooking."

"I don't know anyone who can put breakfast on the table like this."

She almost said, "except Rosa." But she didn't want to even think about her home or her family, much less talk about them right now.

"Well, my mom taught me a few things," he said, dishing eggs onto his plate. "I was the oldest."

Neave ate like she hadn't eaten for days, enjoying every bite, slathering her biscuit with blackberry jam.

"How many kids in your family?" she asked.

"Six."

"Everybody I know is an only child. Your parents were very brave."

"Actually, it was just my mom," he said.

"God, she must be an amazing woman."

"Yeah. Kind of like Jesus with the loaves and fishes. She could take some beans from her garden and our catch from the ocean and make a feast and love doing it."

"And you – what did you used to cook?"

"Scrambled eggs, spaghetti, fried fish, rabbit stew, biscuits, pancakes."

"For a big group?"

"Yeah, but they'd eat anything, you know," he said. "Not exactly what you'd call discriminating clientele."

She tried to picture him with an apron on when he was sixteen, making a huge breakfast for a crowd of kids.

"Tell me about your sisters and brothers," she said.

He took a bite of bacon and looked as though he were deciding what to say.

"Well, I've got two brothers and three sisters. The next oldest boy is Charlie. Named for Charles Dickens, though we should've called him by his middle name, because if Charlie was anything, it was a dickens."

Which made her laugh. Everything made her laugh this morning.

And he proceeded to tell her about the others – all named after famous authors – Toni Morrison Galloway, Jazmin Lopez Galloway, Naguib Mahfouz Galloway and his baby sister, Isabel Allende Galloway.

Which she found fascinating. And then it occurred to her to ask: "So who are you named after?"

He pumped his eyebrows and grinned.

"Will…Will…" she said. "Oh my God. William Shakespeare?"

"Madam, you bereft me of words, only my blood speaks to you in my veins."

"From?"

The Merchant of Venice.

"So, your middle name is Shakespeare?"

"Forsooth."

"Don't tell me – you've read all the plays."

"We were all required to read works by the author we were named for and share with the others – dramatic readings, acting out scenes."

"I can't even imagine a family like that. It must've been so stimulating!"

"Although there were times I wished I'd been named after Ralph Ellison or Harper Lee."

"A lot less to read."

"Correct, milady."

She took the last bite of her bacon and munched happily, envying his childhood.

He nodded and sighed and then reached across to wipe something from her cheek.

"You've got egg on your face," he said, chuckling.

"Not the first time or the last, I'm afraid."

She smiled, trying to maintain the light tone, although the familiarity of his action – removing food from her face – seemed somehow to suggest they'd reached a new level of intimacy. And sitting across from him, naked under his bathrobe, with his lotion on her skin and his eyes locked on hers, it was as though she was a character in a romantic movie. A full orchestra should be playing behind them as her heart raced.

Instead of withdrawing his hand, he caressed her cheek. That touch ignited a spark deep inside her and without thinking, she took his hand and kissed his palm, closing her eyes. She wanted to put her mouth all over his body. She was embarrassed at the intensity of her lust and released his hand, looking down. And this time, she realized she wanted to be the aggressor. With her light coloring, there was no way to hide her blush. One thing was certain, the floodgates had been opened and a torrent of hormones was surging through her body.

She sipped her juice, hoping it would cool her down, keeping her eyes on the table.

"Neave..." he said.

When she looked up he was watching her intently. She swallowed several times, trying to settle herself.

He reached across the table again, until the tip of his forefinger touched the tip of hers, sending a white hot current directly into her bloodstream and to her heart, her lungs and a part of her brain she'd never known existed. And when she spoke, her voice sounded alien to her.

"Now I want to make love to you," she said.

He pulled off his shirt as he stood up and drew her to him. She put her mouth on his chest, nibbling and kissing as his chest hairs tickled her nose. She shrugged the robe off and then pulled his shorts down so he could step out of them and led the way to the bed.

Chapter 15

If their time in the cave had been a dream, the trip back to Atlanta was a nightmare. Each mile they traveled seemed to put more distance between them.

The negative vibes started after he came out of the shower. It's like the passion had washed down the drain with the soap and shampoo. When she tried to kiss him, he gave her a perfunctory peck on the lips and turned away, intent on making notes for his insurance agent. Then he was busy getting the truck ready to go. And then he was busy driving as space music played in the background, refusing to allow the onboard computer to drive. His forehead was pinched and he sighed every few minutes. Finally, she couldn't stand it any longer.

"Will, what's wrong?"

"Nothing."

He refused to look at her, just shaking his head slightly as he stared straight ahead at the highway.

"You're lying," she said.

He looked at her then, dead serious, but swallowed and focused again on the highway.

"I'm just distracted. Worried about my losses."

She turned and looked out her window at the dusty landscape as they sped along the freeway. Was the passion they'd shared just a casual affair for him? Had she read too much into his touch, his kiss, the look in his eyes? She realized he'd never said he loved her. But, damn, she thought she'd felt it. Was there something about men she didn't understand? But, then again, maybe she was a bad lover. Maybe she didn't compare with other women he'd known. Had she made a fool of herself? Her whole body felt weak.

"I think we've got communications again," he said.

He clicked on his iCom and picked up an internet signal, transmitting it to the truck computer so they could see a newscast. There were horrifying images of the tsunami. The towering wave that struck Morocco had killed hundreds of people, even with the tsunami warning system activated. The wave there was so monstrous, it looked like it had been computer enhanced.

Video of the wave that came ashore along the east coast of the U.S. paled in comparison. About seventy people were unaccounted for, but emergency officials had no idea yet whether they might have reached safety or whether they were dead. Will had nearly been one of them and Neave cringed at the thought. Tsunami waves had lashed parts of Europe as well, and inundated low-lying parts of southern Britain.

After watching for a few minutes, he clicked off the internet and made a call.

"Hi Mom," he said. "Just wanted to let you know I'm all right, though my XT was swamped when the wave hit. My communications were down. Everyone okay?"

He made it sound like no big deal, Neave thought.

"Good. I'm on my way to Atlanta to talk with Jackson," he said. "Any other work sites damaged?"

He listened for a moment and then told his mother he'd call again later.

Neave messaged her mother that she was on her way back to Atlanta. She said she was very tired and would need to sleep when she got home, hoping her parents wouldn't rush over and give her the third degree.

He clicked back on the news coverage in time to see her father on the screen. She wished the networks wouldn't call him about everything. Why did they do that? There must be other experts to call. She suspected he made himself extremely available and the media knew they could always get Robert Alvarez to fill air time. An easy "get," as they called it in the news biz.

"It was bound to happen," her father was saying. "As the oceans get warmer, the water expands, putting more weight on fissures in the earth's crust. And that increases seismic activity. It was only a matter of time before Cumbre Vieja blew its stack. And if we don't do something soon to cool the oceans, it's going to get worse."

"Are you referring to the shade ring?" the news anchor asked.

"That's the fastest way to cool the oceans," Dr. Alvarez said. "No doubt about it."

"So that's what you'll be telling senators during your upcoming confirmation hearings?" the anchor asked.

"Yes," said Dr. Alvarez. "And I've got plenty of evidence to back me up."

"Your father is one smooth operator," Will said, clicking off his iCom. "I guess the tsunami will make Senate confirmation a breeze. Good timing."

She was surprised by the intensity of his disgust.

"His only rival for Climate Secretary kicks the bucket," he continued, "and now a tsunami..."

"You've been reading too many of those mystery novels,"

she said. "I know you don't like my father…"

"Or your mother," he said.

She wanted to slap his face. If he hadn't been driving, she might've done it.

"It's a wonder you could stand being in the same room with me, much less…" she said, trailing off.

She closed her eyes tightly, seething with anger and frustration. It was like he was two people. There was *this* Will – the attack dog who wanted to hold her responsible for her parents – and there was the tender, passionate, funny Will, who made her want to waltz with him and talk with him and make love to him. Maybe it was true – maybe there was something different about clones. Maybe their brains were wired differently. Maybe they didn't have a soul. Tears welled up but she ordered herself not to cry.

They didn't speak again until they turned onto Peachtree. In the bright sunshine, the rotating skyscrapers now reminded her of giant metallic robots towering menacingly over the city.

"Neave, I'm sorry," he said, as he pulled up to the curb in front of The Cordoba. "Have dinner with me this evening?" His voice was strained.

"What's the point?"

She jumped out, slammed the door and hurried into the building. Her iCom buzzed before she could even get to the elevator. She ignored it. Then a message arrived. "7pm Hilton lobby." She deleted it.

~~~

"So what was I supposed to do?" Neave asked.

"Call the authorities," her father said.

She hadn't been in her apartment fifteen minutes when her parents arrived.

129

"I did. And they insisted everyone had been evacuated."

"Well, you should have kept calling and explained the situation more clearly," he said.

"I tried. But when it became obvious they weren't gonna do anything, what was I supposed to do? Just let him die?"

"You should've called me," he said. "I'm sure I could've handled the people at FEMA."

She sighed dramatically and walked to her living room window, gazing out at the skyline. She didn't want to talk anymore. She could see Stone Mountain in the distance. It looked like a lonely, distant cousin of the Appalachian Mountains to her now.

"You do understand," Dr. Alvarez said, "that my confirmation hearings begin next week?"

She whirled around and looked first at her mother, whose eyes were closed and lips pressed tightly together, and then at her father.

"Well, too bad I didn't drown in the tsunami so you..."

"Neave!" her mother cried.

"Well, why not, Mother? If I'd died in the tsunami, then Father could've..."

"Enough!" Dr. Alvarez barked.

"I would've been doing you a favor, Father. Adding dramatic evidence to your argument for the shade ring."

"Callaté!" he snapped. "Don't be ridiculous!"

"Why not?" Neave replied. "Because I certainly feel ridiculous."

Without another word, she turned and sprinted from the apartment, making a quick exit into the stairwell as her mother called her name. She trotted down nine flights and then took the freight elevator to the ground floor and left by the rear door. She wasn't sure where she was going but it didn't really matter.

Smitty Al's was the jazz bar she'd walked by a hundred times. A trio was performing to a mostly empty room. They were dressed in black and seemed totally into their music. And by her third drink, she was too. She closed her eyes and tried to let the music fill her consciousness. She wanted to crowd out all her anger and hurt – to medicate herself with salty margaritas and old-fashioned jazz. She focused on the piano, bass and drums, wishing she could stand up with them in a slinky black dress and make her voice into an instrument. She would sing sad songs of lost love, of men who'd done her wrong.

When the waiter suggested she might want to order some food she checked her iCom. It was 6:47. Will's message had said seven o'clock. How very presumptuous of him to think she'd want to have dinner with him. She realized she was talking to herself as she looked into her half empty glass.

"Who the hell does he think he is – the asshole – using me for his own pleasure after I saved his life! Then bad-mouthing my family, casting aspersions, suspicions – slanderous aspersions and suspicions – the nerve of him! I oughta give him a piece of my mind! I already gave him a piece of my ass."

Her voice had gotten loud enough that people were staring. A couple at a nearby table looked away, shaking their heads. They thought she was drunk. She'd show them.

She paid her tab and left, making a supreme effort to walk casually.

Standing at the entrance to the hotel lounge, she heard her name called. It was Macho, Will's buddy.

"Hey, Neave. Qué pasa?"

"Where's Will?"

"He asked me to tell you he's running a little behind. He

said you can go up to his room if you want. He's in 304."

If she wasn't mistaken, a look of disapproval lurked behind his grin. She glanced down and realized she still had on the blue climate suit she'd been wearing for two days. Will had put it through the wash during the time she'd spent in his robe. Of course, it was irrelevant what she was wearing since she had no intention of actually going to dinner with Mister Hot-and-Cold Galloway.

She had imagined herself making an ugly, embarrassing scene in a big dining room in front of a bunch of people. But she was afraid if she waited for him to come down, she'd lose her nerve. So she took the elevator to the third floor, ready to let him have it with both barrels.

When the door opened, there he stood, with only a white towel wrapped around his waist – that trim, muscular body she'd explored with such pleasure only hours before on display. Just as she opened her mouth to speak, she heard a woman giggling from inside the room. He gave her a guilty look but said nothing. And Neave said nothing, since there was really nothing to say after all. A woman called his name in a high pitched voice and Neave turned away, suddenly stone cold sober.

~~~

She installed a new security code on her door and ordered two cases of her favorite wine chillers from a web bar and settled in to watch old movies. She spent three days drinking, watching movies and sleeping. Every time she started to cry, she would open another bottle. Every time she tried to figure out how she could've fallen in love with a dipshit, she downloaded another movie. Besides being heartbroken, she was a dope, a dimwit and a boob. It was beyond her why she'd ever thought Will loved her. She must've been so desperate, so blind, that she just saw what she wanted to see. The look she thought she'd seen in his eyes must've really been the look in her own eyes reflected back at her. Maybe that was the nature of clones – they were *reflections* of real people.

The evening of the third day there was a knock at the door. She was furious with herself when she realized a part of her hoped it was Will coming to beg her forgiveness. How absurd! When she didn't answer, a man's voice called her name.

"Neave, open up!"

She remained on the couch, staring at her movie. She'd chosen *Bar None* because it had won an Academy Award but it was too violent and she decided to watch something else.

"Neave, it's me – Nat."

She touched her iCom, scanning down a list of "romantic tragedies of the twenty-first century."

"I know you're in there," Nat called. "Please let me in."

Losing Ground would do. She hit "select."

"I brought pizza from Pizza Pedro," he said.

The music began as her stomach rumbled. It was true, she was hungry. She didn't know when she'd last eaten.

"It's got pepperoni, tomatoes, black olives and green peppers," he continued.

She stood up, considering. She carried her drink with her to the fridge, opening it to see if there was anything decent inside. There wasn't, unless you counted the bag of salad she'd paid a pretty penny for, but which had turned to green mush, and two frozen entrees that tasted like seasoned biofoam. Standing in the kitchen, so close to the door, the spicy aroma of pepperoni and garlicky tomato sauce was making her mouth water.

"I'll behave like a gentleman, I promise," Nat called

through the door. "What's that old American expression? Cross my heart, hope to die, stick your finger in my eye. Something like that."

She hadn't forgotten the last time she'd seen him. How he'd demanded payment for his help. Were all men assholes?

"Neave, are you okay?"

On the other hand, she was miserable, lonesome, drunk and hungry. He was the only person who cared enough to actually come and see her in person. Oh, her mother had messaged her. Kwan had messaged her. Rosa had called. But Nat had come. With pizza. She opened the door.

He took one look at her standing there in her baggy pink pajamas and stringy hair and hurried in before she could change her mind. He set two bottles of Coke and the pizza box on the table, opened it immediately and pulled a chair out for her.

She sat down and without even saying hello, lifted a slice of piping hot pizza from the pie, strands of melted cheese stringing out like a spider web from the pizza box to her mouth. She closed her eyes as she chewed.

"When was the last time you ate?" he asked, sitting across from her.

She shrugged.

"Here, have some Coke," he said, sliding a bottle to her.

She ignored it and gobbled down two large slices without pausing.

"Eat up," he said, pushing another slice towards her.

But she took a swallow of her wine chiller.

"You're the only person I know who never answers her iCom," he said. "Do you have any idea how many times I've tried to reach you?"

She closed her eyes.

"And, by the way, you look like frog feces," he said.

She looked at the bottle in her hands, studying the fruity design on the label.

"So you saved that worthless clone's ass," he said.

She didn't want to share her hurt and humiliation with anyone, especially Nat Patel. But her face crumpled and hot tears rolled down her cheeks.

"I'm sorry," he said, all traces of sarcasm gone. He took her hand and led her into the living room. They sat next to each other on the couch and he put his arm around her shoulders in a comforting way. There was nothing demanding in his manner and her tears flowed as he handed her tissues. He picked up the remote and turned off the t-view, leaving the room quiet except for her sniffling. He didn't ask any questions. He didn't need to. When she'd cried herself out, she sat limp beside him.

They were quiet a long time before he spoke.

"I've got one spot left on an expedition to Greenland," he said. "Maybe you'd like to get away for a while."

He looked over at her.

"We leave Friday. Might keep you busy, maybe give you a chance to see another side of climatology," he said. "Lena's going. Kwan too. And me. No pressure, though. You can think about it and let me know tomorrow."

She blew her nose and wiped her eyes.

Chapter 16

This time, she paid attention during the expedition briefing. But she still wasn't prepared for how cold it was. Living and working on ice, her feet were perpetually frozen. Lena said it was because she was too thin.

At least she fixed her hair and bathed every day, which is more than she could say for Lena. She'd never seen Lena look so awful. Like she'd just fallen out of bed, all day, every day. Messy, flat hair, circles under her eyes, no makeup. And she smelled like she'd stopped using deodorant. Besides the unkempt appearance, the sparkle was gone from her eyes along with the constant smart-ass banter. Neave hadn't seen her smile since they were at the beach - before Osley's death. Which said a lot.

While she had jumped at the chance to vamoose out of Atlanta, this field expedition was not the escape she'd hoped for. Because Lena was so morose, Kwan was quiet and irritable. There wasn't the usual friendly, joking comradery the group had shared in the past. Dr. Osley's death seemed closer now that they were together again.

And although Neave had complained about the hot, sticky experience at the beach, that climate now seemed preferable to the unrelenting cold of the Hanson Research Station. Their job was to measure the ice dam at the tip of what was left of the Nunatakit Glacier. As Nat explained it, they were developing a 3D representation of the leading edge of the glacier to get a clearer picture of its dynamics.

Tramping across the dam was much more challenging than she'd expected. The surface was pitted and uneven and required great care navigating on foot. They positioned themselves, holding antenna wands in front of them – triangulating them along the surface to get their measurements. The wands were connected to digitizers in backpacks they lugged around. The data obtained through a combination of ultrasound and radar emissions was then transmitted to Nat, bundled up in a warming blanket in the Research Vehicle – a specially equipped Jeep – along the edge of the ice dam, where he processed and stored it for re-transmission to the Climatology Center. Occasionally, he'd get out of the vehicle and aim his iCom at them, using those images to spice up his daily reports.

He said opinion was divided on how long the dam would last. Melting had increased over the last year. Sometimes it worried her that they were walking along the top of this dam as if it were made of concrete. But she reminded herself that the ice was as wide as a two-lane road and their daily monitoring would certainly give them warning if there was some deterioration.

The view was breathtaking. On one side was Storstrommen Lake, sparkling in the sunshine, mirroring the sky. The sun danced on the water so intensely it was hard to look at, even with their protective sun goggles on. The glacier swept down from the north and fed the lake with glacial melt. It was the tip of the glacier that wrapped around the lake on the south side that formed the dam. On the other side, the dam dropped some forty feet to a snow-covered valley.

Their third evening there, after a long, tedious day of moving their instruments along the ice dam and freezing their feet despite the high-tech ice boots and warming socks, they collapsed in the common room to watch a movie Kwan chose from his personal iFlicks. *Doppelganger* was a horror movie about clones who took over the Earth. Neave didn't like it but she sat wrapped up in a warming blanket and watched anyway, too tired to move. Lena disappeared without a word about twenty minutes into it, missing out on the fight to the death between the ruggedly handsome good guy and the ruggedly unhandsome bad guy.

When it was over, Kwan stretched and yawned and dragged himself to bed, leaving Neave wrapped snugly in her blanket and Nat typing on his iScreen. The light tapping of his fingers was lulling her to sleep, nestled cozy and warm on the couch.

"Are your feet still cold?" he asked softly.

"Not as long as I stay where I am," she whispered.

"Let me give you a foot rub."

"I'm going to crawl in bed and wrap them in my warming blanket. Once I can force myself to get up, that is."

"Reflexology is an excellent way to get the blood flowing."

He'd been so nice to her, she'd really begun to relax around him. And she was seriously considering his offer.

"Of course, a hot toddy helps warm the feet too," he said.

"A hot toddy?"

He set aside his iScreen and ducked into the kitchen for a moment. She could hear him pouring and heating and then he was back with two steaming mugs.

"It's been proven scientifically," he said, mock serious.

She took the cup and held it under her nose. The liquid was a deep reddish brown and smelled enticingly of apple cider and wine. The first sip was quite good. It warmed her throat going down and very soon, she could feel the alcohol tingling in her veins. If she'd been relaxed before, she was positively languid now. They sat quietly, sipping from their mugs.

She didn't protest when he took the cups into the kitchen and made a second round. Sleep would come easy tonight.

"Now, slide a foot out from under that blanket," he said.

She hesitated a moment and then complied, closing her eyes as she held the mug in front of her face.

He rubbed it with a sure hand, working over the ball of her foot with his thumbs. She'd never had a foot rub and was pleasantly surprised. Then he patted it in dismissal and motioned for her to extend the other one. She obeyed, sipping her hot toddy as he massaged her left foot. She was like butter melting on a baked potato.

Since arriving with the group, she'd stayed busy enough that she mostly avoided thinking about Will, which was a good thing, since thinking of him had a tendency to either make her furious or reduce her to tears. Nat acted as though they were friends and she was in an appreciative mood when she realized the massage had changed. He was gently rubbing her toes, one at a time. And then he lifted her leg and rubbed his chin over the sole of her foot before kissing it softly, looking at her from under his dark lashes.

"Na-at," she sing-songed, wagging her finger at him.

He sighed and resumed the massage, giving her a resigned, but friendly shrug of the eyebrows. He had been so kind, she realized her feelings towards him were changing. Maybe she'd unfairly held his relationship with her father against him. When she stopped and thought about it, it made sense for a man in his position to align himself with her father. It was possible the rap against Nat was mostly professional jealousy by those who wished they were lucky enough to be Dr. Robert Alvarez's right hand man. She'd heard the gossip that Nat was good with politics but sloppy with his science. But she'd read enough to know that just like politicians, scientists sometimes found the evidence they needed to support their theories.

She pulled her foot back inside her cocoon, drained her mug and set it on the table beside her, and closed her eyes. And then his lips were on hers, warm and gentle. She didn't fight him, hoping to feel some stirring of hormones.

"Gotta sleep," she said quietly when the kiss was over.

There was no surge. But, then again, that old feeling of revulsion didn't well up to make her chest tight.

Chapter 17

The mood was sour the next day. The novelty of an expedition to Greenland had worn off completely. It was cold, exhausting work – setting up the monitors, checking to make sure they were properly positioned, waiting for the sensors to do their thing and then moving the equipment one meter and doing the whole thing all over again. And again. And again. All the while, carefully watching their step so they wouldn't slip and break their necks.

Of course, it didn't help that today Nat had them loading new monitors into the truck. He said the new ones also had seismographs, which he thought would be reassuring, but Neave begged to differ.

Kwan was cussing in Korean again. At least, that's what it sounded like. His cussing in Korean routine usually had the effect of lifting everyone's spirits. Not today. Lena was in no mood for laughter.

"We could use a day off," she said, tucking her e-cig in her pocket.

"But, Lena, you know our job is very important," Kwan said. "They want us to hurry up and tell them the goddam dam is getting goddam thin."

"Por que?" she asked.

"Because, a certain V.I.P. scientist is going through Senate confirmation hearings as we speak," he said.

"And what's that supposed to…" Neave started.

"It means," he said, "that if Nat can provide some real time evidence that global melting is getting worse, it's great for the dog and pony show."

"Mierda!" said Lena. "We're out here on this Godforsaken wall of ice, risking limb and life, freezing our culos off, not getting paid one lousy peso, to funnel Neave's big shot father some high-powered ammo?"

"I'd say you've boiled it down to the essentials," said Kwan.

Neave was surprised at the intensity of this little exchange.

"What're you looking at?" Lena snapped at her.

So Neave studied the blinding reflection of sunlight bouncing off the ice.

"God, what a cold, shitty day!" Lena whined, slamming the monitor into the vehicle.

"Actually," said Kwan, "shit is about 98.6 degrees Fahrenheit. Not cold at all. Fresh shit, that is."

He looked from Lena to Neave, but no one laughed.

Lena was definitely not herself. But she refused to talk about it. And, after several attempts, which only resulted in angry outbursts, Neave stopped trying.

Nat and Lena rode in the Jeep. Kwan and Neave followed on a snowmobile.

And then, when they got to the dam, Nat told Neave he wanted her to stay in the research vehicle and help process the data because of the new monitors. Which caused more unpleasantness. Lena argued she should get first dibs at the cushy job of sitting in the truck, staying warm. Neave took her side, hoping to make peace. She was uneasy about getting preferential treatment from Nat.

"I'll give you a turn tomorrow," Nat told Lena.

"Let her do it, Nat," Neave pleaded.

But he ignored her.

"You'll be glad tomorrow when you get your turn and Neave is freezing her butt off," he said, trying for a jocular tone.

Lena rolled her eyes before heading out. So Neave got a respite. She covered herself in a warming blanket as she sat in the passenger seat facing the computer console built into the dash. It was tight quarters in the Jeep – just two seats – with all the electronic equipment. Kwan and Lena made the laborious hike halfway across the dam, planting their steps carefully, to set up the new monitors. Nat, dressed as usual in a black parka, stood beside the truck, iCom in hand, like he was shooting a documentary for SciWeb. He shot video of them, of the valley below the ice dam, and then he turned the camera on the lake.

As she waited for them to begin transmitting measurements, Neave's gaze followed the direction of Nat's iCom – something she didn't do while working on the dam. It made her nervous looking at that frigid body of water so close by. The water seemed to swirl a bit, reflecting the cirrus clouds floating high above. A shiver made her draw in her breath and look for her friends, so small on that slab of compacted snow. She could tell them apart by the color of their jackets: Lena was green and Kwan was blue. Her own parka was brown, which suited her mood.

Then the data was incoming and she monitored the scanner, uploading the measurements. Nat climbed into the vehicle with her, pulling off his gloves and hat.

He said nothing, just stared at the gauges and then at Lena and Kwan. Just as she raised her eyes to look through the windshield again, she felt a vibration. It was very slight, but there was no missing it.

"What was that?" she said, craning to see her friends.

Nat pulled his iCom from his pocket, presumably to check the seismometer readings.

The others had obviously felt it too. They were standing stock still. Lena was on the valley side, Kwan on the side closest to the lake. Without putting her gloves or hat on, Neave climbed out of the vehicle. Nat yelled at her to shut the door just as an awful rumbling filled the air. She watched in horror as a big chunk of ice fell away from the dam just behind Lena, crashing in slow-motion to the valley below. Lena lost her balance, her feet slipping out from under her. She was on her back at the very edge of the newly created gap. Kwan immediately started towards her. Neave could hear their muffled, faraway voices, but not what they were saying. She held her breath as she watched. When he got within a few feet of her, he lay down on his belly and slid closer. But just as it looked like his hand was about to touch Lena's leg, she disappeared from view. Neave could hear the echoing scream.

As she squinted into the sun she heard another cracking noise that sent chills down her spine. A second slab of ice broke off – this one about twenty feet beyond where Lena had been standing. Neave reached inside the Jeep and grabbed her sun goggles, hat and gloves. By the time she turned around to look towards the dam again, Kwan had disappeared. She didn't know if he'd fallen or climbed down after Lena. Either way, she knew she had to move fast because there was no doubt in her mind that the dam was about to give way.

"Nat!" she shouted. "Bring the truck!"

He looked where she was pointing as she jumped on the snowmobile and took off. He was yelling something but Neave couldn't hear him over the roar of the engine. There wasn't a second to lose. She drove parallel to the valley, heading away from the dam until she reached a slope she could negotiate. The air was freezing her nose and cheeks as she pushed the snowmobile as fast as it would go. Down on the surface of the valley, she had to zigzag across the ice because of all the crevices and icy outcroppings. She went airborne several times and nearly lost control when she hit one bump that turned out to be a bigger than she expected. But she held on. It seemed to take an eternity, but finally, as she approached the base of the dam, she could see Lena's green jacket. She was sprawled on her back and Kwan was just reaching the valley floor, after rappelling down the side of the dam, which, from the bottom looked a whole lot taller than forty feet.

When she roared to a stop, he had reached Lena and was kneeling beside her. He motioned for Neave to move the snowmobile closer. She accelerated slowly, sliding to a halt only a couple of feet from them. She noticed a stream of water close on her left. Her eyes followed it backward, looking for the source, moving up the side of the dam itself to a spot about halfway up. Water was leaking from cracks in the ice. Kwan saw the fear in her eyes and looked too.

"Shit," he said and hurried to carry Lena to the snowmobile.

Neave craned her neck, looking for Nat. But he was nowhere to be seen. Then she glanced at where they'd been parked and could see him standing by the Jeep, his iCom in front of his face, looking like a black shadow against the stark white of the ice and snow. He was shooting the action.

"Damn him!" she shouted, getting off the snowmobile to help with Lena.

She was relieved Lena was conscious but it was obvious

she was in a lot of pain. Under normal circumstances, they wouldn't consider moving her after such a fall. They'd wait for medical personnel. But these were not normal circumstances.

"Kwan, you drive," Neave yelled over the idling engine.

They hoisted Lena onto the seat.

"Help me strap her in," Kwan shouted, handing her a bungee cord and using another one to strap Lena to the backrest. Neave followed his lead, then climbed on behind Lena as Kwan jumped in front and grabbed the handlebars.

He started off slowly so he wouldn't cause Neave to slip off the back. It was a two-man snowmobile and wasn't designed to carry three people.

They picked up speed and headed down the valley at an angle, navigating around the depressions and bumps. They'd only gone a short distance when she heard a low, growling sound like a huge monster was after them. Kwan yelled something but she couldn't make out his words between the engine noise and the wind rushing past them. But she knew what he was saying even before she glanced over her left shoulder and saw the crack where water had been leaking a moment before had now ruptured. A big hunk of ice had fallen and water was gushing through the gap.

She yelled "faster, faster!" But they couldn't get up the side of the valley until they reached the spot where she had come down. The walls were too steep. He was going as fast as he could, but there was too much weight. She looked again over her shoulder, knowing full well it was useless to do so. As she gaped at the water rushing towards them – gaining on them – they hit a small bump, and she lost her grip. She bounced off the back, landing hard on her butt and sliding about fifteen feet. She came to a sudden stop when she slammed into a ridge of ice jutting several feet from the snowpack.

She instinctively looked back just in time to see the dam burst open, crumbling as the full weight of water from the lake surged through the huge gap. A wall of frigid water raced through the valley as though it were a giant demon from Hell.

A scream was fighting to get out as a jumble of thoughts galloped through her mind: "I'm going to die; they'll turn around to save me and we'll all die; I'll freeze to death before I drown; and I'm gonna kill Nat Patel!" All this, as she scrambled to her feet, looking first at the water thundering towards her and then at the snowmobile zooming away. And then she heard another sound – another snowmobile sweeping around from the left. The driver's face was hidden by a helmet with a dark, reflective mask. He pulled alongside her, slowing just enough for her to leap on board behind him. A nanosecond later he gunned it and they roared off towards the side of the valley, following the other snowmobile.

Part of her wanted to look back but she tightened her grip on his waist, putting her cheek against his grey parka, hoping to reduce the wind resistance. She expected the water to overtake them at any second. She closed her eyes and held on tight. Then she realized they were climbing and opened her eyes just as they hit a bump and both of them went airborne. She thought they were done for, but they both landed hard on the seat and he regained control in time to avoid crashing into a large chunk of ice protruding from the snow. The eerie roaring noise grew louder and closer behind them as the snowmobile strained to climb the valley wall. Finally, finally, they were on top of the bank but they didn't slow down. Neave glanced behind her and understood why. The water was spreading out, spilling out of the valley onto the embankment. They veered left, heading towards the science station, and finally, the water gave up its pursuit and they were able to slow down to a safer speed. The other snowmobile was directly ahead of them.

They didn't stop until they reached the science station where they found the Jeep parked at an angle out front, not in its usual parking space in the garage. They followed Kwan slowly into the garage and finally, it was quiet, as first one, then the other engine died. Kwan gently carried Lena inside.

Neave's legs were shaky as she dismounted and pulled off her gloves and goggles. Even when her driver turned around, she didn't know who it was. But as he removed his gloves, tucked them under his arm and reached up to pull off his helmet, she realized just before his face was revealed that it was Will.

She stood there with her mouth open, puffs of warm breath filling the air in front of her. It didn't compute. And then he wrapped his arms around her and pulled her close.

"You know, there's a fine line between courage and stupidity," he said. "And I think maybe you like to straddle that line."

His voice was husky and for a moment she wanted nothing more than to let him hold her, to feel the protection of his arms. But the last time she saw him came rushing back – towel around his waist, giggling girlfriend behind him, after that torturous drive from the coast – so she pulled away and hurried inside.

Lena was lying on the sofa, Kwan sitting in a kitchen chair beside her, talking on his iCom. Neave kneeled on the floor by the couch and took Lena's hand.

"Oh, Lena, I thought…"

"I was a goner," Lena whispered.

Neave nodded.

"I slipped down, bit by bit."

"Where does it hurt?"

"My back, my feet, my knees," she said, wincing.

Will walked in, took off his coat and hung it on a hook by the door.

Kwan's voice filled the room as he talked on his iCom. "Mm-hm. Right. Okay." He stood up and paced around the room, running his hand through his hair over and over.

"Sooner would be better," he said.

Neave ran to the kitchen and brought Lena a bottle of water and helped her sip through a straw. Finally, Kwan was able to give them an update.

"A chopper'll be here in about an hour to airlift her to the hospital in Tasiilaq," he said. "We give her pain medicine from the first aid box until they get here and keep her warm."

Kwan found a warming blanket to wrap her in and Neave got the meds.

"Where's Nat?" she asked when she returned.

She got blank expressions in reply.

"He was shooting us with his iCom," she explained.

Kwan stormed down the hallway towards the office, Neave right behind him. He didn't bother to knock, opening the door so hard, it slammed into the desk where Nat sat at a computer, manipulating video files on a PC.

"You get a good price?" Kwan snapped.

"Price?" said Nat, jumping up like he'd been caught down-loading porn, trying to hide the screen with his body.

"How many networks?"

"What're you talking about?"

"Don't play dumb," Kwan snarled. "How many networks? You get big money?"

"What the hell," Nat said.

"You were up there shooting video while the rest of us were rescuing Lena, man!"

Nat was shaking his head like they were all crazy but Kwan closed the distance between them until he was right in Nat's face.

"You rushed back here to sell the fucking video, didn't you?" Kwan said, pushing Nat's shoulder.

Nat towered over him but that didn't seem to make any difference at the moment.

"I didn't sell anything to anyone!" Nat yelled, sitting back down in his chair.

Neave looked from Nat to the computer screen where she could see the U.S. Climatology web page.

"You sent it to my father," she said softly.

He stared at the screen.

"You've been shooting video ever since we got here," she said.

"And sending it to Alvarez every day?" said Kwan.

"It's part of my daily report," Nat said.

"You need a visual for every report?" she asked.

Nat just sighed.

Neave felt like she was standing too close to radioactive material. Prickly, uneasy. She looked at the computer screen as it processed the video images. They were zooming past so that the collapse of the ice dam and their race to escape the rampaging water played like a silent film from the dawn of moving pictures. All herky-jerky motions. No sound. Herself falling from the snowmobile. Being rescued by Will.

"Let's check C-web," said Kwan.

It only took a moment to get the live feed from the Senate floor, where her father was speaking. Kwan turned up the volume.

"I hadn't planned on having such dramatic evidence to present today but I have just received some video from my assistant who is with a group of young scientists in Greenland. They have been measuring an ice dam on the tip of the Nunatakit Glacier. And while they were doing their measurements today – just moments ago, actually – the dam broke and they just barely escaped with their lives. I could overwhelm you with data but I think this one brief video clip tells the story. May I?"

Senator Jefferson nodded and Dr. Alvarez clicked his iCom and transmitted the video to two large view screens in the Senate chamber.

Surreal. That's the only way Neave could think of to describe the experience of watching her father show senators in New Washington the video of their narrow escape that Nat had just uploaded. Her stomach felt cold and empty watching the violence of the bursting dam. She could see now how close they'd actually come to being swept away to certain death.

The senators were obviously mesmerized. And so was everyone in the cramped Research Station office.

The video ended as the two snowmobiles hurtled up the hillside to safety. Her father clicked his iCom, disconnecting the transmission so the screens went dark again. He took a moment to speak.

"I have to tell you, I'm still a little weak in the knees. My own daughter was in that video," Dr. Alvarez said. "She nearly lost her life due to runaway global melting."

And he looked down for a few seconds, pulling on his earlobe.

Neave stepped forward and turned the feed off.

"This whole field expedition was a setup. You knew the ice dam was about to break," she said, looking hard at Nat.

Kwan stared at her.

"One way to find out," she said. "Let's call Dr. Baynard and ask him about the status of the ice dam."

"No need." It was Will, his tall frame filling the doorway. "That's why I came. They said you were on an expedition to Greenland. So I was referred to Baynard at the Climate Center. And he said you guys wouldn't be here because they'd ordered a halt to ice measurements once the dam got too thin to be safe. Which was about six months ago. And he said even before they suspended the measurements, they'd been using robots, just in case. But the university," he said, looking at Nat, "told me you were here."

There was silence in the room as the full meaning of his words sank in.

"You fucking knew!" Kwan hissed, turning on Nat.

"I...." Nat said.

"And you didn't care if we were on it or not!" Kwan shouted, lunging at him.

The chair tipped over and they both landed on the floor, Kwan on top, throwing punches like a madman.

Suddenly, there was a crashing noise down the hallway, which put a halt to the attack. Will was first to the common room, Neave and Kwan right behind. They found Lena awake and in pain, a broken lamp on the floor beside her. Neave wondered if she'd knocked it off to stop the fight.

Just before the chopper arrived to fly her to the hospital Kwan checked his iCom and saw a headline saying Dr. Alvarez had won Senate confirmation with only a handful of dissenting votes. Which further depressed everyone's spirits except, of course, for Nat. But no one went to see how he was celebrating the news.

Kwan accompanied Lena to the hospital, leaving Neave

alone at the research station with the two men she hated most in the world.

Chapter 18

Neave hid out in her room, taking a hot shower to try to relax. It didn't work. Her mind kept rehashing everything. She was furious with herself. She'd allowed Nat to con her into joining this phony expedition – supposedly to take her mind off Will. Turned out Nat had ulterior motives. Then Will showed up anyway. Of course, if he hadn't, she'd be dead now. And it galled her the whole thing had been arranged to give her father a leg up in his Senate confirmation hearings.

She dressed in her baby blue flannel pajamas, wrapped herself in her heating blanket and sat in bed, knowing full well she couldn't sleep. She tried reading but couldn't focus and ended up staring at the white walls of her tiny room, which made her feel like she was in a prison cell.

And then there was a knock on the door.

"Go away," she said, not caring which asshole it was.

"It's me – Will."

"Right," she whispered to herself.

She did owe him a thank you. He risked his life for her. Of course, she saved his life too.

"Can I come in?"

She didn't move.

"Please."

She unlocked the door and hopped back onto the bed,

wrapping the blanket around her again. He stepped into the room and closed the door behind him. And then there was an uncomfortable silence, until they both started speaking at once.

"After you," he said.

"Thank you for coming to my rescue," she said, looking at the floor in front of him. "Of course, I don't know what the hell you're doing here."

He stuck his hands in his pockets and nodded his head.

"I wish I could say I knew you were in mortal danger and I rushed here to save your life, like you came to the coast to save mine. But that would be a lie. I tracked you down because I had to talk to you. And it was only after I tried to find you that I suspected you might be in danger. But the reason I came was because I had to tell you something."

He moved closer but she just pulled the blanket more tightly around her, studying a cobweb in the corner.

"I don't think there's anything to say," she said, trying to sound aloof, but coming across as angry and hurt.

"Yes. Yes, there is. I came to ask you to forgive me, to say I'm sorry – sorry as hell. And I need to tell you something – something I should've told you before." He took a deep breath before continuing. "I need to tell you... that..."

He looked down, then closed his eyes.

"I have to tell you something about myself... that... I'm... I have to tell you that I'm..."

And he stopped again and sighed.

"A clone," she said.

Dead silence. And then he breathed again.

"You know?"

She nodded, not looking at him.

"How? How long?"

She sighed.

"When did you...?"

"When I begged Nat to help me get the heli-scooter, he told me."

"But..." his mouth hung open as he squinted in concentration. "You knew when... you knew when we...?"

"Yes, I knew you were a clone *then*. I just didn't know you were an ass!"

"You knew!"

"A heartless ass."

He sat on the bed in front of her, his brows in a knot, looking like he was in pain.

"Neave..."

She turned towards the wall.

"You have no idea what this means to me. The women I knew before all thought of clones as lepers. Worse than lepers. The scum of the earth. Evil. Once a girl finds out I'm a clone, we're history. The first girl I fell for when I was sixteen, she was all sweetness and light until she found out. Then it was like I didn't exist. I became invisible. Do you know what that's like? When I was twenty I dated a girl I liked a lot. Same thing. Worse, actually. When she learned I was a clone, she was disgusted. She acted like she'd kissed a maggot."

"You just hung out with the wrong girls."

"You have no clue."

He tried to take her hand but she jerked it away.

"So I was sure when you found out the truth, you'd hate me too – just like they did. You'd be grossed out when you realized you'd made love to a clone. See, I knew it wasn't just casual sex. I could tell it was your first time."

"So?"

"So if it was your first time, that meant it was important.

156

Most girls have had plenty of sex by the time they're your age. Not you. It was important to you. Don't deny it. The next morning, you wanted to get to know me, asking questions about my family. And when I thought about how much you risked flying to the coast to rescue me – Christ! A woman wouldn't do that unless she was pretty damn serious. And when it finally sank in that it wasn't just a fling, I knew when you found out about me, you'd be filled with regret. God. I really, really wanted to avoid that. Because I was so in love with you. The thought of you turning your back on me – hating me, loathing me – was too much. So I made you dump me."

"Made me dump you?"

She was looking at him now, fire in her green eyes.

"Yeah, it all came together in my head as I was showering that morning. So, as we were driving to Atlanta, I concocted the scene in the hotel room. It was Jaz. I asked her to play the part when you came to my door."

"So I would dump you."

He blew air out of his mouth as he looked down.

Her hands had balled into fists while he was talking.

"You bastard!" she cried. "You broke my heart so I wouldn't break yours?"

But before he had time to answer she slapped his face hard.

"You... you... heartless coward!" she said, her voice cracking.

She hit him again but instead of backing off, he wrapped his arms around her. She tried to push him away as tears streamed down her face.

"You knew," he said over and over, holding her close as she struggled. "I'm sorry, Neave. God, I love you."

"Damn you, you..."

"Neave, I began to wonder if people were right – that clones don't have a soul – until I fell in love with you. I could feel the spark when I was with you. When you looked into my eyes, there was this hot thrumming in my ears. It felt like our souls touched."

She stopped thrashing.

"But I was so afraid you wouldn't want me if you knew the truth."

She'd never thought about what it was like to be a clone. She'd heard the clone jokes and she'd heard people make snide remarks. Even her own friends. But she hadn't taken it a step further and thought about what it was like to actually *be* a clone. About the humiliation, the rejection, the pain.

"God, can you forgive me?" he whispered into her hair.

And forgiveness welled up inside her. She couldn't seem to stop crying, though it had started in anger and frustration, now they were tears of joy and relief.

He wiped her tears with his fingers and kissed her, soft and sweet. Then he kissed her again, more passionately this time. She returned the passion and held him tight in her arms.

They undressed each other then and made love, re-establishing the bond they'd forged in the cave.

"Hear my soul speak," he whispered later, "Of the very instant that I saw you, did my heart fly at your service."

"Shakespeare?"

"*The Tempest.*"

~~~

Their first two days back in Atlanta were like a honeymoon – late morning visits to the coffee shop, drinks at Neave's new favorite jazz club, back rubs. And, of course, sweet, passionate sex.

She loved looking at him – watching him shave, watching

him walk, watching him cook. And when she gazed into his eyes, she was always startled by the somersault in her stomach. He made her body buzz at the subatomic level. Sometimes it felt like her heart muscle was being tickled. And when that happened, she would lean in close and kiss him, closing her eyes so she could concentrate on his scent.

He was entranced by her as well, taking the brush from her and stroking her hair as he stood behind her, holding her hand as they walked along the street, watching her taste the food he prepared – scrambled eggs, banana bread or lasagna – waiting for her moan of pleasure. They talked about her love of theater, his love of Shakespeare, her love of music, his interest in expanding his family's business.

On the third day after their return Rosa said Lena was up to having visitors so they agreed to meet Kwan at the hospital. She'd already had two surgeries. While they knew it could've been much worse, she was in for a long, painful recovery.

The three of them entered her hospital room together. Kwan set a bouquet of pink flowers on the window ledge alongside two other fresh arrangements. Neave put the small art deco container of cookies Will had made on the tray by the bed.

"How ya feelin'?" Kwan asked, leaning over and giving her a kiss on the forehead.

"Like shit," Lena answered.

And, it was true, she looked pale and weak. And irritable.

"Are you in a lot of pain?" Neave asked.

Lena rolled her eyes and shook her head slightly as if she were surrounded by a bunch of idiots.

"Is there anything we can do for you?" Kwan said, as they forced themselves not to look at each other in dismay.

"Yeah, you can bring me an e-cig."

159

"Will do," he said. "Anything else?"

"Yes. You can stop all this irrelevant small talk and tell me how Nat did it."

"Did what?" Neave asked.

Again, the look of condescension and exasperation, as though she'd been plunked down in the middle of a pre-school class.

"How Nat made the ice dam break!"

"You think..." Neave began.

"Oh, noooooo. Of course not. I'm sure it was just a coincidence that we were out on that ice dam the same week of your father's Senate confirmation," Lena said, dripping with sarcasm. "Oh, and it was just a coincidence that the dam just happened to go boom the very day he was testifying. And, yes, it must've been a coincidence that Nat specifically told you to stay in the truck that day – you know, the daughter of his big boss and mentor, and the woman of his wet dreams. And no doubt it was just a coincidence that the ice gave way right after we started using those new monitors. Mm-hm, I'm absolutely sure it was just a series of coincidences."

"The monitors," Kwan said, looking at Neave.

"You think they were rigged to..." Will asked.

"To cause the ice dam collapse," Lena said. "There's no other explanation."

"Other than complete coincidence," said Will.

"What about proof?" Neave asked.

"Find the monitors," Lena said.

"They're probably in tiny pieces at the bottom of the ocean," said Kwan.

"Come on, guys." Lena shook her head and sighed deeply. "Worthless." And she laid her head on the pillow and closed her eyes, her brows pinched in pain.

"I guess we better go," said Neave. "Anything we can do for you?"

"Yeah, you can cut Nat's balls off and feed 'em to those goddam poison dart frogs he keeps in his terrarium."

"I like it," said Kwan.

"Are you gonna try and find them?" Neave asked as they left the hospital.

"I don't know," Kwan said. "How would we go about looking for a piece of a monitor? It would be like looking for the proverbial needle in a haystack."

"But she's got a point," Will said.

They looked at him.

"Nat's not my favorite person," Neave said. "And while I do think he broke the rules to feed my father the video, I can't believe he'd actually try to kill you guys."

"Well, you have to admit that's a lot of coincidences," Will said.

Kwan said he'd start by tracking down the company that made the monitors.

Chapter 19

She considered declining the dinner invitation from her parents, but finally decided getting the introductions out of the way might be a good thing. She wasn't sure who was more nervous – her or Will.

"It's okay if you don't like them," she said as she slipped into a short, peach-colored dress. She wasn't trying to impress her parents, but wanted to look pretty for Will. "I actually don't like them much myself, but they are my parents."

"You really don't like them?"

"That sounds bad, doesn't it?"

He shrugged.

"Well, growing up, it was kind of like living in a lab refrigerator," she said.

He crossed the room and wrapped his arms around her, looking down into her eyes. He kissed her forehead and held her close, swaying slowly back and forth, rubbing her back softly as though she needed his body heat.

"We'll get through it," he said.

"Together," she said, and kissed him.

~~~

Her parents' home was in an old neighborhood where the street names were throwbacks to an earlier time – Oak Grove Lane, Azalea Court and her street, Maple Avenue. From the front, it was a modest adobe bungalow with a charming screened porch, as though someone might actually sit there in winter to enjoy a glass of tea. The small front yard was landscaped with white gravel, orange gazamias and a six foot tall saguaro by the front walkway. No one would've guessed that two of the nation's pre-eminent scientists lived here. Of course, it was not as humble as it appeared, nor as welcoming.

The few friends she'd been allowed to bring home were surprised when they discovered how big it really was. Most of it was underground, hidden from view. That's where her old bedroom was. She'd always wished for a window to let the sunshine in. Instead, her parents had floor-to-ceiling view walls installed so she could link to live cams around the world. She could choose a view of Niagara Falls on one wall and a scene of snow falling in Canada's Northern Forest on another.

They pulled into the driveway a few minutes after seven. Neave laced her fingers through his as they walked to the front door, admiring how handsome he looked in his jeans and tan shirt. She gave him a peck on the lips just as the door opened.

"Hi, Rosa, this is Will," she said, smiling happily. "And Will, this is Rosa."

"I've heard so much about you," he said, extending his hand.

Rosa stood gaping at him. She finally swallowed and shook his hand, giving him a weak smile.

"Welcome," she said. "Come in."

She'd never seen Rosa lose her composure like that. But before she could ponder any further, they were ushered into the living room where they found not just her mother and father – Nat was there too. And they were all three staring at a picture on a huge view screen on the far wall.

Neave hadn't expected to be greeted with open arms but her parents' reaction was totally unexpected. They both had perplexed looks on their faces, as their eyes fixed on Will. She started to make introductions but the giant image on the wall stopped her cold. It looked like a picture of Will and herself. But the hair on the man in the picture was short and uncharacteristically neat. And he was wearing a suit and tie, standing in front of a house with his arm around... but it wasn't her. His arm was around a beautiful young auburn-haired woman. It looked like her mother when she was young. Neave glanced at Nat standing off to the side and detected a smugness in his expression, although she didn't understand it. Then she turned to Will, whose face changed from confusion to recognition.

"What's going on here?" she asked.

When her mother and father didn't answer, Nat stepped forward.

"We were looking at family pictures," he said.

Neave looked again at the image on the wall and then at Will.

"That's not you," she said. "Is it?"

He shook his head.

"That's your grandfather," said Nat.

She could hear the self-satisfaction in his voice as she looked hard at the picture and then at Will, noticing they both had vivid blue eyes.

"Will's grandfather?" she asked.

"No, *your* grandfather," Nat said, triumphantly raising his eyebrow at her.

"My..."

She was still trying to process the scene, trying to figure out what was going on. Her father was looking at her mother who was openly staring at Will.

"How many clones did you make of your father, Dr. Sullivan?" Will asked.

"I..." Dr. Sullivan said, her eyes locked on his as though in a trance. "He... he cloned himself. But, yes, I... I helped." She looked down, putting a hand in front of her mouth.

The look on his face when Will turned to Neave was like he'd just learned of a death in the family – the death of someone he loved. He gazed for a moment into her eyes and then turned and walked out.

"Wait!" she cried.

He ignored her and disappeared through the front door. She looked again at the picture on the wall, noticing the man in the picture looked like Will's twin, except his smile. There were two dimples, while Will had only one.

"Neave, sweetheart," her father said, reaching for her arm.

But she stepped back and turned towards Nat, who made the mistake of shaking his head slightly in a "what a shame" gesture.

"I'll never forgive you for this," she said and slapped his face.

The driverless hub car was backing out of the driveway when she dashed down the front steps. When it stopped at the street, she jumped in beside Will.

"I'm so sorry. I had no idea. Nat should be whipped," she blurted. A sheen of sweat coated their faces as the AC struggled to cool the car.

"Why?" he asked.

"I'm sure he..."

"He's not the one who cloned your grandfather," he said, as the car backed into the street.

"No, but..."

"And it would've come out eventually."

"Will…"

"I'm a clone of your grandfather, Neave," he said, as they headed towards town. "That's a rather significant problem." The stony look on his face was unsettling.

She closed her eyes and sighed.

"Will…"

But she couldn't think of what to say. So they rode the short distance home in silence as she tried to think. Once inside the apartment, he immediately pulled his bag out of the closet.

"What're you doing?" she asked, her voice barely above a whisper.

"Packing."

"I can see that. But why?"

"I have to leave."

"Leave?"

He kept moving.

"We need to talk," she said.

"Talk about what?" he said, tossing shoes into another bag.

"The I-love-you, you-love-me stuff."

He reached in the closet and quickly pulled several shirts from their hangers.

"Will, don't ignore me."

He rolled the shirts into a ball and crammed them into his bag. Then he strode into the bathroom. Neave followed, becoming frantic.

"Will!"

He gathered his shaving gear and toiletries and dumped them into a small zip bag.

She stepped close behind him and wrapped her arms around him.

"I love you," she whispered.

"I've gotta go."

"But you love me too."

"It's not allowed!" he yelled, pulling away.

"Not allowed?" Her voice wavered.

"You think I like this? You think I *want* to leave?" He hurried back to the bedroom. "I'm sick of being reminded I'm a clone every time I turn around. I'm sick to death of people treating me like I'm not a full-fledged human being. I started to think that, just maybe, with you, I wouldn't have to feel that way anymore. And then the shit really hit the fan. I don't want to see that look in your eye. I can't take it."

He picked up his bags, slinging one over his shoulder.

"I'm not gonna live my life like some pathetic imitation," he said.

"You can't just walk out on me."

"I have to. I'm a clone of your grandfather. And you would always have that in your brain. You'll always remember that picture. You'll poke around until you find other pictures so you can see how much I look like him. It'll gnaw at you. And it'll gnaw at me until...."

"Stop it! We're two people. You're Will, I'm Neave. And we love each other."

The pleading was thick in her voice, but he ignored her and headed for the door. She darted in front of him to block him.

"All of a sudden, you're Mister Morality?" she yelled. "This isn't the Victorian, Shakespearean era!"

"Those are two very different centuries."

"You get my drift!"

Her hands were balled into fists and part of her wanted to use them on him, like it would do any good.

167

"I've gotta go," he said softly, looking down.

"Where?"

It was clear he was struggling.

"Home."

She didn't remember stepping aside. Maybe she did or maybe he lifted her up and set her on the bed. She wasn't sure of anything except that she was now sitting alone on the bed where they'd woken up together that morning. She knew the apartment was empty and she was back in the cool, dark refrigerator.

Chapter 20

She sat for a long time, eyes unfocused, listening to herself breathe. Finally, she rose and went to the fridge, pulling out a wine chiller. She poured it into a tall glass and took a sip, but it tasted bitter, so she dumped it down the drain. She paced around the apartment from room to room, trying to make sense of the evening's events. Thinking back to the scene at her parents' home, she was infuriated all over again. Nat did it to punish her. It was his way of getting back at her for rejecting him.

And she had questions for her mother. The look in her mother's eyes as she stared at Will was one of shock and something else she couldn't name.

She saw the picture again in her mind and wondered why she didn't recognize her grandfather, why she had no idea Will looked like him. Then she realized her mother had never had any family pictures on display. At her friend J'nai's house, pictures were everywhere. Framed photographs, view screen digital images that changed every few seconds. She'd seen pictures of J'nai's parents when they got married, her grandparents on both sides, great-grandparents, aunts, uncles, group photos, portraits. At every house she'd ever visited, she'd seen family pictures. But not at her own house. At the Alvarez/Sullivan home there was original art purchased at expensive art galleries. There was sculpture and folk art her parents picked up on their travels. There were view-walls with scenes from all over the world. But there were no family pictures on display. She'd seen a few pictures of her father's family on the computer, but there were no collections of photographs of his family to show her friends. It was like he wanted to hide his relatives, like they weren't good enough. And there were no pictures at all of her mother's family. None. She thought it was normal when she was growing up, but now she knew her mother hadn't wanted her or anyone else, she guessed, to know what her father looked like. Neave had seen a picture of her grandfather as an old man in an online encyclopedia article but he just looked like an old man to her. He died before she was born and her mother had rarely mentioned him. And when she had spoken of him, there was no warmth in her voice. Neave had assumed that was their way – a distant family by nature.

Twenty minutes later she was once again walking through her parents' front door. Her father tried to give her a hug, but she brushed past him.

"Is that asshole still here?" she asked, peering through the door to the living room.

"If you're referring to Nat," her father said, "he's gone. But you should be thanking him for being concerned about your welfare."

"Right," Neave said, glaring at him. "He might be concerned about *his* welfare and he's probably concerned about *your* welfare but he's definitely not concerned about *my* welfare."

Dr. Alvarez cocked his head back so he was looking down his nose at her. When he spoke, his voice was calm.

"I happen to know Nat is very concerned about you."

"To hell with Nat!" she shouted, her eyes ablaze. "I didn't come here to talk about that, that... putrid pustule!" Then, more quietly: "I came here to talk with Mother."

She'd only raised her voice to her father one time but she had never yelled at him and he was momentarily taken aback. She could see the indignation in his eyes and the flaring of his nostrils.

"You do know, of course," he said, "that you cannot continue to see Mr. Galloway. Bad enough you were involved with a clone, but I won't stand for..."

"Where's Mother?"

"I won't stand for my daughter to have a relationship with a clone of her grandfather!"

Neave started towards the back of the house.

"I won't tolerate the family name being dragged through the mud like that!" he said in his booming voice.

Her mother stepped through the back door from the garden, wearing an emerald green caftan, a light sheen of sweat on her face and a Japanese fan in her hand.

"Do you understand me?" Dr. Alvarez roared.

"Robert," his wife said.

"I will not have the daughter of Robert Alvarez consorting with..."

"Robert!" Dr. Sullivan said, her voice sharp. "I think Neave and I need to have a mother-daughter talk. You mentioned earlier you had to go by the office this evening. Now might be a good time."

Her voice was calm and quiet but Neave knew her mother had just dismissed him. Which was shocking. She'd never seen her stand up to him. Never. And apparently, neither had her father. He stood there gawking at her like he didn't know who she was.

Without waiting for a reply, Dr. Sullivan took Neave by the elbow and led her towards the kitchen.

"How about a glass of wine, dear?" she suggested.

She chose a bottle of Chardonnay from the cooler and filled two wine glasses, setting them on the white table.

Neave watched the doorway, expecting her father to come barging in. Instead, she heard the front door slam.

They both took a sip at the same time and smiled their approval. Neave tipped her glass again and took a bigger drink, hoping it would help her relax.

"So," Dr. Sullivan began.

Neave nodded and took another sip before she spoke.

"First, I assume Nat engineered that, that... ambush."

"He called your father yesterday to congratulate him on his Senate confirmation and asked if we had seen you and your 'new friend' since you got back from Greenland. When your father told him we were having you over this evening, Nat asked if he could drop by for a few minutes beforehand."

Her mother took a big swallow of wine, then slowly twirled the glass by the stem as she continued.

"I wanted him to leave before you arrived but he and your father got into a long conversation about the shade ring. Then, as he was getting up to go, he said he had recently run across a picture of my father as a young man on the web and was taken by surprise because he strongly resembled your friend. Robert was intrigued and said he'd only seen my father in his later years and wasn't sure he would recognize him as a young man. Nat had just transmitted the picture to the view screen when you and Will arrived."

She drained her glass and touched the corners of her mouth with her finger.

"I'm not the praying type, as you know, but I was doing

172

something akin to praying as I heard the two of you come through the door. Praying Nat was wrong."

Neave sat quietly, waiting for her mother to continue.

"And when I saw that strong, handsome face, well... my heart was racing."

Neave refilled their glasses as she tried to recall what she knew about her grandfather. Dr. Jack Sullivan had been a pioneer in genetics and had created quite a stir when he successfully cloned human organs when he was only in his thirties. She'd read in an online biography that he had even cloned his own liver and had it implanted when he developed cirrhosis. There had been speculation that he succeeded in cloning humans, but he never admitted it and died in his nineties in an accident at his home.

"How many clones? And why?"

Her mother sighed.

"Two. As for why – my father decided organ cloning wasn't enough. He didn't want to be a healthy *old* man. He wanted to be a healthy *young* man. A virile, healthy young man. So he spent years working on brain transplants. The older he got, the more delusional he became. And when he felt he was getting close, he cloned himself. I was a geneticist by then – a field he chose for me – and he insisted I help him. Out of all our attempts, two embryos survived. He paid two different women to carry them and give birth to them and then nurse them. He never visited them."

Dr. Sullivan took another swallow and sighed.

"But you did?" Neave said.

"They were just like real babies," she said dreamily. "They *were* real babies. They laughed. They cried. They learned to walk and talk. They played with toys. They clung to their mothers like all babies do. And I..."

Neave had never seen emotions get the better of her mother this way.

"I couldn't allow him to use those little boys. They were human beings, not lab rats."

"So you…" Neave said.

"Intervened."

"How?"

"I couldn't figure out how to hide them, how to spirit them away. Their surrogate mothers were well paid for their services. I was afraid if I approached them, they would tell my father what I was up to. And, besides, I knew that if I was somehow able to save them, he would just make more clones. And I couldn't allow that. He had decided to implant his brain in one of the boys when they reached the age of fifteen. He was already in touch with a surgeon in China he'd worked with on brain transplants. It was pure insanity."

Dr. Sullivan had a faraway look in her eye, as though she'd been transported back in time to a very ugly place.

"So what did you do?" Neave asked.

"Well, I brought his old golf cart out of the garage."

Which was the last thing she expected her mother to say.

"He wanted to drive it," Dr. Sullivan went on, "which I fully expected. I told him he was too old to drive, which made him furious. I told him I was going to drive him to the clubhouse, which was adjacent to his property, that I thought he would enjoy being back on the links again. He called me names in front of the cook and chauffeur. And then he drove himself to the clubhouse. And he started driving himself regularly. He loved driving that golf cart. Sometimes I rode with him and cautioned him to be careful, to stay away from the cliff along the fifth fairway. I knew he hated being nagged by anyone, especially me. And I knew him well enough to know he was a risk taker. Sometimes, just to scare me, he drove close to the cliff on purpose. He couldn't play golf anymore but he loved getting out in his golf cart. So I bided my time, waiting for just the right opportunity. And one day, when no one was around, I rode along with him, begging him not to drive near the cliff. He laughed at me, telling me, as usual, that I was a sissy. He drove to the very edge, trying to scare me. And I was ready."

Neave sat transfixed, hardly breathing. Dr. Sullivan drank again from her glass and then a steely look came into her green eyes.

"I had a remote control in my hand that looked like my iCom," she said. "I clicked 'accelerate' and I jumped."

Neave stared at her mother, trying to imagine her as a murderer. It didn't compute.

"I dismantled the remote and placed the components in recycling containers far from Father's home. No one ever suspected me. His cook, his driver, his lab assistants and even Robert had all heard me warn Father about driving the golf cart."

She closed her eyes and leaned forward, putting her hands on the small of her back, as though in pain.

"And the boys?" Neave asked.

"Adopted by two different families."

Dr. Sullivan refilled her glass again, which she then carried with her as she paced around the kitchen, finally coming to rest leaning against the counter. She sipped in silence as Neave digested this terrifying story. It finally occurred to her to ask why she didn't adopt them.

"Your father," Dr. Sullivan replied.

"He said no?"

"I didn't ask him." She appeared to struggle over what to

say next, running her fingers through her hair and sighing. "Your father is an ambitious man – very much into status and appearances. We've never talked about it, but I always knew he was consciously raising the cachet of the Alvarez family name when he married me. He married a distinguished name, connections, and a bit of money. He was never in love with me. It was what you might call a business transaction. He was interested in his career and other things – not having a family. Especially that kind of family. He would never have accepted them. As you know, he wasn't exactly a model parent for his own flesh and blood. Of course, it's probably a miracle he's as decent as he is, considering how he was treated as a child."

"How was he treated?"

"His own mother was psychotic. And a drug addict to boot. She never gave him love and affection and abandoned him when he was nine. His grandparents took him in, but the damage was done."

For a moment, Neave imagined a sad, lonely little boy with dark hair. She'd never really thought of her father as a child. It came as a bit of a shock.

"And I never saw the boys again and always hoped they were adopted by loving families," she said.

~~~

She stopped at a Coffee Casa rather than heading home. She knew the emptiness of her apartment would be overwhelming. So she sat at a table by the window, a Danish and a mug of café con leche in front of her. She picked up the mug and blew softly, causing steam to swirl in front of her face. The delicious smell reminded her of that morning when she and Will had gone for a late breakfast after he had kissed her awake and made the most passionate love to her. God, she had been so happy sitting across from him drinking coffee, talking about everything and nothing. She had felt then like a big, shiny party balloon floating on a string. Now, she was deflated, limp.

Without taking a drink, she set her cup down and gazed out the window. It was after eleven and the sidewalk was full of people. But she looked past them, her eyes unfocused. She saw his handsome face, his dimple, his long, straight nose and his thick brown hair which she loved to run her fingers through. But his resemblance to her grandfather was unnerving. She couldn't deny it. They had the same deep blue eyes. That must've been why he looked familiar when she met him. It wasn't often that she saw blue eyes. They'd become few and far between with intermarriage but were more common when her grandfather was born.

Sitting in the coffee shop wasn't helping her think so she decided to walk instead. Her mind flitted about, like a butterfly that didn't seem to really know where it was going, only that it needed life-sustaining nectar.

She thought it would've been worse if she'd actually known her grandfather. At least she'd never met him, which was good. But still, she was back to wondering about the nature of clones. She knew enough to know he had the same DNA as Jack Sullivan, but he didn't have the same gene markers. And he'd lived a different life, been raised by a different family. The whole "nature versus nurture" debate came back to her. How much of a person is based on his genes and how much stems from his upbringing, his environment.

It also bothered her that he was one of two clones. Was there another Will out there? Would she be able to tell them apart?

Perspiration soaked through her dress as she continued walking. She wanted to sweat. She wanted to flush the unpleasantness from her body. But she wished she had someone to talk with. And she realized that someone was Will. He was the first person in her entire life she'd felt close enough to really talk with about things that were truly important to her. And he cared what she said. He cared.

He might be a clone of her grandfather, but he was obviously not her grandfather. He was no megalomaniac. He didn't use people for his own ends. He was the man she loved. He was Will Shakespeare Galloway. He was the man who loved her. And he was the man she wanted and needed. Tears overflowed as she realized she couldn't even imagine life without him. He'd walked out of her apartment to give her the freedom to move on, if that's what she needed. He'd given her a way out of their relationship. But she didn't want out. She wanted in.

Chapter 21

When she finally turned onto the coastal highway, she was exhausted. She'd driven the car herself rather than using the autonomous mode. Her GPS told her she was almost there and she recognized the landmarks from what Will had told her. The sun would be coming up soon. It was too early to arrive unannounced at the Galloway home so she drove slowly past it. It was bigger than she'd imagined, a yellow house with gables, at the end of a tree-lined driveway – like something out of long ago. She parked a short distance down the road on the beach side and decided to watch the sunrise. She followed a path between two large dunes covered with sea oats and pulled her sandals off, carrying them in her hand.

The water was calmer than she'd ever seen it. It looked more like a giant lake of silver mercury the way it curled and swirled, the water and sky seeming to merge into one. Maybe it was because the Gulf of Mexico was calmer than the Atlantic here on the Florida panhandle. The sound of the surf was peaceful, nothing like the last time she'd been to the coast. The hissing of the wavelets lapping on the sand had a muffled quality to her ears and there was no sunken city nearby to dirty the landscape. She looked first to the west and then to the east.

And there, in the distance she could see a man holding a

long pole out over the water. He was too far away to see clearly but there was something about the way he held his body that convinced her it was Will. Small crabs darted into their holes as she walked towards him. Instinctively, she scanned the beach for larger ones, but saw none.

The sand gave way beneath her toes and a light breeze lifted her hair from her shoulders as she squinted, trying to make out his features. She was still wearing the short, sleeveless dress she'd put on for dinner the evening before and the breeze felt wonderful on her bare legs and arms. She closed the distance slowly, not knowing what she would say. She just knew she had to keep walking.

As she got closer, he turned and saw her. But then he cast his line again. Standing on the wet sand, he was barefoot and shirtless with his jeans rolled up to his knees, holding what looked like an antique rod and reel. There was a bucket sitting on the sand a few feet behind him.

She thought he might speak as she approached but he held his gaze on the ocean. She came to a stop behind him, noticing a cleaned fish in the bucket. She leaned against him, laying her cheek on his back, slipping her arms around him and sliding her hands in his front pockets. It felt so good to touch him, to breathe in his scent, sweaty now from long hours on the road mixed with the smell of fish and the beach. She breathed deeply and closed her eyes.

After a few moments he jerked slightly and pulled on his fishing rod. She stepped away so he could reel in his catch. Silvery grey and nearly a foot long, the fish thrashed about on the line as he lifted it from the water and removed the hook. He pulled a hunting knife from his pocket and expertly slit it open, cut the head off and dumped its guts into the waves. He dropped the fish in the bucket, picked up the pail along with his pole, nodded for her to follow and led her to a spot near the dune.

He stacked small pieces of wood and struck a match, using dry bits of kindling he'd gathered to get a fire going. Then he opened a pack and spread a blanket on the sand, motioning for her to sit. He pulled the tan shirt he'd worn the night before from the pack and put it on before retrieving a black iron frying pan, a bottle of oil, a bag of cornmeal, and salt and pepper shakers.

She sat on the blanket, hugging her knees, watching him as he filleted the fish on an old cutting board.

"Fish," he said, finally, "is a great breakfast food. People around the world have eaten fish for breakfast for thousands of years."

He rolled each piece in cornmeal and laid it in the hot oil. Four portions, side by side. The smell was heavenly. The sizzle from the frying pan intermingled with the lapping of the waves on the sand. She watched as he deftly turned the fillets with a fork.

A glow to the east announced the rising sun and she looked out over the water in time to see low clouds far out at sea turn scarlet and pink. She watched for a moment, then turned back towards the fire. He was looking at her, his hair dancing in the breeze, his face reflecting the warm glow of the sun. He hid the wistful look in his eyes at once, turning his attention again to his cooking.

"I found this frying pan in an abandoned building near old Panama City. Cooks great. Handle gets hot, though," he said, wrapping it with a towel and setting the pan on the sand by the fire.

Then he lifted the fillets onto a plate. They were brown and crispy and Neave was more than ready to try fish for breakfast. She realized she hadn't eaten anything since a late lunch the day before when they'd split a burrito at the apartment. He brought the plate to the blanket and sat next to her.

"It's flounder," he said.

She'd never tasted anything as scrumptious. And it wasn't just because she was hungry. It tasted like real food. And, of course, he had prepared it.

"Mmmm," she said, holding her fish with her fingers and crunching on it like it was fried chicken.

They ate mostly in silence, licking their fingers when they were done. The sun was up and the temperature was rising fast.

"You drove a long way for our farewell breakfast," he said, giving her a tired look.

"What makes you think I came to say farewell?"

"Well, you know, the speech about 'we'll always be friends.'"

"Will…"

"You're an honorable person," he said. "I know you don't want to hurt me. I understand."

"No…"

"Yes, I…"

"No, you don't!" she snapped. "You do *not* understand."

She was sitting on her knees now.

"All right. Maybe I don't totally understand," he said. "But maybe you don't totally understand either."

He got to his feet and kicked sand onto the fire.

"I can't help who I am," he said. "I can't help how I was created. I can't help that there's more than one of me out there."

"Will…"

"And I can't control how your revulsion would bubble up."

He leaned over to put the cornmeal back into the pack, refusing to look at her.

"Will!" she shouted, jumping to her feet.

"And it *would* bubble up. I don't blame you for not wanting to make love to your grandfather."

"Shut up! Just shut up and listen for a minute. You're not my grandfather!"

He straightened up and looked her in the eye.

"Right, well, I'm a..."

"You're as different from my grandfather as I am from my mother! Or my father! You have your own soul just like I do."

"I don't want your pity," he said, lowering his voice as he bent over to pick up the blanket.

"Pity? Pity?"

She surprised herself by shoving him from behind, taking him off guard, and knocking him onto the blanket. He rolled onto his back and started to get up, but she jumped on top of him, pushing him flat on his back.

"You listen to me," she said, sitting on his stomach as she grabbed his shoulders. "I've thought this whole thing through, all night long. I thought about everything! And you know what? I can't even imagine life without you. Do you hear me?"

Her tears escaped then, but she wasn't through.

"Do you?" she yelled.

"But..."

"But nothing! You're the man I..."

"It won't work, Neave."

"Yes, it..."

"No..."

"We can *make* it work," she said.

He stared into her eyes, searching.

She lowered herself until their lips were touching and she

kissed him very gently.

"You're the love of my life," she whispered. "I can feel it in my heart, in my gut, in my soul."

He blinked his eyes several times.

"But, what if you change your mind?" he said.

"Will, do you know how much I love you?"

"I'm positive your family is against..."

"Screw my family."

She closed her eyes and pressed her cheek against his, so that her lips touched his ear.

"You are my heart," she whispered. "There's no way I can live without you."

He closed his eyes and breathed slowly.

"Neave..."

"My heart," she whispered.

Strands of her hair were blown by the wind into his face but he didn't brush them away.

"Are you sure?" he asked.

"God, yes."

And only then did he wrap his arms around her, whispering her name. They rolled over so they were facing each other. He stroked her hair and rubbed his hands over her back. When they were both calmed down, he kissed her softly as the wind picked up, scattering sand over them. But neither of them seemed to notice. She wanted nothing more than to lie here with him and feel his arms around her, feel their hearts beating together.

"I want you," she whispered in his ear. "Forever."

She kissed his mouth, full of longing and his hand traveled over her body, sliding under her dress. But as she pressed herself against him, they were startled by someone clearing his throat.

They looked up to see two young men only a few feet away, staring down at them. Her heart pounded as the worst possibilities flashed through her mind. She didn't see any weapons but there were two of them. The taller one was a handsome young black man about the color of her café con leche, wearing a white, gauzy sun shirt and straw sun hat. The other one was a skinny teenager, nearly six feet tall, who looked Middle Eastern. He was shirtless with a dark shock of hair topped by a cowboy hat.

"Gib wanted to keep on watching," the taller one said, nodding towards his young partner and crossing his arms over his chest. "But I wasn't sure it was a good idea for him to have such a graphic lesson on sexual intercourse at the tender age of fifteen."

The corner of Gib's mouth curled up.

Neave had heard of young men in remote areas attacking people. Sexual attacks too, she recalled. She wished she had her stun gun with her that she used to keep under her bed.

"You scullions! Rampallians! Fustilarians!" Will shouted.

She stared at him like he'd lost his mind.

"*Henry the Fourth*," he explained.

"Is that the best you can come up with?" the taller man said.

Wide grins split the intruders' faces.

"Neave, these are my brothers, Charlie and Gib," Will explained.

Chapter 22

As the four of them strolled to the Galloway home, Neave was struck by its tranquil appearance. It was nestled about two hundred yards off the coastal highway, at the end of a paved driveway with live oaks on both sides, whose branches intertwined overhead, forming a charming tunnel. The trees had been shaped by constant sea breezes so they all leaned towards the house as if pointing the way. The house itself was surrounded by even larger live oaks whose branches seemed to wander up and down so you weren't sure where they started and where they ended. The house was painted a soft yellow with white shutters. A wrap-around screen porch and gabled windows made it look like something out of the 1900's. Pretty white latticework hid sturdy concrete pilings that raised the house off the ground, allowing parking underneath and protecting the home from storm surges.

Will held Neave's hand in his, carrying his fishing pole in the other hand. Charlie had the bucket and Gib carried Will's supply pack. The three had fallen into animated conversation about the valuable antiques they'd scrounged from recent demolition sites. But she knew he was very much with her, the way he caressed the back of her hand with his thumb.

When he turned to look at her, there was an amused glint in his eyes.

"In fact, I actually found Neave at old Charleston," he said, grinning. "I'm climbing down from the XT one evening and I hear a woman's voice screaming bloody murder."

She sighed and rolled her eyes.

"Yeah, and I see this woman in a green cooling suit with her leg in the claw of a coconut crab."

"I didn't know..." she protested.

"It was like a horror movie," he continued. "You know – the creature from the boiling lake."

He dropped his fishing pole and scooped her up in his arms.

"It was like I was a knight in shining armor," he said, looking into her eyes. "And it was love at first sight."

"You couldn't even see my face," she said.

"Okay, second sight," he said.

"I think it was thirteenth sight," she said. "Maybe fourteenth."

And he kissed her until she developed a serious blush.

"You're bound and determined to give Gib a hook-up lesson," Charlie said, touching his vibrating iCom. "Mama says why didn't you tell her you were coming? She's in there fixing buttermilk biscuits without any buttermilk for Sunday breakfast. Just wait till she finds out you brought a guest." And he tapped out a reply.

Neave wasn't sure what she'd expected but she was taken by surprise when they walked through the kitchen door and found a woman sliding a pan of homemade biscuits into an antique yellow oven. The oven door squeaked as she closed it. Then she turned around, a welcoming smile on her face.

She was a light-skinned black woman with charming freckles and large, expressive brown eyes, wearing a printed aqua caftan and matching hoop earrings. She was unabashedly plump, not slender like Neave's mother and every other woman she knew. She wore a short, salt and pepper Afro.

"Come here and give me a kiss," she said to Will, who happily obeyed, hugging her and kissing her forehead.

"Now, introduce me to this lovely young woman," she said.

"Mama, this is Neave Alvarez. Neave, this is my mother, Angela Galloway."

"I'll call you Neave and you call me Angela," she said, moving past Neave's outstretched hand to pull her into a warm embrace. "How nice," she said, patting Neave's cheek.

"I'm so glad to finally meet you," Neave replied.

"Now, everybody wash your hands and let's get some breakfast on the table," Angela said. "Will, you scramble up a dozen eggs. Charlie, you make up a pot of grits, Neave, you can set the table, and Gib, if you'll round up some jellies, honey and butter and put them on the Lazy Susan."

The kitchen was transformed into a hive of activity and a mingling of wonderful aromas. A little girl with shiny black pigtails skipped into the room and helped Neave arrange pretty butterfly plates, napkins and silverware on the table.

"Hi," she said. "My name is Isabel and I'm six years old. Who are you?"

"My name is Neave. I'm a friend of Will's."

Isabel looked like a cross between Latino and Japanese and was prettier than any child Neave had ever seen.

Charlie swooped in with a stack of glasses and proceeded to pour orange juice from a yellow jug, giving the little girl a gentle tug on one of her pigtails.

"This is Charlie. He's twenty-one years old," said the little girl.

"Yes, he and I just met," said Neave.

A few minutes later they were seated at the big, round table, everyone talking and laughing and serving themselves. There was a big basket of fluffy biscuits, a gravy boat with steaming, cream-colored gravy, a huge bowl of scrambled eggs, a big bowl of grits with a pool of butter on top, sliced cantaloupe, a bowl of canned peaches and fresh coffee. The smell made her stomach growl but no one noticed with all the noise.

As the bowls and plates were passed and the Lazy Susan twirled around she could feel the warmth of family, which made her envious. She felt like she was in a period movie set in pioneer America, except no family back then would've looked like this one.

"So how did you two meet?" Angela asked.

"You'll be so proud, Mama," Charlie said.

"Yeah," Gib chimed in, "Will rescued her from some sea monsters." He grinned at his own cleverness, nodded at Will and popped a big spoonful of grits in his mouth.

"Yeah, it's true," Will admitted, telling the story again about saving her from the giant crabs. Everyone laughed as they ate. Neave too.

"I actually didn't know what she looked like during the rescue operation," he joked. "Her back was to me and I've gotta tell ya, it was a big relief when I got her inside and she turned around and I could see my arm had been wrapped around such a beautiful woman." He paused to smile at her and everyone said "Awww" in unison.

When breakfast was over, Angela led Neave and Will upstairs while the others tackled cleanup. Stepping into a bedroom at the east end of the house, she gestured at the sun-filled room. The walls were pale aqua, decorated with a few well-chosen wall hangings, including an abstract sand and surf design above the bed that was actually a quilt made of tiny squares of cloth. The large bed was covered with a summery white coverlet. An antique love seat upholstered in teal and aqua checks sat near the window. Dainty white curtains and small white area rugs completed the airy décor.

"This is a guest room now," she said. "Used to be Will and Charlie's room. You should be comfortable in here."

"It's beautiful," Neave said, walking quickly to the window to gaze out towards the ocean visible in the distance, over the dunes.

"Will, why don't you bring her things in?" Angela suggested.

~~~

After moving her car from the road and parking it under the house, he returned, locking the door and setting his bag on the hardwood floor beside Neave's bag. He stood by the door, staring at her where she sat on the bed. His Adam's apple bobbed as he swallowed.

"There's a nice shower in there," he said, nodding towards the bathroom and pulling his shirt off. "But… I don't know, I kind of wish my smart-ass brothers hadn't interrupted us on the beach." He raised one eyebrow and looked down for a moment. "I really wanted to taste the sweat on your skin." He crossed the room, forcing her not to look away. "I still do."

Her joints seemed to loosen as he held her hands and pulled her off the bed to stand in front of him. He was only inches from her, his head bent towards her. He was waiting, she realized, for her reply – waiting for permission. She paused only a second before unzipping his pants.

They were like two animals, burying their faces in each other's musk, moaning and panting. It was a far cry from the lovemaking they'd shared before. This was more like they were trying to consume each other. And when they were finally spent, she was slightly bruised and he had a couple of scratches on his back. They lay side by side, holding hands. She listened as his breathing slowed and thought he'd dozed off, but he moved towards her then, turning her away and pulling her butt into his lap. He put his mouth on the back of her neck and whispered to her.

"Love is a spirit, all compact fire."

"From?"

"A poem called *Venus and Adonis.*"

With one hand he softly caressed her breast, then rolled her nipple between his thumb and forefinger till its firmness matched his own growing hardness behind her.

"I feel like a wanderer in the desert who finally finds water and can't get enough," he said, kissing her on the shoulder as he pushed against her. "Tell me to stop and I will."

She replied by pressing herself more firmly against him.

Neave didn't know what he'd said to his family, but no one bothered them for the rest of the day, leaving them to take a leisurely shower together and a long nap entwined in each other's arms. When they finally emerged from their room, the air was thick with the tantalizing smell of fried chicken.

"Does your mother cook everything from scratch?" she asked.

"Just about."

The closer they got to the kitchen, the more self-conscious she became. She glanced down at her white shorts and blue tank top and wondered if she should've dressed up a bit. She expected hidden glances but no such luck.

"Well, did you lovebirds finally work up an appetite for food?" Angela asked, laughing heartily as she carried a large bowl of potato salad to the table. She was dressed in a pretty blue and green broom skirt with a light blue top.

Neave felt herself crimsoning as the others converged on the table, laughing.

"Mama decided to fix fried chicken to make sure you two keep your strength up," Charlie said, stressing the word "up" as he glanced conspiratorially around the table.

"It's true," Angela said, "exerting yourself all day can make you weak if you don't refuel."

Will spooned potato salad on his plate and smirked playfully as Gib lifted the platter of fried chicken.

"Breast," Gib teased, "or thigh?"

Everyone roared with laughter. Neave chuckled quietly to herself, glad her hair was hanging over her ears which were getting hotter and hotter.

Finally, little Isabel spoke up.

"What kind of job were you guys doing all day to get so hungry?"

Which sent them all into spasms, leaving the little girl looking innocently around the table.

After dinner they moved to the comfortable living room decorated in pale yellows and light blues. Neave was about to sit in a chair by the window, but Will took her hand and guided her to a nearby loveseat, pulling her down next to him and wrapping his arm around her. Out of the corner of her eye, she caught a momentary expression on Angela's face that reminded her of her own mother when she was concerned about her father saying something unpleasant to Neave. Was it a look of dread? Uneasiness? But it was gone as quickly as it had appeared.

"Cobbler, Mama?" Gib asked, pushing an antique serving cart towards her, loaded with coffee and homemade peach cobbler.

"Heavens, no. I just made it for a room deodorizer," Angela deadpanned, causing more laughter.

He served her first and then made the rounds as though he were a waiter in a fine restaurant, adding a scoop of vanilla ice cream to everyone's cobbler while Charlie poured coffee.

Neave wondered when the family friction would start to show at the seams.

"Well, we've talked your ear off," Angela said, stirring creamer into her coffee. "We've hardly let you get a word in edgewise."

"Oh, I'm enjoying it," Neave said.

"Do you have brothers or sisters?" Charlie asked, setting a mug of coffee on the table beside her.

"No, she doesn't."

It was a husky woman's voice that was familiar to Neave. They all turned as Jaz strode into the room. Isabel squealed and jumped up.

"Jazmin!" she shrieked as Jaz lifted her and swung her around in circles, nearly toppling a floor lamp in the process.

Angela was on her feet too, hurrying across the room.

"Well, you could've messaged me, you know," she said. "But, noooo, everyone's gotta walk in unannounced."

She hugged Jaz close as Isabel clung to her side.

"But you like surprises, Mama," Jaz said, kissing Angela on the forehead.

She towered over her mother like she towered over most people.

"And it's a good thing," said Angela. "First, Will arrives unannounced. Then I find out he's brought a guest. And a lovely guest she is, too," she said, smiling at Neave. "And, now you're here without so much as a howdy-doo!"

Angela hooked her arm through her daughter's and they

made their way into the room.

"And this is Neave," she said.

"We've met," Jaz said, sitting down next to her mother and pulling Isabel onto her lap.

Gib served her a bowl of cobbler and poured her coffee.

"At Charleston," Will explained.

"Although I didn't know you were related," Neave said.

Jaz eyed Will.

"We were just getting to know each other a little bit," said Angela.

"Like what we do? Who our parents are?" Jaz asked, raising her eyebrows.

"So you're an only child," Charlie said.

"Unfortunately," Neave replied.

"You must think we're a rowdy bunch then," he said.

"I like rowdy," Neave said, laughing, between bites of cobbler.

"And our line of work may seem a bit alien to you," Angela said. "Demolition, recycling, selling antiques. Not what you're used to, I'm sure."

"Is the whole family involved in the business?" she asked, trying to delay the inevitable.

"Well, we all work either with the demolition company or the solar/wind company. Or both," Will explained. "We each have a piece of the pie."

"Speaking of pie," Neave said, pointing to her bowl with her spoon, "this is the best I've ever eaten. Do you have a secret ingredient?"

Angela nodded vigorously.

"Top secret," she said, holding her finger in front of her mouth. "Don't tell anyone," she whispered. "Tons of sugar!"

More laughter.

"Have you talked about what *your* family business is yet?" Jaz asked.

"Science," said Neave. "Although I haven't decided if it's for me."

She looked at Will, unsure what else she should say.

"Her father," said Jaz, "is Dr. Robert Alvarez – the world famous climatologist and our new Climate Secretary. And her mother is Dr. Molly Sullivan – a geneticist at Pioneer Genetics."

That quieted everyone down. Charlie gave Will a look. Angela nodded and drank from her mug as Gib glanced from Jaz to Neave as though trying to figure out a mystery.

"And just like us," said Will, "Neave has no control over who her parents are."

Angela nodded her head and smiled reassuringly at Neave.

"Isabel, sweetie, how about you and I show Neave the verandah," she suggested.

A hot breeze greeted them but Neave was glad to be outside, away from judgmental eyes. Angela flipped a switch that turned on several chill fans, so it was tolerable. The porch had a wooden plank floor and was enclosed with dark screening to keep the bugs out. A variety of rockers and settees provided plenty of seating, no matter which side of the house you were on. There were cactus plants here and there on tables and window ledges.

"Wanna swing with me?" Isabel asked, sitting down in a white porch swing and patting the seat beside her.

So Neave sat next to Isabel who pushed energetically until they were swinging rather more forcefully than a porch swing was designed for, the chain squeaking rhythmically. Angela told her to slow down a bit.

"Are you and Will gonna get married?" Isabel asked, looking up at Neave.

"Isabel, sweetie, you shouldn't ask personal questions like that," her mother said softly.

"Oh, sorry," Isabel said. "I was just wondering."

"Quite all right," Neave said.

"It's just that Will hasn't never brought a lady home before."

She stopped pushing and the swing gradually slowed.

"That's right," said Angela. "This is a big event."

Neave didn't know what to say.

"I've never seen him so happy," Angela continued, sighing. "But..." She cocked her head thoughtfully and chewed her lower lip. "Do you know," she said, finally, "that all of my children are clones?"

Neave shook her head slowly, taken by surprise.

Angela leaned back and gazed into the distance.

"I was married to a woman I loved a long time ago," she explained. "We both loved children and planned to have a family together. But her family disapproved of our relationship. Told her she would be disowned, banished forever, never allowed to see them again. So, she left me. Broke my heart."

Neave could see pain and regret in her eyes.

"Then one day, a couple of years later, she messaged me, saying she needed my help. When we talked by phone she asked if I still wanted children. I said 'of course.' Though my original plan had included two parents, not one. She said there was a little clone boy who badly needed a home and would I be willing to take him in? She said it had to be hush-hush and that she couldn't give me any information except that his life might depend on it. I didn't hesitate. And less than a week later she brought this little tow-headed boy to me. Great big blue eyes. Sweet smile. Though he didn't smile much at first."

She stood up then and strolled to the edge of the porch, looking towards the ocean. The setting sun painted the puffy clouds a pale peach color.

"I loved him from the moment I saw him," she continued. "Decided to name him William Shakespeare Galloway because I loved Shakespeare. Believe it or not, I actually got to play Juliet and Ophelia when I was in college."

She chuckled to herself but then turned towards Neave and looked her in the eye.

"I started doing research on cloning, making contacts. Turned out there was a growing number of scientists cloning humans. Some rich couples have two or three clones created and just keep the one whose appearance they like the best, or whose personality they like the best. You probably know that clones are not exact replicas."

She smoothed her top, pulling the hem lower over her skirt.

"So I kept adopting until I had a wonderful family. I loved them and nurtured them and taught them, but I can't protect them from everything. They still face a whole barrel full of rejection."

She folded her arms across her chest and sighed.

"Like right now, Gib is going through a tough time. He's fifteen, you know. And he's a very handsome young fellow, as you may have noticed. He's from Egyptian - Iranian stock and could be a model or an actor. But that's another story."

She picked up a fan lying on a table and fanned herself as she continued.

"Well, he fell in love with a pretty girl he met. But she just strings him along, smiles at him, gives him hope, then goes out with some other boy. Then flirts with him again – teasing him. She knows he's a clone and she apparently has no qualms about using him for her own entertainment."

She shook her head and sighed deeply.

"It's tough, you know. So you can see why we're very concerned about geneticists who…"

"My mother isn't involved in cloning," said Neave, deciding to avoid her mother's past.

Angela nodded thoughtfully, touching her upper lip with her finger to blot a bead of sweat.

"Toni says she's gonna have a baby the old-fashioned way," Isabel piped up. "But what *is* the old-fashioned way, Mama?"

Which prompted some chuckles and relieved the tension.

"Toni will be home in a few days, sweetie, so you can ask her, okay?" Angela said.

"Where is Toni?" Neave asked.

"Oh, she's in Colorado looking at some stuff," Isabel said. "Me and Toni and Jaz and Mama are goin' to the mountains for a vacation pretty soon. And we're gonna stay in a log cabin right beside a mountain stream! Jaz says it's for girls only."

"Wow, that sounds like fun," Neave said.

"Let's go back inside and cool off," Angela said. "I'm sweating like a pig out here."

They wandered through the deserted living room, gathering dessert bowls and coffee cups to take them to the kitchen when they heard Will's voice in the hallway, as though the door to the office had just opened.

"…the best thing that's ever happened to me."

And then he was in the kitchen, followed by Gib and Charlie, both wearing uncomfortable expressions. Jaz was a few steps behind. Will made a beeline for Neave, wrapping his arms around her waist from the back and pulling her close, causing her to nearly drop the dishes she was carrying.

Will kissed her on the cheek, smiling at Jaz, who shrugged in reply.

Chapter 23

"Okay… so why didn't you tell me Jaz was your sister?"

They were making the bed before heading down for breakfast the next morning. Neave was in a short white robe and Will was in his boxers.

"Well, it's not something I broadcast, you know. It raises eyebrows. Raises questions."

"Yeah, but later…"

He finished smoothing the bedspread.

"When I'm with you, I forget about my family."

They were on opposite sides of the bed.

"Like right now," he said. "I don't want to put my clothes on and go meet Charlie and Jaz. I want to…" and he crawled across the bed, pulling her down with him. "I want to…" and he untied her robe, pulling it open in front. "I want to…" and he rubbed his face over her breasts.

She closed her eyes and smiled.

"It's like I'm a deer in rutting season," he said. His hands glided over her bare skin. "You must think I'm an animal."

"I think you're ridiculously handsome and irresistibly sexy," she whispered, leaning closer to kiss him.

But they were interrupted by a sudden knock at the door.

"Will?"

It was Isabel.

"What's up?" he said, grinning.

"Mama says men don't live by bed alone. She won't tell me what it means, so it must be a secret code."

Which made them chuckle.

"Is it a secret code?" Isabel called.

"Yes," he replied. "It means I need to get to work. Tell her I'll be right down."

"Okay!" she cried.

They heard her skip down the hallway and clump down the stairs.

Neave kissed him, giving him a playful tweak lower down.

~~~

The warehouse was only a short walk from the house. It had been a school at one time – tan brick, one story with a curved driveway out front. The windows were covered over with sheets of plasteel. The A-frame roof was lined with thin solar panels and micro wind turbines.

"This was our first installation after we bought the solar/wind company," Will explained. "It provides enough power to air condition the building and run the security system, computers and lighting."

Isabel took Neave's hand and led her to the third room on the left where the toys and dolls were stored. Angela had given her permission to choose something to take back to the house. Will stood at the door for a few seconds for a security scan, which opened the door. He left the two of them to their toy shopping and joined the others in another room to discuss a shipment for a museum in Colorado.

The family might've thought she was just humoring her, but she was actually enjoying Isabel's tour. They looked at outdoor toys first – a rusted red metal wagon with a tag identifying it for restoration; a plasteel riding horse for toddlers that had been repainted in black and white; a set of gardening tools for small children made of wood and metal; and a variety of Frisbees. They worked their way through train sets, building sets and superhero figures and finally reached the shelves that held what Isabel longed for: dolls. There were decorative Japanese dolls in kimonos, teenaged dolls with stylish outfits, dolls that looked like little girls from around the world and baby dolls. Isabel picked up a baby doll with brown skin and black hair wrapped in a pink blanket and held her close.

"This is a newborn baby doll," she said, looking up at Neave. "Isn't she pretty?"

The doll had a tiny, puckered mouth with a little hole in it so you could give her a bottle.

She laid the doll on the floor and unwrapped the blanket.

"See? She has a diaper. And when she drinks her bottle, she pees."

She pulled the diaper off to show Neave the hole in the doll's bottom.

"Just like a real baby," said Neave.

"Yes!" Isabel said, smiling happily. "But where's the bottle?"

"Oh, I'm sure we can find one somewhere."

She rummaged through doll clothes, doll furniture, and other baby dolls until she found a toy diaper bag. Inside was a toy pacifier and a tiny bottle.

"Let's try this one," she said, handing it to Isabel, who was again holding the doll in her arms.

"It fits! It fits!" she cried. She ran from the room, calling "Mama, Mama!"

When Neave found her, she was giving the others a demonstration, her voice loud and happy as they stood in the center of a room filled with antique credenzas, China cabinets and cupboards.

"And the pee comes out here!"

The laughter was infectious and Neave laughed too. Isabel looked up at her.

"Neave, are you and Will gonna have a real baby?"

Which caught her so off guard that she coughed and laughed at the same time. Now that she and Will knew he was cloned from her grandfather, having a baby was out of the question. And while she hadn't dwelled on it, there was a tiny part of her that suffered from that loss. But now she'd seen firsthand that adopting children could mean a real family. And she knew that as long as she and Will were together, she would be happy. Of course, at this point she had no idea whether that was really in the cards. She didn't actually know what their future held.

"Isabel," Angela said. "I thought you weren't going to ask any more questions like that."

"Sorry," Isabel said.

"No problem," Neave said.

Her contraceptive vaccine was good for another six months so she didn't have to worry about getting pregnant. All the years she'd taken it without needing it, and now she finally needed the protection.

On their way back to the house, Isabel walked next to Neave, talking about her baby doll. She had decided to name her Seussilla, after Dr. Seuss. And she wanted to sleep with her at night and her mama said she could get a baby bed for her and on and on. And then as they mounted the steps to the house she piped up with another question.

"Are you and Will going to live here now?"

"Yeah, what's the plan?" Jaz asked.

"Don't have a plan," Will said.

When Neave looked his way, he was smiling at Isabel and she had the distinct feeling he was avoiding looking at her.

He spent the afternoon working on a sale to the Denver History Museum. So Neave took the opportunity to call her mother. She'd let her know where she was when she first arrived but decided it would be a good idea to touch base.

"Classes start next week," her mother said.

"Yeah, I know."

"Are you..."

"I don't know."

There was an awkward pause.

"Neave, dear, I..."

And then nothing for a moment.

"I'm glad we talked," Dr. Sullivan said. "And I hope we can talk again."

"I'd like that."

"We need to talk again."

"Is there something wrong, Mother?"

"No, no. Nothing's wrong. It's just... when you come back, let's talk again."

"We can talk now."

"No, nothing urgent. We'll open another bottle of wine sometime."

She'd never felt close to her mother and wasn't sure what to make of this conversation. She detected something in her voice, but didn't know what it was. But a relaxed conversation – just the two of them – over a bottle of wine would be a good thing. She suddenly wanted to know her mother better.

Supper was fruit salad and design-your-own pizza. Afterwards, Charlie produced a shiny red antique accordion, sat down in the living room and started playing polkas. Which, of course, meant that Neave got her first polka lesson, once the furniture was pushed out of the way.

Will grabbed her firmly and they bounded one way and then the other until she was out of breath. And she thought the waltz was exhausting! It was sedate compared with the polka. When they collapsed, laughing, on the love seat, she was holding her sides. But before she could catch her breath, Gib was standing in front of her, his hand outstretched and a hopeful look in his eye. She started to beg off, but after hearing about the sorry state of his love life, she jumped up and gave it her all.

"Where'd you learn to do the polka?" he gushed as they skipped and twirled around the room.

She laughed and rolled her eyes.

"Really," he said. "I didn't think anybody had even heard of the polka."

"Your brother just gave me my first lesson," she said, glancing over at Will, who was now taking a turn with Jaz.

Finally, Neave and Gib plopped down on the couch.

"I don't suppose you have a younger sister," he said. "No, of course not. You said you're an only child. That's too bad."

"Yeah, it is."

They clapped their hands as Angela took the floor with Isabel. Angela was surprisingly light on her feet and was quite the polka dancer! And then, when it was Isabel's bedtime, the accordion was retired and the sweaty dancers wandered off in different directions, leaving Neave and Will alone together for the first time since they'd taken a leisurely shower for two that morning, before Isabel's untimely knock at the door. He brought them both an ice cold beer and groaned as he sat down next to her on the loveseat.

"God, your family is amazing," she said.

"What about me?"

"You are the most amazing person of all."

And she leaned over and kissed him on the mouth, teasing him by rubbing her breasts against his chest. He set his beer down and tickled her, burying his chin in her neck, causing her to thrash about.

"Stop, you brute," she cried, still laughing.

"Only if you promise to..." he raised his head and looked around the room to make sure no one was there. "Only if you promise to tickle my fancy once we get to our room."

"Your fancy?"

"Mm-hm. Let's pick up right where we left off this morning before we were so rudely interrupted."

~ ~ ~

The following morning, she knew before opening her eyes that she was alone. Will had slipped away so he, Charlie and Jaz could attend a meeting in Tallahassee with a client. She hugged his pillow to her face and breathed in his scent. She knew he would have to return to work soon and the thought of sleeping in a bed without him depressed her immensely. She tried to imagine herself returning to Atlanta to begin classes, as her mother and father expected. Lots of couples lived that way – commuting on weekends. But she could feel the loneliness of a long distance relationship filling her heart already. She hugged the pillow tighter. He said he loved her and she believed him. And it was obvious he wanted her. A lot. But he had never said anything about marriage. And he'd never said anything about living together. And he'd avoided answering Isabel's question. What if he only wanted the kind of relationship where you both go about your business for a couple of weeks and then come together for a passionate weekend? She only knew that she wanted so much more.

When Will, Jaz and Charlie finally returned, supper was

on the table. Neave kissed him and pulled him excitedly to his chair. She thought he seemed a bit nervous when his mother announced that Neave had prepared the dinner.

"Don't worry," she said. "Your mom kept a close eye on me."

Which prompted Angela to sing her praises. Still, she noticed he seemed distracted during dinner – a little slow on the uptake, not throwing himself into the conversation like he usually did. And as they began to clear away the dishes Charlie spilled the beans.

"Great last supper together," he said.

"Last supper?" Neave asked, looking from Charlie to Will.

Charlie gave his brother an apologetic look.

"Well, we've got to get back to work tomorrow," Will explained.

"Another hurricane's on the way," Jaz added. "Gotta move some equipment."

"Of course," Neave said, stacking plates and bowls to take to the dishwasher.

"You two go on," Angela said, shooing them from the kitchen. "We'll clean up."

So they strolled arm in arm to their room where he pulled her onto his lap on the loveseat. She wrapped her arms around his neck as he buried his face in her hair. They sat quietly.

"So," he said.

"So."

"I've gotta get back to work and your classes are starting soon."

"Yes, but…"

"You enrolled, right?"

"Yes."

He sighed and held her tighter.

She never wanted to leave him. It hurt her heart to even consider it. But what if he had other plans? What if he liked his space and freedom?

"Well, I don't want to keep you from your classes," he said. "Will you miss me?"

"That's an exceedingly stupid question," he whispered.

She blinked several times, forcing herself not to cry. She wanted him to beg her not to go.

"No, it's not. I need to know."

He pulled back enough so he could see her face.

"Neave, don't you know by now how I feel?"

"Yes... sort of."

He shook his head incredulously as she heaved a big sigh.

"What's wrong?" he whispered.

"I can't bear the thought of not seeing you every day."

"But you're going back to..."

"So I enrolled to take classes online," she said.

"Online?"

She searched his eyes.

"Do you mind?" she said.

"Do I mind?"

"I mean, do you mind if I stay with you?"

He answered by laying her back on the couch and kissing her cheeks, her nose and forehead and then her mouth.

"Do I mind," he said finally, shaking his head. "I've been so afraid. Afraid I couldn't survive without looking into your eyes, without holding you in my arms every night. I was scared you wouldn't be satisfied staying with me, so I forced myself not to beg. And you thought I'd mind if you stayed?"

He kissed her deeply.

"You know what I really want?" he said. "I want you to marry me and stay with me always. But I don't have the kind of status you're used to. I stay on the edge of society so people won't covet what I've got. I'm not sure I'm good enough for you."

"You are so full of shit," she said, slapping his shoulder. "Say the part about wanting to marry me again."

"Neave, do you think you'll still love me fifty years from now?"

"Oh, Will."

He lifted her in his arms.

"Marry me?"

"Yes, yes, yes."

He carried her to the bed without taking his eyes from hers. They held their gaze as they undressed each other.

"God, you are the most beautiful woman," he whispered. "I n'er saw true beauty till this night. But it's not just your lovely green eyes or this heavenly body. My soul craves your soul." He paused, holding himself above her. "It has to be you and only you. I love you, Neave, more than words – even the poetic words of Shakespeare."

He trailed off, his eyes glistening. And she looked deeply into the windows of his soul.

Chapter 24

As she pulled clothes from the closet of her Atlanta apartment, she realized she should've hired someone to do this. That way, she wouldn't have had to leave Will for even one day. None of this stuff mattered. She just wanted to get the movers in and out, put most of her things in storage and return to the coast.

She would join him at his work site in Mobile as soon as she wrapped up loose ends here. She couldn't wait. She already missed him intensely, aching to hear his voice in her ear, to feel his hands touching her, to look into those loving eyes. It made her tingle just thinking about him.

They had yet to talk about a wedding, but she knew she wanted a small affair. His family would be there, of course. As for her family, she would want her mother there, she thought, but not her father. Which was awkward.

The two moving men had been coming and going for more than an hour when she heard a familiar and unwelcome voice. It was Nat saying hello to the movers as they carried her sofa out the door.

He glanced around at the mess and walked in uninvited. He looked thinner, she thought, in dark grey slacks and an even darker grey polo.

"So it's true," he said.

She had hoped to get out of town without seeing him. But knowing she was leaving him behind forever made her relax. He was no more than a mosquito buzzing in her ear. She sighed in answer.

"You're dropping out of grad school?"

"Taking courses online."

She had the impression he was only half listening. Then he lifted a bag he was carrying and pulled out a bottle of Cabernet.

"I thought we could toast your new life," he said, carrying it to the kitchen where he opened the bottle and poured the wine into two biofoam cups.

"Are you sure you know what you're doing?" he said, handing her a cup.

"Positive."

"Your father's upset. Says he's not supporting you anymore if you do this."

She gave a small shrug.

"I wish you'd let me make a counter offer."

And he stared into her eyes and shook his head slightly.

"Nat, I wouldn't marry you if you were the last man on earth. And even then I wouldn't marry you. I'd change my sexual orientation instead."

It felt good to say it. She thought it might anger him but he smiled as though she'd said she preferred riding a scooter over a bicycle.

"Well, then, to your future," he said, holding his cup towards her as if they should touch them in a toast.

She only tipped her cup in his direction, just wanting to get this over with. While she didn't believe Lena's wild ravings about him breaking the ice dam on purpose and trying to kill them, she knew he'd engineered the Greenland trip to

211

boost her father's political ambitions, risking their lives in the process. And he'd arranged the ugly scene at her parents' home the night she and Will arrived for dinner, even if Will was right, that the truth had to come out sooner or later.

He took a big swallow and smacked his lips slightly. She didn't want to drink a toast with him but decided if it would speed his departure, she'd play along. So she took a sip, then drank it down and carried her cup to the recycle chute in the kitchen.

"By the way," he said as she returned to the living room, "I found the date that picture was taken."

She breezed past him and busied herself stuffing towels in a storage bag.

"The picture I was showing your mother and father the day you and Mr. Galloway arrived."

She turned around slowly as he crushed his cup in his hand.

"It was taken in 2045," he said and pumped his eyebrows.

She just stared at him.

"You can check it out yourself," he said.

The movers returned then, passing through the living room to the bedroom. They exchanged a few words in a language she didn't recognize.

"Well, I can see you're busy," he said. "So I guess I'll wish you good luck and be on my way." He looked at her for a moment before picking up his bag and walking out the door. "See ya later," he called as he headed for the elevator.

"Fat chance," she whispered under her breath.

She closed her eyes and recalled the image on her parents' wall. She'd been so focused that day on the man in the picture that she couldn't recall clearly how the woman looked. She'd thought at first that it was her and Will, then realized it was her mother as a young woman. If it was true, that it had been taken more than seventy years ago, then obviously it had to be her grandmother standing there with her grandfather. Of course. He was young, she was young. His arm encircled her waist. That's the way Will pulled her close when they were together. Neave would ask her mother to see the picture again. She wanted to see the grandmother she'd never known, who obviously looked a lot like her daughter.

Nat was a born trouble maker. Her instincts had been correct all along.

Her iCom dinged. She started to ignore it, thinking it was him, but then changed her mind. She was surprised to see it was a call from Rosa.

"Neave?"

Rosa's voice was shaky and breathless.

"Rosa? What's wrong?"

Dear Rosa was crying.

"Catalena has... she's..."

Neave was alarmed at Rosa's sobbing.

"What is it?"

"Catalena is dead. She... they say she killed herself."

Rosa sniffled, mumbling in Spanish as Neave stood in her empty living room, staring out the window at the sunbaked city. She tried to ask some questions. Was she sure? How did she learn about it? But Rosa didn't hear her. She said something about a message from Lena and hung up.

She pulled her iCom from her ear, staring at it in disbelief. She had to call her back. But there was a message from Kwan. It was actually a video message from Lena that Kwan had forwarded without comment. Lena had apparently set her iCom on the nightstand by her hospital bed so she could look into the tiny camera as she talked.

"Right, Kwan. Easy for you to say. No – everything's *not* gonna be ok," she said, leaning against a pillow, her hair unwashed, no make-up on. "It's like I'm in a cage with no door. And I think you'd better keep your distance. I just wish I'd told the truth. But now I'm in so deep, I'll never get out. I've tried to kick it, but I can't. No matter how hard I try. You don't know what it's like. And he keeps sending it to me. And, yes, I know it's what caused Osley's death. There are times I wish I could kill Nat. Take a giant rock and bash his head in! I can't sleep because I keep having nightmares. I see myself closing my eyes as the D hits me, sends me floating, while Nat's got the controls. He said 'no problem,' you know. No problem. He planned it. Dump Osley out of the chopper. He must've loosened the bolts or something. And I'm wanting the D so bad. I was desperate, you know? I'd run out, you know, while we were at the beach and he kept putting me off. By the time we were flying home, I was going nuts. So he pulls it out – the cartridge – and says 'Here ya go. Here's your fix. I'll take the controls for a minute. So, like a complete idiot – like a drug addict – I popped the cartridge in my e-cig and took a big drag. I wanted it so bad! I closed my eyes and inhaled until I felt the D in my veins.

"God, I'm sorry, Kwan. I've gotta figure out a way. But they have so much on me now. It's not just Osley's death. Not just the D. I've done stuff for them. Things you don't know about. And it would kill Rosa if she knew. I'm not even a student anymore. I flunked out. But they keep using me, keep paying me, keep giving me Discretion even though I want out. Nat even had me playing Cupid with Neave, trying to get her to go out with him. Ordered me to shoot video while I had sex with Osley but Osley told me to get lost. He made me do it to get my D. I don't wanna go to prison, Kwan. I don't know what I'm gonna do. But, you're wrong if you think it's easy to tell the truth. Estas equivocado."

The message was dated the day before.

Neave leaned against the wall and closed her eyes. She was stunned. But it was unthinkable that Lena would commit suicide. She loved life. Wanted to get married and have kids some day.

She clutched her iCom, considering who to call.

Kwan answered right away.

"Kwan..." she said, but her voice didn't work.

It only took about fifteen minutes for him to get there. He gave her a long hug. There was nowhere to sit, so they stood by the big window, alternately staring out at the endless blue sky and their shoes.

"Do you really believe she killed herself?" she asked.

He looked at her like she was dense.

"Well," she said, "I know she was depressed. I watched the message and things were bad. She was very low. But it's so hard for me to believe."

"Maybe you should watch it again. She was more than just 'very low.'"

Neave sighed and looked out the window again, thinking how desolate the landscape looked with the hot sun broiling everything as far as the eye could see.

"How'd she die?" she said.

"You've heard of Discretion?"

"But how'd she get it in the hospital?" she asked, walking slowly to the other side of the room.

Kwan shrugged.

The movers came through again with two carts loaded with boxes.

"She said Nat was her supplier," she said. "That he kept

sending it to her. What if he engineered an overdose."

"You think Nat…" Kwan said.

"Well, Rosa certainly didn't bring it to her," she said. "And we didn't bring it to her."

Neave was pacing, trying to think.

He put his hands on top of his head, lacing his fingers together.

"I brought her the e-cig," he said.

They looked at each other.

"We thought she was nuts," said Kwan.

"If Nat knew she wanted to come clean," she said, "he might've decided to shut her up. If he really did kill Osley like she said and if he really did try to kill you guys that day on the ice dam, then he wouldn't have any qualms about killing Lena."

They stared at each other with pained expressions.

"And he was just here," she said, her hands shaking.

"Who?"

"Nat."

"Today?"

"Yeah."

"What for?"

"To try to talk me out of marrying Will, I think. Although he didn't try very hard."

"Well, you know what? I think we can officially consider him dangerous. And I think you need to get the hell out of Atlanta."

"I'm gone as soon as the movers are done."

"And I think I need to catch a flight to Greenland. Some kind of proof about what happened on the ice dam would help. Can you call the police? Tell 'em it might not be a suicide? Tell 'em to find her e-cig. Maybe find out if Nat came to visit her?"

She nodded.

"And forward them her video message," he added.

And he was gone.

She was beginning to feel prickly. Her emotions were all jumbled and she was finding it hard to think. She couldn't believe Lena was gone. There was a growing lump in her throat that hurt so much, she could hardly swallow. And then tears were streaming down her face. She lowered herself to the floor where she sat on the pale blue rug her parents had given her when she moved in, head propped on her knees, eyes closed, completely drained. She didn't lift her head as the moving men made another trip to the bedroom. But she had to call the police.

She didn't know how long she'd been sitting there when the men returned, saying they needed to take the rug. She scooted over a few feet to the wall, watching as they rolled it into a tube. Then one of them handed her his e-board to sign and they carried the rug out the door and were gone.

She would call the police. But she was so tired... drained... nauseated. She lay down on the bare floor, staring up at the white ceiling, but the ceiling was undulating like white caps on the ocean, which made her dizzy. Her eyelids were heavy. She was so hot. Very hot. She unzipped her green climate suit trying to get some air to her skin. She needed a tiny rest... just a bit of rest before she called.

Chapter 25

She was in the middle of a river – floating, bobbing. But the air around her was so stiflingly hot, she could hardly breathe. She pulled at her clothes. And then something cool was on her forehead. Maybe a fish, she thought. There were voices around her but they seemed to be speaking in a foreign language. And then the water moved more slowly and she twirled around, as though caught in an eddy, round and round. And then she drifted away to a quiet, dark place – like a cave.

When sounds began to penetrate her mind again, she couldn't tell how long she'd been in the cave but she was hot and pushed the cloth from her body.

"Neave…"

It was a man's voice.

She opened her eyes just enough to see Nat's placid face above her. He pulled a sheet over her. But she felt like she was a piece of meat roasting on a spit so she pushed it down, desperate for relief. Before she could make sense of anything, she slipped away again, her mind floating in circles.

At length, she heard hushed voices, familiar men's voices. But she couldn't open her eyes. She tried to concentrate but her head and body were so heavy and warm, she felt like she was sinking into a bowl of Rosa's warm banana pudding.

Finally, she emerged from the cave again, trying to fight her way out of this horrible dream. But it was Nat's face she saw again when her eyes winked open. He laid a cold wet cloth on her forehead.

"Good," he said. "I think the fever's eased a bit."

He held a cup close to her mouth and guided a straw between her lips.

"Have a sip," he said.

She drank a little, wetting her parched mouth.

"Don't worry," he said. "You'll be all right."

"I want you to meet someone," he said, stepping aside so she could see a man standing behind him.

It was Will! She was so relieved, so glad he was here. But when her eyes focused, she noticed a small scar on his left cheek and very short hair. And his eyes – they were blue, but they were not Will's eyes. And she knew this was not the man she loved.

"Neave, this is Curt Maddux," Nat said.

She had to escape so she closed her eyes.

"She was one hot babe, y'know."

His voice. It was as though Will was pretending to be an evil character from a Shakespeare play. *Richard III*, maybe?

"Shh," Nat hissed.

"She's totally zoned, man."

"Shut the hell up," said Nat.

"You owe…" Curt started.

"Zip it!"

The disembodied voices stopped. Neave couldn't tell if the quiet lasted a few seconds or an hour.

"Neave, wake up."

Her heavy lids opened again, only to find Nat staring down at her.

"I'm sure you've already guessed – Curt is Will Galloway's twin, for lack of a better word," said Nat unnecessarily. "The other clone of your grandfather." He gave her a self-satisfied smile. "It took me a while to track him down. Tell her a little about yourself," he said, nodding to Curt.

"Look, man," Curt said, glaring at Nat. "I just want my money. The job's done. Where's the cash?"

Their eyes locked for a moment, as if in battle. Then Curt cleared his throat and turned towards Neave, although he was staring at the wall above her bed.

"I got out of prison three months ago."

The timbre of his voice was disturbingly like Will's, but his accent and intonations were different, hard edged.

"Tell her what you were in for," Nat said.

"For accidentally killing someone." He drew his face into a mock smile, nodding slightly at Nat.

Strange, Neave thought. He had two dimples. Not one, like Will. Two dimples, like her grandfather, Jack Sullivan.

"Who'd you kill?" Nat said.

"None of your fucking business."

"And that wasn't the first time you were in prison, was it?" Nat asked, unfazed.

It was like a nightmare she couldn't escape from. She wished she could wake up and find she was snuggled up with Will. He would hold her close and reassure her that everything was all right. But she couldn't. So she escaped the only way she knew how – by drifting back into her feverish dream world and the depths of the cave. But as she drifted off she heard Curt's insistent voice.

"She's fucking asleep. I want my money. I didn't ask why the Latina chick had to die. I just did my job – took her the cartridge. She popped it in the e-cig right away, just like you said."

~~~

She was about to tumble over Niagara Falls. The roar of the waterfall filled her senses. But then she realized it was the view wall in her old bedroom. The small desk lamp was the only source of light besides the wall, which she couldn't stand to look at. The water cascading over the precipice made her head swim.

"Turn it off," she whispered.

She had awakened again not knowing whether it was day or night. Not knowing how long she'd been lying in bed.

"Turn it off," she croaked.

"You're awake," Nat said, his face appearing above her.

"Turn it off," she said again.

"Turn what off?"

"The wall."

She clamped her eyes shut.

"How long?" she asked.

Nat crossed the room to a touch screen by the door and the view wall went dark.

"You've been sick since yesterday," he said, returning to the chair by the bed. "But you're gonna be all right. The doctor's been here twice. We've got you on some good meds. Don't worry."

Every square inch of her body ached.

"Where's Mother?"

"She's in Texas for Lena's funeral. Your father's in New Washington for the treaty signing."

"Rosa?"

"She's in El Paso too."

"Of course."

That her parents had left her in Nat's care was very

troubling.

"Where's my iCom?" she asked.

"I don't know," he said, turning his back to her. "I'll have to look for it. Time for your pill."

He sat on the bed and held a white capsule in front of her, a glass of water in his other hand.

"What is it?" she asked.

"Your antibiotic."

"I feel awful."

"It'll make you feel better."

She took the pill from his hand and put it in her mouth, then emptied the small glass of water. That small exertion was exhausting and she closed her eyes. She'd never been sick a day in her life and this weakness and dizziness were completely alien. She hoped Rosa would be there next time she woke up. What kind of illness was it? What did Nat say? She couldn't remember.

She heard him moving about the room as she drifted helplessly back down to her subterranean vault and into a nightmare. It was a horrifying dream in which a giant octopus enveloped her, its suction cups attached to her breasts. And then a tentacle slid between her legs. She wanted to escape, to wake up, but the dream went on and on, until, finally, the monster released her, leaving her feeling cold and slimy.

She hurt all over. It took her several minutes to remember where she was. When she opened her eyes, she was alone. Her hands glided down her belly and she realized with surprise that she was naked. She instinctively reached between her legs and confirmed what she already knew – she was bruised and sore. And the awful dream came back to her. She didn't realize she was crying until tears puddled in her ears. And then the doorknob turned and she wiped her tears on the sheet and closed her eyes.

"Good morning."

Nat's voice was chipper, as though he was on top of the world.

"I'm gonna move you this afternoon to a private care facility. So don't be alarmed when you wake up in a different room."

He sat down on the bed beside her and laid his hot hand on her arm.

She could feel him staring at her but she refused to open her eyes. She didn't want him to see the red hot anger that burned inside her like an August forest fire in the Georgia mountains. She didn't want him to see how shaken she was either.

"Time for your pill," he said. "Open up like you did last night."

His fingers touched her lips and she opened her mouth so he could slide the capsule in. He took her hand and placed a small cup of water in it. Barely opening her eyes, she took a tiny sip and handed the cup back.

She closed her eyes again and lay very still, breathing slowly. She could hear him typing on his iCom as though he were messaging back and forth with someone. And then he grunted under his breath.

"I've got to meet someone but I'll be back later," he said. "I'll give you a sponge bath then."

Then he was typing again and moving to the door. As he pulled it closed behind him she spit the soggy capsule into her hand.

Chapter 26

"When she finds out he's dead, she'll turn to me," Nat said. "But I've gotta fly to New D.C. for the signing so I need to move her first. And I don't have much time."

Neave shuddered and leaned against the wall. She was in the darkened hallway outside her father's home office. Her mind was muddled. When *who* finds out that *who* is dead? She looked through the doorway from her hiding place in the shadows and a sick feeling crept over her, starting in her gut, moving up through her chest and into her throat.

"You want me to move her?"

It was Curt Maddux, but he didn't look much like Will now. The right side of his face had a nasty scrape, his neck was bruised and his knuckles were raw.

"I can handle it," Nat said.

She was reminded of a nature program she'd seen where two Bighorn Sheep circle each other before locking horns. She held the stun gun tightly, afraid she might drop it. She'd found it where she always kept it – under her bed. But her mind was in a thick haze and her legs felt like rubber. She leaned against the wall, letting her warm cheek rest on the cool plaster.

Curt stood as though to leave.

"I can find my way out," he said.

She was about to hide when Nat reached into the top drawer of the desk and pulled out a gun.

Curt froze, looking from the gun to Nat's face.

"I no longer need your services," Nat said.

"I can be very useful."

"You know too much."

"I don't know anything."

"Yeah, you do. You know we had to kill Lena because she was about to spill a lot of beans, including Dr. A.'s part ownership of Chang NanoTec and Beijing Space. And I had you get rid of Galloway because he was trying to steal my fiancée. Dr. A. promised me his daughter and I'm gonna collect on that promise. I already told my family we're engaged and they're giving us big bucks for a wedding present." He nodded his head in a bragging sort of way. "And you've probably figured out what happened with Osley. Once he learned about Dr. A.'s financial interests, we couldn't let him blab to the president. Of course, that one took a couple of tries." He shrugged his shoulders. "So, you see? You know way too much."

Will was dead? She felt as though she'd been punched in the stomach.

Nat extended the weapon, finger on the trigger, ready to murder his hired assassin. Part of her wanted to let him do it, let him kill this low-life piece of garbage. But Nat was the one who'd hired him, and he was in cahoots with her father. If she wanted revenge, she wanted it against all three of them. And, besides, she couldn't stand by and watch someone kill another human being. Curt had Will's DNA. There must be some good in there, she thought. She forced herself through the doorway, pushing herself with adrenaline. She had no other strength left.

Both men turned in surprise. Nat pointed the gun in her direction for an instant, until he realized who it was. Then he quickly aimed at Curt again.

"Neave, what are you doing up?" he said, alarm in his voice.

She had no idea how awful she looked or that she was swaying as she stood there. She was dressed only in a thin white nightgown she'd found at the foot of her bed, her hair was in knots and she had dark circles under her eyes, accentuated by the pallor of her skin. Her lips were dry and cracked.

"You need a chair," Curt said, reaching for the one he'd just risen from.

She aimed the stun gun at him. She was taken aback by the expression on his face and had an overwhelming feeling of déjà vu. But, naturally, she would. The look in his eyes at that moment made her think of Will. Amazing, she thought. It made her wonder whether that look was genetic, whether her grandfather had the same look. If they made a hundred clones of him, would they all have those eyes that appeared to plumb the depths of your soul?

"Neave..." Nat said. "I think you need another dose..."

"You hired..." she said.

"You need to go back to..." he said.

"I'm not going anywhere. I heard what you said."

The effort of standing was taking its toll.

"You're too sick," he said.

"Thanks to you!" And she leaned against the door frame.

"I didn't want you to learn about it like this, that's for sure, but Curt saw Will Galloway fall to his death yesterday at his job site."

"Liar!" she cried. She felt as though she might faint. "I heard everything."

"Neave…" Curt said, rising from his chair.

"You killed him," she said, pointing her stun gun in his direction. "Just like you killed Lena."

Curt stepped closer.

"Don't move!" Nat barked, his pistol pointed squarely at Curt's chest.

Neave knew she had to do something before she ran out of steam. She wasn't going back into that cave again. She knew now that Nat was not only dangerous, he was deranged. And what kind of man would kill someone for money? So she aimed her stun gun and fired. Curt's face drew into a fleeting grimace – a pained smile – and then went slack as he collapsed unconscious on the floor.

Nat stepped around the desk, his pistol still aimed at Curt. But his expression went from relief to surprise when he looked up and saw Neave was now aiming her stun gun at him.

"Neave, let me help you back to bed. You're too sick to be up and about."

"You're the one who's sick. You degenerate!"

Just as she was about to fire, he lunged at her. She dodged to one side and her shot went wild, but she kept her finger tight on the trigger and waved the stick in his direction as he pivoted and lunged again. His arm slapped the stun stick out of her hand and she pounced on it, falling hard on the floor, using all her remaining strength. She grabbed the handle and swung it towards him again. But he was unconscious, sprawled on the floor beside her.

Her heart was pounding as she struggled for breath. She lay there only a few seconds on the cold, hard floor, then forced herself to sit up. She stared at the two inert men, not knowing how much time she had before they regained consciousness. The full weight of what she'd just learned was beginning to spread from her brain to her heart, and there was a part of her that wanted to take the gun Nat had brandished and shoot both of them dead where they lay. A vision of red blood oozing across the hardwood floor formed in her mind.

She held on to the desk and pulled herself up, then pried the pistol from Nat's fingers. She wiped her nose on the back of her hand. She was filled with rage and weaved as she pointed the weapon at his head. Then she aimed it at Curt. They were animals! Worse than animals. She wanted to empty the gun into their worthless bodies.

A groan made her jump. Nat's eyes fluttered. She was shaking. And then she pulled the trigger of the stun gun in her other hand. Another dose would keep him unconscious long enough for her to get away. And she zapped Curt too. If the double dose killed them, well, it couldn't be helped.

She collapsed in Nat's chair and closed her eyes, still holding the stun gun in one hand and the pistol in the other. She had no idea what Nat had drugged her with – whether she'd been infected with an actual virus or bacteria, or whether she'd been anesthetized with a narcotic – but she was weak. She didn't know when she'd last eaten. It made her dizzy to stand. On top of that, her soul was weary. She had never understood why some people committed suicide. But now she finally had an inkling. The emptiness that clawed at her insides wasn't physical hunger, it was her desire to turn back the clock. Such a cruel fate – to find the love of her life and then to lose him.

Will's face appeared before her as she closed her eyes. His dimple just starting to show, as though he was about to break into a smile. His eyes were so full of life. She could gaze forever into those eyes. And his voice. She longed to hear his velvet voice, a baritone's voice. She hugged herself, but it was *his* arms around her that she needed. There was no balm for her soul. There would never be anyone to love again.

She didn't know how long she sat staring into space. A minute? Ten? But she finally thought of the treaty signing. What a travesty. A treaty between two countries for the purpose of enriching those who would get the shade ring contract. That had been her father's goal all along – power and money. He'd never been concerned about the earth or his country. It was all about himself. And he would apparently stop at nothing, including murder, to get what he wanted.

She'd have to wait till later to figure out how to go on living. Or whether she even wanted to. Right now, there were some immediate obligations she couldn't ignore.

Leaning down, she took Nat's iCom from his wrist, grabbed his backpack and slung it over her shoulder as she walked from the room, barely able to put one foot in front of the other.

The door on her mother's car opened when she pressed her thumb on the keypad. She drove a couple of blocks before pulling over. When she dumped Nat's backpack on the passenger seat, out fell her own iCom. She called the police, telling them where they'd find Nat and Curt and that the two should be locked up on murder charges for killing Will, Lena and Dr. Osley. They wanted her to come to the station but she didn't have time for that now.

As she hung up, Nat's iCom vibrated. It was a message from "A." Her father, no doubt. It said: "Signing 4p, then u get yr D." Then the message disappeared without a trace.

D. Discretion. So Nat was hooked too. And her father was his supplier. For half a second, she felt sorry for Nat. But it passed quickly. She had no time to waste. She had to stop them. But she needed help. She clicked on her mother's code.

"Mother?" Her voice cracked.

"Neave, dear, what's wrong?"

"Mother..." but she was unable to speak.

"Neave, are you all right? Neave?"

"No, I'm not all right. Nothing is all right." And she sobbed as she tried to talk. "They killed Lena. And they killed..."

"Killed Lena?" Her mother's voice was all anxiousness. "Neave, are you ill?"

"Yes. And Nat did it. He drugged me. Infected me or something."

"Neave, dear..."

"And it was Nat and Father! They're..."

"Who drugged you?"

"They had him murdered. Oh, Mother..."

"Who drugged you?"

It took several minutes for her to calm down enough to explain everything, which she realized she wasn't doing very well. Still, she stumbled on. But her mother was in El Paso. What could she do from there?

"Mother, I'm too tired and I don't have time. I'll find another way. I've gotta go now."

"Neave..."

"I have to find a way to get to New Washington."

And she hung up.

Another message was coming in on Nat's iCom. It was an automated reminder of his scheduled flight on a jet from Peachtree DeKalb Airport. It was scheduled to take off in an hour. Well, if Nat was indisposed, she wouldn't waste the ticket. Since her mother couldn't help, she decided to call someone else.

~~~

When they met in the parking lot at the small airport, Yong's normally careful expression crumbled when he saw her. She could only imagine how she must appear. The reality was much worse than anything her tired mind could conjure up. Her hair hung limp and sweaty on her shoulders. The dark circles under her eyes and her sallow face made her appear as though she'd risen from her death bed. And she was still wearing the thin white muslin nightgown with nothing underneath. She needed a shower, food and sleep, but there was no time.

"We must purchase clothing," he said with some urgency. "And..."

He stared at her face and hair.

"Wait in the vehicle," he said, glancing at her feet. "I shall return immediately."

Sitting upright with her hands on the steering wheel, she dozed off. If Yong hadn't returned, she might've slept for days.

He turned his back as she donned a sleeveless yellow mini-dress, panties and pink leggings he'd bought at a tourist shop in the airport lobby. Surprisingly, the clothing fit, though the outfit was not her style. She slid the pink flip flops he'd bought on her feet. They were a tad big, but tolerable. Then he handed her a tube of pink lipstick and hurried her to the gate. If they missed the plane, they had no other way to get to New Washington in time. She was surprised when he dropped behind her and began brushing her hair as they walked. Just before they reached the ticketing area, he stopped her long enough to apply some Erase beneath her eyes, rather like a mother wiping dirt from a child's face. He rubbed it gently with his index fingers, then deposited the tube in the backpack Neave was carrying and escorted her to the agent's desk, apparently satisfied that she no longer looked like she'd contracted a highly contagious disease.

The gate attendant asked immediately where Mr. Patel was.

"Unfortunately, he's come down with a virus," said Neave. "So I'm going in his place, taking Dr. Yong here to be my father's translator."

The middle-aged woman with short brown hair studied her computer screen, looking up at Neave and Yong. She feigned indifference, but Neave knew better. And then she felt a vibration coming from her bag and knew it was Nat's iCom. The attendant must've called Nat's number from her computer.

"You see," Neave said, "Mr. Patel was going to New Washington to act as my father's interpreter for a treaty signing involving the Chinese government. Mr. Patel is fluent in Mandarin Chinese. But when he was taken ill, my father asked me to bring Dr. Yong to help translate. Dr. Yong, of course, is fluent in Mandarin Chinese."

She could still feel the device vibrating and was alarmed the attendant would hear it too.

"Actually, I speak several Chinese dialects," Yong piped up. He must've heard the buzzing as well. "Mandarin Chinese is my native language, but I also speak Cantonese, Hakka, Shanhainese and, of course, English. These fluencies will be most helpful during the official signing ceremony today in your capital."

Now the lady was looking annoyed, as though she didn't appreciate their chatter. But Nat's iCom was still buzzing so Neave continued talking.

"You've probably heard of my father – Dr. Robert Alvarez? He's the U.S. Climate Secretary? And he's been involved with negotiations on launching a shade ring into space…"

"The reservation is in the name of Nat Patel," said the woman. "And it was for one seat, not two."

Nat's iCom had obviously rolled over to his message center because it finally stopped buzzing.

"Well, I can assure you," Neave said, "that Nat cannot come and that Dr. Yong and I are going in his place. You can charge the extra seat to my account."

But failure was beginning to look like a strong possibility.

"Miss Alvarez!"

It was a pilot stepping into the gate area from the tarmac steps. She racked her brain trying to remember his name. He was the one who'd flown them to New Washington for the state dinner.

"So Mr. Patel's under the weather, huh?" he said.

"Unfortunately," she said. "But, lucky for us, Dr. Yong is fluent in Chinese."

She nodded towards Yong standing beside her.

"Yong Li," Yong said, extending his hand.

"Hi, Yong," said the pilot. "Rob Sanchez."

He vouched for them and once their e-tickets were issued, ushered them through a short boarding tunnel and onto the plane, smiling mischievously at the matronly gate agent.

Chapter 27

The view from her window as she looked down below was a sea of white fluffy clouds. The sun shone so brightly, she found herself squinting and wishing the plane would descend through the clouds for some relief from the unremitting sunshine. She understood humanity's worship of the sun throughout history, but in her lifetime it was something to be escaped from, something to be avoided. She had a wardrobe of hats – not to look fashionable – but to protect herself. She loved clouds and rain. Such weather conditions used to be called dreary by those who took rain for granted. Of course, there were still places where clouds were the norm and she'd often thought about moving to NY2 for the beautiful grey skies and the cool raindrops, in addition to the thriving world of theater. She'd always thought she wouldn't even use an umbrella, but would enjoy getting wet as she walked to the subway. She would just carry small towels in her bag to dry off with. But now it hardly mattered.

She gazed out the window until she drifted into a dream-filled slumber where she saw Will. He was holding a door open for her, gesturing for her to enter. Soft, white light emanated from the door. It looked warm and inviting. Not the kind of warmth that made you sweat, but the kind that made you feel safe and loved. A broad smile brightened his handsome face and there was love in his eyes. She moved instinctively towards him, anticipating the touch of his hand in hers.

And she came suddenly awake, panicked and disoriented. It was difficult to clear her mind. She needed to recall something of importance in her dream. She closed her eyes, remembering whiteness, like the cumulus clouds beneath the plane. And there was something else, but it was gone, something important she wanted to retrieve from the recesses of her mind.

"Are you feeling ill?" Yong asked.

She didn't know how to answer.

"You are overly fatigued," he said.

She sighed and nodded slowly.

"Thank you for coming," she whispered. "I just hope we can get to the signing."

She was deeply indebted to her new friend. He had come instantly and without question when she called. He had believed her when she told her incredible story.

"During your sleep, I researched the Chinese companies you spoke of and found one name on both boards of directors: Wu Jin."

"That must be him."

"My estimation is that the Chinese government knows of this. It is beneficial to China if the shade ring comes to fruition. My country could continue to use coal and gas for many decades into the future."

She checked the time.

"I don't know how the hell we're gonna pull this off," she said quietly.

"While you slept I also created an identity document for myself to prove I am official translator," he said, gesturing towards his iCom. "I believe it will pass mustard."

She almost corrected him, then realized he'd made a joke, which caused her to smile a little.

"My mother had great proficiency to put her tongue in her cheek," he said. "My surrogate mother."

"Is she dead?"

"I do not know. They took her away when I enrolled in Beijing Science Academy when I reached eight years. My assumption is she received generous stipend to disappear."

It made her sad to think Yong had been treated so coldly, denied affection, groomed to serve his country.

"I'm so sorry," she said.

"I have memories," he said, clearing his throat. "We land soon. We must disguise ourselves to avoid detection."

Which brought her back to the present. But a troubling shadow of the dream remained. It was like there was a secret message she needed to decipher but the dream had fluttered out of reach.

A part of her wished she'd killed Nat when she had the chance. And she knew Yong was right. The danger was very real.

"How do we avoid detection?" she said.

"We will trade clothing."

If anyone had been watching, they would've alerted the flight attendant about something fishy going on in 5a and 5b. But the other passengers were either napping or engrossed in their iComs. So Neave and Yong succeeded in swapping clothes, piece by piece. Either no one noticed or no one cared. She removed her pink leggings as Yong slowly peeled off his black slacks. Then she pulled his pants on under her short, yellow dress as he struggled into the leggings. He loosened the knot on his tie and pulled it over his head, handing it to her, then he shed his suit jacket and white shirt and held the jacket up while she stripped off her dress and donned his shirt. He pulled the dress on, then traded his black loafers and socks for her pink flip-flops. The transformation took less than five minutes.

Yong looked her over, then grabbed a small disposable airline pillow and had her stuff it inside her shirt and pants to give her a thicker profile. Then he turned around in his seat and asked an Indian woman sitting behind them if he could buy whatever makeup she had, pulling two one hundred dollar bills from his wallet. He explained that Neave had a role in a play at the Lyric Theater and might be able to make it if she was dressed and made up when she arrived. He also bought the scarf she was wearing.

As the little jet taxied to the gate, Neave and Yong rushed to the front, eager to exit first, telling the passengers and flight attendant they were late for Neave's performance, which seemed to satisfy them.

She was the first one through the door to the concourse, doing her best to walk like a man. Yong's handiwork wouldn't withstand close inspection, but from a distance, she looked like a small Middle Eastern man in a black suit, white shirt and tie. Yong had used the obliging passenger's compact to powder her face to a light brown color. He had drawn a thin mustache above her upper lip using an eyebrow pencil. And on her head was a small, tightly wrapped navy blue turban made from a strip of a disposable airplane blanket. She was thankful for the small backpack over her shoulder, which gave her something to hold on to. She looked straight ahead but her peripheral vision focused on every person she passed.

She wished Yong was by her side, but they agreed to separate until after they exited the airport, figuring if Nat had made it to New Washington, he would be looking for the two of them together after finding out who had taken his flight. They hoped their disguises and their solo departures would buy them some time.

As for Yong, the pink leggings covered up his dark leg hair and the yellow dress was a snug fit. He wore the newly acquired rose-colored scarf on his head, tied so the ends hung on his shoulders. But it was the way he puckered his painted lips that completed a truly amazing transformation, although his toes were a bit hairy for a woman. He waited a few seconds before heading down the concourse.

Neave felt as though everyone was staring at her. She was sure she'd be grabbed at any moment and had to force herself not to break into a sprint. Time was running short – the signing was less than an hour away – and she was beginning to doubt her own sanity. They still hadn't figured out how to get inside the Climate Department building.

As she stepped off the people mover to enter the baggage claim area her skin began to crawl. She felt him before she saw him. It was Nat, not twenty feet away, leaning on a post, holding an iNotebook in front of him, pretending to read.

Chapter 28

How had Nat gotten here so fast? Had the police ignored her? What about Curt? Was he on the loose too? And where was Yong?

She kept her eyes straight ahead as she hurried down the concourse, but monitored Nat's presence with every nerve ending in her body. No doubt, his goal was to prevent her from ever making it to the treaty signing. But she was also terrified that he had much more in mind than just keeping her from reaching today's big event.

Someone coughed. There was an uncomfortable flutter in her stomach. It had to be a signal. Just as she decided to make a break for it, a hand gripped her elbow.

Instinctively she pulled away but the hand tightened its grip. There was no emotion on his face as Nat's dark eyes looked down into hers. A scream welled up from her gut. She would not go peacefully. As she opened her mouth, he yanked the turban from her head, her auburn locks tumbling onto her shoulders.

"Excuse, sir," a falsetto voice sing-songed.

Nat turned towards the voice and there was Yong in that outlandish woman's outfit. Yong gave Neave a fleeting glance, sending her a very clear message.

"Need assistance," Yong said, turning to Nat, his voice surprisingly like a woman's.

And while Nat's attention was momentarily diverted, Neave jerked herself from his grasp and ran towards the nearest baggage turntable. She threaded her way through the crowd, bumping against several people before making it to the other side of the carousel. She knew Yong's diversion would only give her a couple of seconds and she searched frantically for an escape route as bags tumbled from two conveyor belt openings on either end of the carousel. If she bolted for the door, his hot hands would be squeezing her arms again before she reached the transit station. So she leaped into the conveyor belt opening.

But her escape plan was flawed. She scrambled as fast as her limbs would take her without making any progress. The belt was an efficient machine that swept all those suitcases inexorably towards the place she was trying to escape. And it was a tight squeeze. The conveyor was in a tunnel specifically designed for the transport of baggage – not people – so she had to remain horizontal as she clambered frantically over bag after bag after bag. She was quickly running out of steam and about to be spat out onto the carousel again like an overstuffed duffel bag when she noticed a cleft in the side of the tunnel – an indentation in the wall. She clawed her way into position and threw her body into the space, struggling to straighten her legs as more bags hurtled past her. A large grey, hard-sided Pullman caught on the edge and twirled around, nearly smashing her in the face. She stiffened, but forced herself not to cry out.

Her heart was pounding and her mouth was so dry, it was hard to swallow. But she couldn't just hide out in this underground maze forever. Her mission was too important.

Quickly, she assessed her options. She could continue climbing over suitcases, hoping her strength would hold up until she reached an exit in the bowels of the airport; she could wait for the conveyer belt to stop – but who knew how long that might be; or she could ride the belt back into the baggage claim area, hoping Nat had run elsewhere searching for her. She needed to contact Yong.

Finally, there was a gap in the suitcases so she could hold her iCom in front of her face, her elbows and arms tight against her body.

"safe to come out?" she typed.

And then she waited. Her worst fears crawled through her head. Nat would drug her again and this time he would make sure she never escaped; her father would succeed in his personal quest to become rich and powerful at the expense of… well, at the expense of everyone in the world; and Nat and Curt would get off scot free for their awful crimes. She clutched her iCom, willing it to vibrate. But nothing happened. Where was he?

When the device buzzed, she nearly dropped it, realizing to her amazement that she had dozed off for a few seconds. How on earth could she fall asleep at a time like this?

"yes hurry," was his answer.

The conveyer squirted her out and sent her tumbling down the slope of the carousel as people stared. Using all her strength, she jumped onto the floor before a finger was ripped off. She immediately dropped to a crouch, scanning her surroundings as she pretended to search her small bag. She sensed someone approaching from the left and clenched her fists, ready to fight to the death. But, thank God, it was Yong.

Without a word, he slipped his arm through hers, helping her to stand, and held on tight like they were sweethearts as they walked through the door to the transit station. The doors on a train bound for the government complex were about to close but they just made it through. All the seats were taken so they stood at the back of the car, holding onto a bar above them. He stood close behind her, one arm wrapped around her waist as though they were a horny young couple who couldn't keep their hands off each other. In reality, Yong was holding her up, sensing correctly that she might topple over otherwise. Until she saw their reflection in a window, she didn't realize they looked like an odd lesbian couple – she, with her hair down, but still sporting the pencil mustache and men's clothing – and he, dressed in a short dress with a scarf on his head and bright lipstick on his mouth.

Then her attention was drawn to a view screen showing a large protest underway outside the Climate Department. A reporter was interviewing unruly demonstrators waving signs that said things like "No shady ring," "No more space junk," and "Don't sweep it under the rug."

As they watched, Yong unbuttoned the black coat Neave was wearing and removed it, leaving her in the white shirt and black slacks. Then he pulled her shirttail out, causing the little pillow to fall to the floor. She hadn't realized until that moment that she was drenched with sweat. She was now acutely aware that she smelled like her parents' yard man after he'd been pulling weeds on a hot August night.

"Who do they think they're kidding?" a woman asked on the TV. "We know what they're doing. They're selling out to the Chinese."

At the third stop, a man vacated a seat near them and Yong quickly deposited Neave in the space before anyone else had a chance. He squatted beside her, unbuttoning the top two buttons of her shirt and rolling up her sleeves to give her more air.

A message began scrolling over the announcement screens that the train would not stop at the government center, obviously because of the protest. They would either have to get off one stop before or one stop after.

Yong moved behind her and braided her hair to get it off her shoulders. It wasn't pretty, but it was cooler.

The protesters were now chanting "no shade ring, no shade ring."

They exited the train at the last stop before the government center station. Yong immediately took her into the ladies restroom. They entered adjacent stalls and swapped clothes, handing them over the dividing wall. Neave ditched the pink leggings into the nearest trash can, deciding the yellow mini-dress was sufficient. He stopped her for a second on their way out and wiped the remains of the pencil mustache from her face with his fingers.

Now all they had to do was walk two blocks in searing heat, avoid being seen by Nat, somehow get past the protesters and the heavy security, and miraculously convince the guards to let them inside the Climate Building. All, in less than thirty minutes.

Yong checked the GPS on his iCom before they started out. Then, like an old hand at barter and trade, he bought a wide-brimmed straw hat from an older woman by transferring money from his account directly into hers using their iComs. The hat was a godsend and Neave made a mental note that she truly owed Yong more than she could ever repay. He bought a man's sunhat from a guy they met shortly afterwards.

The hats weren't luxuries. It was 118 degrees under a blistering sun. The capital was in the grip of a heat wave.

Perfect timing for a deal to launch a shade ring, Neave thought.

A delicious aroma ambushed their nostrils and Neave tugged on Yong's arm and nodded towards the fast food kiosk.

"No time," he said, paying cash for two bottles of water.

She guzzled hers as they walked.

The news coverage hadn't done the protest justice. There were people everywhere, chanting and shouting and waving signs in the air. Police in blue climate suits and AC helmets had cordoned off the streets and activated a retractable eight foot fence around the Climate Building.

"Shit," she said under her breath.

"Now is not a good time," said Yong.

She turned towards him to explain, but saw a hint of a smile around the corners of his mouth. Cuttin' up and goin' on. That's what Angela called it. And the memory of her sojourn at Will's home, getting to know his family, brought the heartache to the surface.

"We will find a way," he said.

But as she looked again at the fortress they were facing, she noticed a tall man with black hair walking towards the line of police officers.

"Nat," she whispered, turning away and shifting her hat so the brim covered her sloppy braid in the back. Yong turned too and they headed towards the reflecting pool nearby. The shallow water was filled with protesters, some sitting waist-deep in the water, some standing and occasionally dipping their hands in the water and patting their faces and necks. He pulled Neave along until they were in the middle of the fountain. They sat down in the water behind a group of people standing and holding signs aloft, and they tilted their hats forward so their faces would be partially covered by the broad brims.

And that's when her iCom vibrated. It was her mother. She answered softly, not wanting to raise her voice.

"Yes?"

"Neave! Where are you?"

"I'm in New Washington."

"Yes, I know, but where?"

"Near the Climate Department."

"Where exactly?" her mother said, sounding impatient.

"Why?"

Raucous chanting rose from the crowd.

"Where are you?" Dr. Sullivan's voice was uncharacteristically shrill.

Neave looked at Yong, who raised his eyebrows in question.

"I'm in front of the Climate building, in the fountain," she replied.

And the connection dropped.

They watched surreptitiously as Nat talked with one of the police supervisors who made notes on his PDA.

"God, how can we..." she whispered.

"Neave! Neave!"

It was a familiar voice behind her. She turned as Kwan splashed through the fountain towards them, waving and calling out.

"There you are! I've been trying to reach you! We've gotta stop the signing!"

God, what terrible timing, she thought. She and Yong had done everything in their power to disguise themselves, and then, after Nat caught up with them at the airport, they'd managed to escape and make it this far. And now Kwan showed up to blow their cover.

"I found one of the monitors and he *did* engineer the ice dam break!" Kwan said as he reached them. "It had a special laser beam that was directed straight down into the ice. It was designed to cause vibration and heat. Lena was right!"

She twirled around, scanning the crowd, knowing full well Nat must've heard him calling her name. And then he was right in front of her. Two cops were closing in from the left and three security guards were headed towards them from the right.

"What the hell!" cried Kwan, startled at Nat's sudden appearance. "You fucking murderer!" he snarled and lunged at him. The two of them tumbled into the water, splashing as they struggled for the upper hand.

Everyone backed away, including Neave and Yong. It was mass confusion as Kwan did his best to inflict bodily harm, punching Nat hard in the jaw. Then the police and security guards were on top of them and, as quickly as it had started, the fight was over. An officer attached plastic cuffs while two others held Kwan's hands behind his back.

"You're under arrest," the short cop yelled.

"He's the one you should be arresting, not me," Kwan cried. "He's..."

"Put him in the holding pen," the head cop barked, then turned to Nat. "Is this the woman?"

Nat nodded as the security guards led Kwan away.

"Hey! What's the charge?" Kwan bellowed, but no one was listening.

"Miss Alvarez," said the officer, "I need for you to come with me."

Neave couldn't believe she'd gotten this close only to have Nat pressure the police to arrest her. The rat. Had he paid them off? Had he promised them something? It made her sick to think that Nat, of all people, had influence with the police.

She tried to focus as she looked down at the sunshine reflecting off the water, at her bare feet in her tacky thongs, at the feet of the men around her – all of them standing knee deep in the fountain with shoes on, as if that were perfectly normal. She looked at her hands and arms. Her eyes came to rest on her iCom, so out of place where she'd attached it on her wrist that, for a second, she had the feeling she was looking at someone else's arm. Until this week she hadn't worn it like that since she was a little girl when Rosa taught her how to use it – instructing her on how she could stay in constant contact with her family, how she could find her way home with it.

She crossed her lower arms like a prisoner waiting to be handcuffed and then a horrendous, ear shattering shriek filled the air. Until that second, she'd forgotten the emergency alarm Rosa had told her to use if she was ever in danger and needed help. The cacophony was so harsh, so intense, that the policeman who was about to grab her instinctively covered his ears instead. Hands flew up all around as people tried to block the piercing screech.

Nat reached for her but she dodged to the right and splashed through the fountain towards the unruly crowd, lifting her feet out of the water with each step, struggling to move quickly, not taking time to see who was splashing close on her heels. Just as she reached the group who'd been chanting a moment before, a large hand latched on to her right arm. She squealed and struggled to pull free of the officer's grasp. All eyes were on her, just as she'd hoped. And then two reporters wearing camera glasses were there, shouting questions at the police.

"Why are you arresting her? What did she do?"

Several more reporters converged on them, two more with camera glasses and one with a larger camera attached to a helmet.

Neave touched her iCom to turn off the alarm, to everyone's relief.

"I'm the daughter of Climate Secretary Robert Alvarez," she proclaimed in a loud voice, yanking her hat off and tossing it aside.

The crowd booed.

"But I oppose the shade ring," she continued, prompting cheers and applause.

"You came here today to join the protest against your father's deal with the Chinese?" a reporter asked.

"Yes," she replied. "But these police officers want to deny me my rights. And it's this man who told them to take me into custody."

She glared at Nat.

"His name is Nat Patel and he's my father's chief assistant. Maybe you should ask him what authority he thinks he has to stop me from exercising my right to free speech."

The usually unflappable Nat was at least momentarily rattled. And then something green caught Neave's eye behind the reporters. She peered beyond them and saw her mother in a green suit, standing with Rosa and watching the confrontation. She knew her mother was her only hope of getting to the treaty signing.

"And Mr. Patel assaulted my friend here," Neave continued, looking hard into Yong's eyes.

He stepped forward, quick on the uptake.

"Yes, this man attacked me," Yong said, "because I am gay."

"Is this true, Mr. Patel?" a tall reporter with camera glasses asked.

The whole group focused their cameras on him, waiting for Nat to answer. It was their job to keep viewers glued to their view screens and iComs, and they jumped on this juicy tidbit like flies on warm dog poop.

One cop rolled his eyes at the other. And that's when Neave made her break, hoping Yong could hold everyone's attention long enough. Nat tried to follow but the reporters closed ranks and blocked his exit as the crowd jeered him.

"Attacked a gay man… who does he think he is!"

Nat turned to the officers who were moving away, trying in vain to get their attention. But the crowd was now yelling angrily and he was surrounded.

Neave reached her mother and Rosa who sandwiched her between them. As they walked quickly towards the Climate building, Dr. Sullivan took off the green jacket she was wearing and slipped it over Neave's wet dress. Four armed security guards greeted them at the side entrance.

"I'm Dr. Molly Sullivan, wife of Climate Secretary Robert Alvarez. This is our daughter, Neave Alvarez and my husband's cousin, Rosa Alvarez. We're here for the treaty signing."

"You're a little late," the woman guard said, looking at her iCom, "It's already underway."

Her mother calmly extended her arm to allow them to scan her iCom. Neave and Rosa followed her lead. The head guard took her time scanning each of them and then looking at her iCom. She glanced up occasionally as if comparing each of them with a picture she was looking at. Neave tried to look confident, though it was one of the most difficult things she'd ever done. She was amazed at her mother's poise. Rosa's too.

Finally, the guard waved them through, clicking on her iCom to unlock the door.

The cool hallway would've been welcome after the heat outside, but there was a knot in Neave's stomach and her clothes were wet so she quickly developed goose bumps. She must've shivered because Rosa slipped her arm around her and pulled her close as they walked, their footsteps echoing on the hard floor along with a squishing noise as Neave's waterlogged flip flops slapped the cold granite.

She had no idea what would happen next or what she would say if she had the chance. She wasn't entirely sure she could say anything. Panic was spreading from her stomach to her throat and she swallowed repeatedly. The last time she remembered doing that was when her father forced her to compete in a science competition when she was eleven. She had to stand up in front of a large auditorium full of students and judges from the university and give a detailed presentation on the changes in the Gulf Stream and the North Atlantic Drift, and how those changes had caused cooling of the northern European climate. Her father had chosen the topic himself and, although he didn't write it for her, he demanded she present it to him twice before he judged her and all her 3-D animation effects to be ready. She'd been deathly afraid of humiliating herself in front of all those scientific geniuses, knowing she was not one of them.

Then it dawned on her that, unlike her eleven-year-old self, she no longer had to be afraid of embarrassing herself, or of her father's wrath. Now she had nothing to lose. She'd already lost what was dearest to her. Will's death was like a black hole in her life, sucking all hope and joy into it, so that there was no more future for her beyond this mission. She would get through this, do whatever she could to stop her father and then... well, she'd have to think about that later.

Suddenly they were at the door to the Montgomery Room.

Three soldiers in dress uniform checked their identification as Dr. Sullivan complained casually about the annoying protesters outside causing them to be late. And then they were ushered inside.

The three women stepped through the doorway just as people were taking their seats. A voluptuous young intern ushered them quickly to the back row. Chairs were arranged for about fifty guests to witness the signing.

The Montgomery Room was partly a science museum and partly a special event room designed to impress foreign dignitaries and visitors. It was round and high ceilinged with view walls that displayed maps of the entire globe. Each section also included live, streaming video from a location in that region. So you could see a dust storm swirling over the Sahara or the early morning skyline of Beijing muddied by pollution.

Dr. Alvarez stood behind a mahogany table brought in for the occasion. It was polished to a high sheen so it reflected the lights from the cameras worn by a swarm of network reporters. He was dressed in an expensive dark grey suit and red tie.

Neave looked to her left and right, fearing Nat would burst into the room at any moment.

"Thank you for coming. Xiexie da jia." Dr. Alvarez's voice boomed out over dozens of tiny audio speakers built into the ceiling and walls.

"This is truly an historic occasion," he continued, smiling broadly. "And I would like to welcome our special guests from the People's Republic of China."

At which point he introduced China's Minister for the Environment, Du Zuolin, and China's Ambassador to the U.S., Fu Jiechi, along with several other officials from the two governments, including U.S. Secretary of State Stanley Mintz.

Neave leaned over to her mother and whispered in her ear: "I need a microphone."

Dr. Sullivan immediately removed her iCom. She clicked through several prompts as her husband launched into a pompous speech about the importance of the shade ring and the partnership between the U.S. and China to combat continued melting and rising seas through the use of twenty-second century technology.

She nodded at Neave as she handed her the device, gesturing with her hand to show her how to use it. It was an emergency app to magnify the voice, which she knew her mother used from time to time when she was called on to speak before a group unexpectedly.

"And now, if you will join me at the table, Minister Du," Dr. Alvarez said, smiling at his Chinese counterpart.

Du rose from his chair and strode to the table, taking his place beside Dr. Alvarez. And that's when Neave stood up, holding the iCom to her mouth.

"This signing cannot proceed," she said, startling everyone in the room, especially her father.

Chapter 29

Dr. Alvarez swallowed hard as he pulled nervously on his tie. But he quickly regained his composure.

"My apologies, Minister, honored guests," he said. "As you know, a protest has been going on outside the Climate Department today and one of the protesters has managed to gain entry. And that protester..."

Armed guards converged on Neave's position and she knew she didn't have much time. Her mother and Rosa flanked her like bodyguards.

"My name is Neave Alvarez," she said, speaking over her father. "I'm the daughter of Robert Alvarez."

Glances were exchanged all around and the Chinese officials glared at her father.

"Secretary Mintz, you need to know my father is a major shareholder in both of the Chinese companies that would get contracts for a shade ring if this agreement is signed today."

"I'm very sorry," Dr. Alvarez said, "but my daughter has apparently decided she'll go to any length to block this treaty. I'm afraid she's been hanging out with the radicals outside..."

Neave raised her voice even louder.

"My father – your Climate Secretary – owns seven percent of Chang NanoTec and five percent of Beijing Space and stands to get very rich if the United States enters into this agreement. He used a Chinese alias as his shareholder name – Wu Jin."

"Neave…" Dr. Alvarez began.

But she ignored him as the guards closed in.

"He's used his position as Climate Secretary to convince the U.S. government to go along with a very expensive project that would provide work for those companies for decades to come, obviously making them hugely profitable and…"

Two guards tried to grab her but Dr. Sullivan and Rosa wrapped their arms around her and refused to budge.

"And…" Neave continued, "obviously turning a nice profit for my father."

She had their attention. Secretary Mintz looked from Neave to her father.

Neave opened her mouth to continue, but Rosa grabbed the iCom from her.

"And," Rosa said, holding it so close to her own mouth that her voice boomed through the room, "there is the matter of my niece's murder." Her voice was shaking, but she pressed ahead. "You ordered her murder, Roberto," she shouted at Dr. Alvarez. "You used Catalena, intentionally got her hooked on drugs and then had her killed when she knew too much!"

A guard yanked the iCom from her hand and twisted Rosa's arm behind her back.

"Let her go!" Neave shouted. "You're hurting her!"

"Mr. Secretary," Dr. Sullivan said, looking Secretary Mintz in the eye, "I would recommend you delay the treaty signing for at least a few minutes."

"Yes, yes," he said. "Ladies and gentlemen, please excuse the delay."

With that, he turned and whispered to an aide, who then

gave orders to several other aides and guards. The Secretary led the way into an ante-room, followed by Dr. Alvarez, the Chinese Minister, the Chinese Ambassador, Neave, Dr. Sullivan, Rosa and several guards.

As soon as the door closed behind them, Dr. Alvarez turned to Mintz.

"The signing must go forward, Stan. We can't let my daughter's ridiculous foolishness damage this program. We've worked too long."

"Robert," said Mintz, "I'd like to ask your daughter, your wife and the woman with them a few questions."

"We don't have time for this," Dr. Alvarez snapped.

"Yes, we do," Mintz said, his voice calm, but firm. He turned then to the women as Dr. Alvarez sighed loudly and crossed his arms. "Dr. Sullivan, what's going on here?"

Neave feared that once again, her mother wouldn't stand up to her father. But something had changed. There was no fear, no timidity in her voice.

"What's going on here?" she repeated. "Neave and Rosa have, in all probability, spoken the truth. Robert has succeeded in manipulating the people around him for as long as I've known him. And while I'm not prepared to argue the merits of the shade ring itself, I would suggest you thoroughly investigate these allegations before you go through with any treaty that he says is in the best interest of our country. Because the man I've known all these years has always put his own best interests before everyone else's."

Neave watched as her father struggled to maintain his cool.

"Stan, I'm sorry my family busted in here and created such a scene," he said. "It's amazing to me that they're so upset about the shade ring that they would make all these wild accusations, going to such great lengths to stop the treaty from being signed. I think you can chalk this up to an embarrassing family squabble. But, honestly, we can't let this nonsense…"

"Do you know Robert peed on my birthday cake when I was seven?" Rosa said. "He wanted to punish me because he thought I was our grandparents' favorite."

"This is preposterous," Dr. Alvarez sputtered.

"And he poisoned my cat when I was ten to show me how powerful he was," Rosa continued. "He even forced me to give up the love of my life when I was a young woman. Threatened to poison my sweetheart if the romance continued because he said it would make him look bad. But I knew he just wanted to hurt me out of spite. And now – most unforgiveable of all – Catalena is dead."

"Good God, Rosa! You've obviously lost your mind!" Dr. Alvarez shouted.

"Catalena left messages, audio files and video files about how you used her!" Rosa shouted at him. "I have no doubt you're responsible for her death!"

"And we have proof," Neave jumped in, pointing her finger and glaring at her father, "that Nat intentionally caused the ice dam to break with two researchers standing on top of it, just so he could feed you some video for your Senate confirmation hearing."

"Dios mio! The whole world has turned upside down," Dr. Alvarez said, trying for a chuckle.

"And," Neave continued, undaunted, "you promised my hand in marriage to your lunatic assistant who hired a killer to murder the man I love!" And her face crumpled.

"Are we going to stand here and listen to this crazy babbling?" Dr. Alvarez shouted.

"Rosa and Neave aren't babbling," Dr. Sullivan said. "I have kept quiet all these years, just as Rosa has. And now we're finally ready to speak. Neave showed us you have to stand up for what's right. Even when there's personal risk."

The look in her father's eyes scared Neave then. There was a threatening evil she'd never seen before as he glared at his wife.

"I no longer care, Robert, if you tell people my secret. No more manipulation."

Dr. Sullivan gave him a small, triumphant smile and turned to Secretary Mintz.

"You see, he's held it over my head since before we were married... that I'm a clone."

No one was more stunned than Neave. What the hell was going on? Was her mother making it up to punish her father, to further embarrass him? But Dr. Sullivan wasn't one to lie or exaggerate. Neave's mind flashed from one memory to another, in quick succession, searching for some evidence. She wanted to see that picture again – the one of her grandparents.

"Everyone's gone insane!" Dr. Alvarez bellowed. "Loco! You can't possibly believe these... these tall tales! Because that's what they are!"

His eyes were wide as he pleaded with Secretary Mintz.

"We've got to go through with the signing!" he continued. "We cannot let these..."

"We won't be having a signing today, Robert," Mintz said. "Looks like we need to back up and regroup." And he turned to talk with the Chinese leaders.

Dr. Alvarez stalked towards the door, but two guards blocked his exit.

"Get out of my way!" he yelled. "What the hell do you think

you're doing? I'm the U.S. Climate Secretary! A member of the President's cabinet!"

And that's when Neave's vision went dark. She'd been going on adrenaline ever since she dragged herself out of bed at her parents' house to confront Nat and Curt. And now her fatigue, her empty stomach and her broken heart had finally caught up with her. She fainted, landing hard on the bare floor before anyone could soften the fall.

~~~

A deafening siren yanked her from her quiet envelope. She was flat on her back in an ambulance, an IV in her arm, her mother and Rosa sitting close by. She squeezed her eyes shut again, trying to block out the noise.

She was admitted to the hospital for exhaustion and dehydration. Which was fine with her. There was nowhere she wanted to go, nothing she wanted to do. So she let her mother, Rosa and a nurse buzz around her room, plumping pillows and looking after her every need. Their presence made her feel safe so she could relax and sleep.

When she finally woke up the next day, she was in a full-blown panic, thinking she was back in her bedroom, being held prisoner by Nat. She cried out and her mother was by her side in an instant.

"Where's Nat? Where's Father?"

"Your father is under guard in a cushy hotel until they decide what charges to bring," her mother explained. "I haven't heard anything about Nat."

Neave rubbed her eyes, then put her hands on the sides of her head as if she were trying to keep it from flying apart.

"Where's Yong?"

"Who?"

"He helped me get to New Washington. He's the one who

made the ruckus by the reflecting pool so I could break free. You must've seen him?"

"Yes, yes. But who is he?"

"God, I hope he's okay. What if they put him in jail?"

"I'll find out," Dr. Sullivan said. "But who is he?"

"Dr. Osley brought him to the university to lecture. He's a..." she started to say "he's a clone" but stopped herself. "He's a good friend of mine."

"I remember him – he's a clone of Dr. Zhang Kai. A vocal opponent of the shade..."

"We've got to find him and make sure he's all right. And what about Nat? He's dangerous, Mother. And Kwan – he was handcuffed and arrested because of Nat."

Then there was a tap at the door and Rosa ushered two FBI agents into the room. They'd been waiting to talk with Neave. They got right to their questions, asking how she got the information about her father's involvement with the Chinese companies and about the allegations that Dr. Alvarez and Nat were involved in Lena and Will's deaths. She told them everything she knew, including what Lena had said in her video message about how Dr. Osley died. And then she asked them whether they had Nat in custody and if they knew the whereabouts of Yong Li.

"We're searching for Mr. Patel," one of the agents said. "Your mother gave us his iCom that you had on your person yesterday, so we're hopeful information from his PDA will help us track him down. We posted guards outside your door and we're monitoring all entrances to the hospital."

His attempt to reassure her only made her more nervous.

"And we were unaware of the involvement of Yong Li," the agent continued, typing something into his iCom. "We want to interview him as well. The first place we'll check is the jail. And we'll message the police about your other friend."

~~~

With her mother and Rosa hovering nearby, she dragged herself from bed and into the bathroom so she could take a bath. She hadn't taken a real bath in a tub of water in years. Her mother and Rosa refused to leave her alone and she didn't object.

Dr. Sullivan sat on the toilet, which Neave would've found comical at any other time. Her mother – the sophisticated, reserved scientist – sitting cross-legged on a toilet wearing a navy pants outfit. Rosa took up a position in a chair just outside the open door. Both of them were ready to leap into action if Neave began to slip beneath the surface of the water.

She closed her eyes as she relaxed.

"Mother?" she said, not opening her eyes.

She didn't need to say more. There was something in the tone of her voice. Her mother cleared her throat.

"Well, dear, I told you how my father cloned himself. But that's not the first time he cloned someone. The first time was when he cloned his wife – the woman everyone assumes was my mother. Her name was Shauna Murphy. He cloned her as she was dying, before she was removed from life support. It was a desperate effort to create a new Shauna."

She took a deep breath before going on.

"And I'm that clone."

Neave was dumbfounded.

"Shauna's death was accidental – she was in a car wreck," Dr. Sullivan continued. "My father said she fell asleep while the computer was driving the car home from a conference they were attending. He blamed himself because he thought it was important that he stay and hobnob with all the other scientists, so she went on ahead by herself. I looked up news reports. The car's computer apparently malfunctioned, causing the car to crash. They were still ironing out the kinks in driverless cars back then. He went crazy with guilt and grieving. I was born a year later, on his fourth attempt. He let everyone believe I was their child. And he raised me himself. He made me sleep with him from the time I was little and tried to mold me into the woman he loved. But I wasn't her. Never measured up. And he never let me forget it. He ridiculed me and criticized me and forced me into genetics to help him with his work. I think he decided since I was such a failure at being Shauna, that I had to serve him somehow."

Neave's eyes opened slowly, but she said nothing as she listened to her mother's distressing story.

"I think before Shauna's death he might have actually been a decent person. But afterwards... well, it's like he lost all the goodness in his soul."

She was quiet for a moment. Then she sighed and re-crossed her legs.

"He always threatened to reveal to the world that I was nothing but a clone, telling me that everyone would hate me for it, that everyone would desert me if they knew. And I believed him... believed him completely. He made me feel small. Subhuman."

Neave had always thought her mother was cold. She'd been jealous of friends who had close relationships with their mothers. Now, finally, there was an explanation. Her own mother had no idea how to have a close, loving relationship. She'd never experienced one.

"And then my father gave me to Robert," she continued. "I was part of a deal they concocted. Robert got a connection to the renowned Dr. Jack Sullivan and all of the automatic introductions that entailed. It was an easy way to fast track his career. And, as it turned out, I was also a good cover for his less seemly activities, which I did my best not to know about. And in exchange, my father got Robert's complete support and fundraising skills. Robert always had a way of twisting peoples' arms."

They sat quietly for a few minutes, each contemplating her own thoughts. Finally, Neave had to ask the question that was burning inside her.

"Am I a clone too?"

"You? Heavens, no. Though I did make sure you looked like me. Your father didn't care about having children – thought it was a waste of time and money. But I wanted to have a baby. Partly, I suppose, just to prove I was a full-fledged human being. Turned out that conceiving and giving birth was the easy part. Being a real mother was the challenge. Please forgive me, dear, for failing so miserably on that score."

Neave extended her wet hand and her mother took it in her own, water dripping on the bathroom floor.

"I let your father bully you just like I let him bully me," she said, leaning over and kissing her daughter on the forehead. "And if it hadn't been for Rosa, you would've had a truly loveless life."

"Mother, I'm sorry too," Neave said. "What a sad life you've had."

"Rosa suffered because of Robert as well," Dr. Sullivan said, turning to Rosa, sitting so quietly, hands folded in her lap, that Neave had almost forgotten she was there. "I dreaded the day you'd get fed up and walk out, Rosa. From a very selfish standpoint, that was a terrifying prospect. Why did you stay?"

"You make it sound like I was a saint, Molly," Rosa said, "but the truth is... I was afraid of Robert. Afraid he would carry out his threats. I knew from personal experience that he was capable of it."

"What threats?" Neave asked.

"He said if I betrayed him, the people I loved might have some serious, possibly fatal, accidents."

"What a monster," Neave said.

"I used to daydream about poisoning him," said Rosa, "but I could never bring myself to do it. So I tried to help you," she said, looking at Neave, "and you," she added, to Dr. Sullivan.

They were quiet for a moment as Neave digested the troubling revelations. And then a sad light came on inside her head and she started crying.

"What it is, dear?" her mother asked.

"I just realized Will wasn't a clone of my grandfather. I mean, my grandfather wasn't really my grandfather since you weren't actually related to him by blood. Oh my God."

Sorrow flowed from her heart through her veins to every cell in her body, putting her in a kind of stasis. She knew now that dying from a broken heart just meant that grief immobilized the heart and made it stop beating.

Chapter 30

That afternoon two police officers appeared in Neave's room. They were there to escort her to the New Washington jail.

"Why can't I identify Yong online?" she asked.

"Sorry, ma'am," said the lead officer.

She sighed as she took her seat in a wheelchair the doctor insisted on. Dr. Sullivan and Rosa walked on either side of her like offensive linemen, as a nurse's aide pushed her.

A driverless police van whisked them the short distance to the jail and dropped them off at the front door where the officers led the way to a room on the third floor.

It was an unpleasant room. No windows, no pictures, no decorations of any kind on the institutional green walls. There was a large pull-down view screen on one wall. In the middle of the room was a grey plasteel table with four upholstered green chairs arranged as though friends might sit down for a game of Earthquake. Only there was no game. The room was lit by ceiling LED lights. The floor was covered in a thin, commercial green carpet.

Neave parked the wheelchair by the wall and took a seat at the table, facing the view screen. One of the officers said someone would be with them in a moment and they disappeared.

"Here, have some water," Rosa said, passing her a water bottle.

But the door opened then and in walked the two federal agents she'd talked with earlier and a jail official. Agent Dudnic explained they had indeed found Yong Li in a jail cell – arrested on disorderly conduct charges after apparently getting into a fight with Nat when she made her break. A guard sent a message on his iCom and a moment later there was a tap at the door and Yong was escorted into the room.

He had a black eye and a swollen lip and Neave rushed to him, hugging him for a moment. She could see him blushing as she gently touched the purple flesh below his eye.

"They didn't do this to you after you got here, did they?"

"Not to worry," he said. "My face became bruised in the altercation with Mr. Patel."

"Oh, Li, did he attack you?" she asked.

"Mr. Patel attempted to follow you so I kicked him in a sensitive area," he explained.

"And then he hit you?"

"He is very strong," he said, nodding.

"Was Nat arrested too?" she asked, looking from Yong to the agents.

"A police officer tried to put, uh, restraint devices on him, but he resisted successfully," Yong explained. "He is an accomplished runner."

"We haven't been able to locate him yet," said Agent Dudnic. "But we've frozen his accounts and posted a worldwide APB. We'll find him."

Neave's shoulders slumped as she looked down at the floor and shook her head. The thought of Nat on the loose made her want to crawl into a shell and hide. A tired sigh was all she could muster.

"We need to get her back to the hospital," said Dr. Sullivan, moving to her daughter's side.

The FBI man looked surprised.

"Mr. Yong isn't the person we wanted Miss Alvarez to identify," he said.

"Kwan?" Neave said.

"We released him this morning," he said.

"Mr. Yong, you're free to go," the guard said.

Yong nodded, then turned to Neave.

"Are you improved?"

It looked like he wanted to say more but not with everyone watching.

She sighed and leaned close, hugging him again, but said nothing and patted his shoulder in dismissal.

"Well?" Dr. Sullivan said, as soon as the door closed.

Agent Dudnic strode to the view screen and pressed a button, causing it to slowly retract to the ceiling, revealing a large window. The window gave them a view of a brightly lit adjacent room with an upholstered green chair positioned in the center, facing towards them.

"Miss Alvarez," Agent Dudnic said, "if you'll step this way."

He escorted her to a position a few feet from the window.

"On the other side of this window," he said, "it appears to be a mirror. No one can see us or hear us."

She looked at her mother, who shrugged in reply.

"We'd like to know if you recognize this man," he said, nodding towards the window.

After a few seconds a man in an orange jumpsuit was led into the room. He was handcuffed and wore a sensor collar that would sound an alarm and give him a shock if he tried to escape. He was tall and slender with a buzz cut. The hairs stood up on Neave's arms as she realized who she was looking at.

"Do you recognize him?" the agent asked.

"Yes."

"Who is he?"

"That's the man who killed Lena and Will," she said. "That's Curt Maddux."

She turned away, hugging herself as she hurried to the other side of the room. Her mother followed and embraced her protectively.

"I'm ready to go back to the hospital," Neave said.

"Miss Alvarez," the FBI agent said, "we really need your help."

"I've already told you – it's Curt Maddux. What else do you want?"

"That's the man who gave Lena a drug overdose?" Rosa asked, her eyes filled with hatred.

She turned and rushed towards the door.

"I'm going to kill him con mis propias manos."

"Rosa," said Dr. Sullivan.

A guard blocked the door. She tried to get around him but he was much bigger and stronger. She whirled around and eyed the FBI man.

"I want justice! Comprende? If you don't punish him, I'll find a way to make sure he gets what he deserves!"

Dr. Sullivan was at her side then.

"Don't worry, Rosa," she said. "We'll make sure justice is done."

The agent took a moment to send a quick message on his iCom. Immediately, the door opened and two more guards entered the room. Rosa looked at them resentfully, but forced herself to calm down.

"All right, Miss Alvarez," the agent began again. "If you

would please step this way."

Neave reluctantly returned to her position by the view window.

"Now," the agent said, "the man you're looking at says his name is Will Galloway."

Neave gave him a blank look, thinking she hadn't heard right. But then she realized there was no misunderstanding.

"And you believe him?"

"Well, his DNA matches..."

"Of course his DNA matches! I told you they're both clones of..."

"So, obviously, we need some assistance," the agent said.

Neave just stared at him, her fists clenched.

"Whoever he is," the agent said, "we found him walking the hallways of the hospital looking for you."

"I thought you were protecting my daughter," her mother said. "If I'd had any idea..."

But she was interrupted by a familiar voice coming from the other room. It was broadcast on a ceiling speaker.

"Neave?" he whispered.

Neave jumped back, bumping into one of the chairs, and sitting down hard. Her face was white and her eyes were riveted on the man in the other room.

He appeared to be staring directly into her eyes, which was unnerving, especially since she'd just been told that people in the other room couldn't see them. He looked so rough. The side of his face was scraped and he had a bruise on his neck, just above his sensor collar, like someone might've tried to strangle him. The thought made Neave shiver, just thinking that Will fought for his life with this man and lost. She wanted to look away, but couldn't. He was the same man she'd seen in her father's office with Nat – the same man she'd knocked out with her stun gun. What happened with the call she'd made to Atlanta police?

"Don't be scared, Neave," he continued. "Curt's dead. He came after me while I was on my job site. I was in the cab of the XT - the same kind of machine you rescued me from."

Nat had obviously briefed him, she thought.

"He was waiting when I opened the cab door and pushed me from behind. I almost fell but grabbed hold of the door handle. I've never had to fight like that in my life but I was mad as hell. It was so strange, looking him in the face. It was almost like looking in a mirror."

Neave found herself hanging on his every word, studying his facial expressions, trying to look into his eyes. He ran his hand through his short hair, and Neave wondered whether the gesture was genetic, it looked so much like Will's gesture.

"And then I had him pinned. I had him down and he stopped fighting. Completely, you know, like he was through. And he told me he just couldn't kill me. He said no matter what Nat said, he just couldn't kill me. He said it was like we were brothers. And I wondered how much we might've been alike if we'd grown up together, you know, if he'd lived with my family or if I'd lived with his family. And I must've loosened my grip, because suddenly he lunged and pinned me on the edge of the platform, my head dangling. We were thirty feet up, all those chunks of broken concrete and glass below us. And he was gloating – telling me what an idiot I was. He said I deserved to die for being so stupid. Just like you deserved to be raped by Nat while he had you drugged in your own bed. He said he was going to ask Nat when he got back to Atlanta if he could have a turn with you. And he laughed as he pushed me harder and harder. For a second, I thought I was going to die, but when he said that about you – well, I don't know – I just reached down and latched onto him as hard as I could and I yanked him and threw him over my head."

His eyes were unfocused as he stared into space. And she found herself wanting to believe his story.

"I pulled myself up and looked down below and saw his body lying motionless down there. And I felt sick."

She took a step towards the window, but then she thought about Curt. He would do something like this. He would try to trick her. He could've learned things about her and Will. Nat could've told him about the tsunami rescue. She stepped back again.

"Neave?" he said. "I know you're confused. And I'm sorry about that. I rushed to Atlanta to save you from that, that monster. I disguised myself as Curt so I could get into the house. I had just sat down with Nat when you walked in. God, you were so weak. So sick. But so brave. And Nat pulled the gun, and then you used the stun stick. That was smart. You didn't know who I was. You had to use it. And when I woke up, you were gone and so was Nat. I snuck out the back as the cops were coming in the front door."

He sighed and went on.

"It took me a while to get here and then I saw you on the news in the middle of the protest and Nat right next to you. I thought I was too late. And then you were on the news again, putting the kibosh on the treaty signing, and then I heard reports that you collapsed and were taken to the hospital. I just had to see you, to be sure you were okay. And then they hauled me to jail because they thought I was Curt. So now all we've got to do is to tell these guys who I am."

He took a deep breath as though he was exhausted.

"Well?" said the agent.

She squinted hard at the man in the next room.

"It's Curt," she said.

"Neave," he said, "I know I look bad, but give me a chance to prove who I am."

She stood there for what seemed a long time.

"We'd like for you to talk with him face to face," the agent said.

"I don't like it," Dr. Sullivan said.

"We'll bring extra guards in."

He nodded at the guards by the door.

She wanted to go back to the hospital. Wanted to get away from all this. It was Curt in that room, lying to save his own skin. But just as she was about to refuse to cooperate any further, a tiny bit of doubt settled in a corner of her mind. Was there a wisp of a chance he was telling the truth?

"You've got to tell him not to come close to me," she finally said. "He's got to stay on the other side of the room."

The agent sent a quick message and immediately, a table was moved to the center of the adjacent room. A guard positioned the chair on the far side and ordered Curt to sit in it. Another chair was positioned on the opposite wall, so that the table was an obstacle between them, like a protective wall. Several guards were brought into the room.

"We're ready," he said to Neave, gesturing towards the door.

"I'd like Mother and Rosa to come with me," she said.

He nodded and then the three women, the two FBI agents and the guards made their way into the hallway. It was only a few feet to the door that opened into the other room. She stopped just before she reached it and took a deep breath. Her throat was so dry, she struggled to swallow.

His eyes followed her as she walked to the empty chair. It

was a worried look, a concerned look. Her mother and Rosa took their places behind her. Neave stared at her hands, fingers laced together in her lap.

"Miss Alvarez has some questions for you," Agent Dudnic said, opening the proceedings.

She swallowed and finally looked up. He looked even worse now that she was in the same room with him. So rough, so beaten up. His face was raw on the right side. This could not be Will, she thought. No way.

She sat staring at him for a moment. Then she cleared her throat.

"I can't think of a good question to ask," she said to her mother. "Something he couldn't have found out."

"Why don't you ask me when I fell in love with you?" he said.

She couldn't find her voice.

"It wasn't when I rescued you from the giant crab," he said. "It started when we danced the waltz and I looked into your eyes. And then I knew I was in love with you for sure when you told me what an ass I was for judging you because of who your parents were. That cemented it for me. You were right, of course. It's not who creates us, it's who we become, what we stand for."

She had to hold back the tears that wanted to well up in her eyes. She was trying to figure out if Curt could possibly know that. Or whether he could express himself so eloquently. Was it possible Nat could've told him those things? Or that he could've tricked Will into telling him those things before he killed him?

"And then, when you risked your life to save me in Savannah and our time together in the cave – well, I knew you were my dream come true. And then, when I came to your room at

292

the research station to beg you to forgive me for being such a bastard and I started to tell you I was a clone... God, you said you knew. You already knew when we made love in the cave. That's when I knew I wanted you forever. I just wasn't sure you would want me. But, of course, I underestimated you. More than once. And you didn't give up. You never give up. That's one of the things I love about you."

She clamped her teeth on her lower lip to keep it from quivering.

"Neave," he said, his voice soft as burgundy velvet, grimacing in concentration.

And it was at that moment that the dream on the airplane came back to her. She'd never been able to figure out what she was supposed to remember. Until now.

"Smile!" she commanded him.

But he only looked at her quizzically.

"I need to see your smile," she said.

And she remembered now the split second after she used the stun gun in her father's office. Before Curt crumpled to the floor, he grimaced. It was a pained smile. And that's what her dream on the plane was about. After she stunned him, when he grimaced and fell to the floor, she realized now there had only been one dimple, not two. The man she zapped with her stun gun was Will, not Curt. And if her mind hadn't been so muddled from drugs at the time, it might've registered.

So he smiled. But his face was scratched and bruised. She couldn't see a dimple at all.

"Bigger," she said.

He obeyed. His face was so banged up it was hard to tell. So she stood and walked halfway across the room so she could see better. It was true - there was no dimple on his left cheek, just the one on his right cheek. She could see it through the scratches.

She sidestepped the table and ran to him. He got up in time to catch her as she threw her arms around his neck. The guards were on them in an instant but Neave waved them away.

"It's really you," she whispered.

"Are you absolutely sure, Miss Alvarez?" said the FBI agent.

"Yes," she said, gazing up into Will's eyes. And they were definitely his eyes. She could see the love. She could see his soul. And she put her hand behind his neck and pulled him down so she could kiss him. The tears flowed freely along with her nose. A tissue appeared in her hand from somewhere. But she couldn't peel herself away. She needed to touch him. She couldn't let go. And she kissed him again, oblivious of the hubbub around her.

And then she laid her cheek on his chest and closed her eyes, breathing in his sweaty musk. She smiled to herself, his arms wrapped snugly around her. The empty feeling in her gut that had been there for what seemed an eternity was suddenly replaced with an emptiness in her stomach that left her craving crackers and peanut butter in a cave near the coast, naked under a man's robe. And she began to cry, but they were tears of joy and relief. She had her life back.

He seemed to sense her exhaustion, because he gently pulled her with him to the chair he'd been sitting in a moment before and sat down again, placing her carefully on his lap. She rested her head in the crook of his neck as he held her close. Finally, the tears stopped and she sighed and shivered. She'd forgotten about the others in the room until she heard her mother's voice.

"She really needs to lie down."

"Only if Will comes with me," Neave said.

"Before we release you," the agent said to Will, "we need for you to speak with your mother. She's waiting for us to call."

"I'm ready," he said.

The agent placed the call and linked it to a portable view screen he placed on the table.

"Mrs. Galloway, I'm Agent Dudnic. As we explained, we need to verify the identity of the man we have here in New Washington who says he's your son. We'd like for you to talk with him and satisfy yourself of his identity."

He stepped back and turned the screen towards Will.

"Hi Mom."

Angela studied Will and Neave for a moment before speaking.

"Why didn't you call me?"

"I lost my iCom in the fight and I was in kind of a hurry to get to Neave. Sorry."

"Are you two okay?"

"We are now," he said. "How'd you like to have some company?"

"As soon as we get this over with. Tell me your brothers' and sisters' names."

He ran through all the names of famous authors, not missing a beat.

"And tell me why my house is painted yellow."

He paused for a moment, which caused Neave to hold her breath.

"I think..." he started, then stopped. "I think you were planning to paint it white, but we came across a supply of yellow paint at that abandoned paint warehouse when I was eight or nine."

They stared at each other on the view screens.

"Anything else?" she said.

"Well," he said, "once we started painting, you said it was probably fate because yellow was the favorite color of someone in your past you loved very much."

She nodded.

"And that's why you liked that old American folk song *The Yellow Rose of Texas*," he said.

A sad smile crossed her face.

"The guest room is ready," she said.

And then Neave saw Rosa walking towards them from her position beside Dr. Sullivan. It all came together in her mind as she crossed the room – the yellow top she was wearing, the bright yellow kitchen in their house – Rosa's kitchen – the yellow daffodils she grew in pots. She said Dr. Alvarez had threatened to hurt someone she loved. And, of course, it must've been Rosa who took Will to Angela when Dr. Sullivan decided to save the little boys. She was the Yellow Rosa of Texas.

Rosa stood behind Will and Neave, putting her hands on their shoulders, and stared into the view screen.

"Angela, I don't suppose you have two guest rooms, do you?" she asked.

~~~

It was Will who pushed her in the wheelchair as they left police headquarters. They rode the short distance to the hospital sitting close together in the back seat. There was so much to say but her mother, Rosa and two officers were with them and she was too tired to talk. She was happy just holding hands. She'd agreed to return to her hospital room on the condition that they set up another bed. She would rather have gotten a hotel room, but she knew better than anyone that if

Nat was free, he might very well want to pay her a visit. The police and FBI had reassured her they would find him, but she wasn't so sure. Which made the police presence at the hospital comforting.

Two officers were positioned at the hospital entrance, though the agents had theorized Nat would hide out, at least for a while, maybe even travel to another country. They'd already alerted the airlines and airports, in addition to posting reports and pictures on international police websites and news websites.

Neave didn't know what he might do. No doubt he was a madman, but she felt safer now that Will was with her.

When they arrived at her room, there were no guards stationed at her door. Incensed, Dr. Sullivan was on her iCom immediately as she hurried back towards the nurses' station.

Neave, Will and Rosa went on into the room.

"I have to powder my nose," Neave said, rising from the wheelchair.

She closed the bathroom door and glanced in the mirror to see how bad she looked. She hadn't cared about her appearance all the time she'd thought Will was dead. But now she did. As she took in her gaunt face and the dark circles under her eyes, she heard a swishing noise behind her. She spun around as a tall man lunged from his hiding place in the shower. It was Nat.

Chapter 31

Neave screamed as Nat grabbed her arms and yanked her around so that he was holding her from behind. He quickly reached over and locked the heavy door.

"This needle contains a poison that will kill you in sixty seconds!" he hissed in her left ear. "It pays to keep poison dart frogs as pets."

She continued to struggle.

"All I have to do is stick you anywhere on your body and you're dead," he said. "Understand?"

"Let me go!"

"If you think you can just walk away from me, you're badly mistaken. And if I can't have you, nobody can!"

He was holding her so tight, she could hardly breathe.

There was banging on the door and someone was trying to turn the doorknob.

"Back off!" Nat yelled. "I'll kill her if you come through that door!"

"Nat!" Rosa called. "Nat, please let her go. I'll help you."

"I don't need your help!"

"Nat, don't do this," Rosa cried. "You know you don't want to hurt Neave."

And then he whispered in her ear.

"I'm going to make love to you one last time. Now…"

"What you did to me before wasn't making love," she said. "I don't think you know the meaning of love."

"Oh, yes I do. I've loved you almost from the moment I met you. And you've been cruel to..."

"You don't love me. You just want to own me. You want me for a prized possession. That's not love."

"Bullshit! I do love you. And now we're gonna die in each other's arms. If you won't have me in life, you'll have me in death. Now, unzip your pants."

Instead, she yanked his hand and arm, trying to free herself but his strength was magnified with anger.

The door knob rattled again, causing him to back away, dragging her with him.

"Nat!" Rosa called. "I'll help you get away. Just let Neave go."

He ignored her, putting his mouth to Neave's ear. "Pull... down... your... pants."

She knew in her gut that he would kill her and then himself, which made her blood run cold. No one had any leverage with him. No offer would entice him. There was nothing that she, herself, could offer him either. Even if she promised to go with him, he knew the police or the FBI would track him down sooner or later – probably sooner. With her father headed for prison and his get-rich-quick scheme in ruins, Nat no longer had a powerful patron. He had put all his eggs in the Robert Alvarez basket. Now his own family would reject him. He would be a pariah.

Her only hope was that someone could break open the heavy door. Or was there possibly another way to get into the bathroom? Maybe an air vent? A ceiling tile? Her eyes darted frantically around the room, careful not to turn her head. There was a small air vent in the middle of the ceiling. Way too small. Whether someone could even use it as a window to shoot through was doubtful. It dawned on her that she might be the only person capable of saving herself.

"All right," she said, putting on a brave voice. "I'll go with you. I'll stay with you. I'll marry you. I'll…"

"The time for talking is over! You don't give me any thanks, any credit. I saved you from marrying a fucking clone. I made sure you were safe before I shattered the ice dam. I…"

"Murderer!" she cried.

She'd been waiting for someone to burst through the door, thinking that's when she would try to wrench herself free. But there was no sound to indicate anyone was even trying. Struggling to break free wasn't likely to succeed. Nat was much too strong. So she decided on another strategy.

She went completely limp, as though she'd passed out. He had to use both hands to lay her on the floor, her left cheek landing roughly on the cold, hard tile. She opened her left eye a crack – the eye he couldn't see – and saw he was now holding the dart like a cigarette between his index and middle fingers. She remained limp as he got on his knees behind her, fumbling to pull her pants down. And that's when he let go of the needle. She lunged for it and just barely got her fingers around it before his big right hand clamped around her wrist, squeezing it in a vise grip. She groaned in pain and frustration as he slammed her wrist hard on the floor twice, forcing her to let go of the dart. It skidded away, coming to rest by the shower stall. Just as he reached for it, they were both startled by the loud metallic clatter of the doorknob crashing to the floor.

Will rushed in, a bedpan in his hand. Neave thought for a second that it was over but Nat reached in his pocket and produced a second dart, flipping a safety cap off. He sat on

Neave's butt, holding the point close to her lower back. The left side of her face was now chilled by the cold floor as she stared helplessly at Will, whose eyes burned with loathing.

"Don't come near me," Nat barked. "Get out!"

"Nat," Will said, "We'll..."

"You heard me!"

"If you agree to testify against Dr. Al..."

"Get out!"

Rosa stepped into the crowded bathroom.

"Nat, Robert manipulated me too. I know what he's capable of doing," she said, her voice surprisingly calm and sympathetic. "Now that he's locked up, you're probably not getting your drug, are you?"

"I don't need it where I'm going!" he shouted. "Now, get out! Everyone out! I have one last piece of business to attend to and I..."

But before he could finish, Will charged forward and swung his right leg in a mighty arc, catching Nat under the chin, lifting him up and making him lose his balance. Then Will kicked again, aiming to knock the needle from his hand. But Nat pulled back just in time and grabbed Will's foot and yanked his leg upwards, causing him to fall, the bedpan clattering to the floor. He landed hard on his back, his legs coming to rest on top of Neave's legs as they lay at odd angles on the floor. Nat reached in his left pocket and withdrew yet another needle, now holding darts in both hands.

There was a demented look on his sneering face. He stared down at Neave, who was struggling to get away, and started to bend down, his arm outstretched, ready to plunge the needle into her flesh. But then his whole body jerked in surprise. He turned his head and looked down at Rosa whose hand still gripped a dart in his lower back – the first dart that he had knocked out of Neave's hand. While Nat's attention was diverted, Will grabbed Neave and dragged her towards the door. Nat struggled to follow. But Rosa retrieved the bedpan from the floor and slammed it hard on his right arm, causing him to lose his grip on one needle. As soon as it hit the floor, Rosa kicked it across the room. Then she swung the bedpan again, but Nat blocked the blow with both hands, knocking it out of her hands. It clanged to the floor but he ignored it and turned again towards his target. His movements were those of a man trying to walk through water, every motion slow and labored. And then he held his one remaining needle in front of his chest, the point away from his body. It was all too obvious that he would throw himself towards Neave so his remaining dart would be driven into her body as he fell on her, like a hammer pounding a nail. But just as he took the one step he needed to reach his goal, his head jerked back and his neck muscles tightened as though he'd been tackled from the rear, his large frame crumpling. He fell in slow motion, first landing on his knees, teetering for what seemed an eternity, and finally crashing to the floor, face first, as Will dragged Neave through the doorway to the bedroom.

The two guards who were supposed to be protecting Neave made their entrance then, rushing in with weapons drawn. Dr. Sullivan was right behind them, looking all around, trying to make sense of the terrifying scene. Will lifted Neave from the floor and carried her to the bed, wrapping his arms around her as they sat side by side. The room quickly overflowed with police investigators and medical staff. A doctor in green scrubs knelt beside Nat's limp form. He quickly surveyed the scene and asked aloud if anyone knew what was in the needle protruding from Nat's back.

Neave opened her mouth, but no words came out. And no one else spoke either.

~~~

She heard a high-pitched trilling. At first, she thought it was a bird. But as the chirping continued in rhythmic spurts she knew it was a frog. He was calling for his mate. She turned towards the golden frog, his body glistening in the eerie artificial light, and looked into his black eyes and realized he was calling *her*. He raised his head up and down and leaped in her direction, quickly moving into position behind her. His forelegs stroked her arms urgently. And she screamed at the top of her lungs. The scream sounded like gurgling, as though she were drowning on her bile.

"Neave, wake up!"

She slapped at him, trying to free herself.

"Neave, everything's all right. It's me – Will."

And she opened her eyes to find Will lying next to her in bed, his hand on her arm.

"You were having a nightmare. But you're safe with me. We're here in the hotel room."

She shuddered.

"It's all right," he said softly. "Everything's all right. I'm here."

"It was Nat."

"Nat's dead," he said. "He can never hurt you again."

She nodded slowly, wondering how long it would take every last recess of her psyche to absorb the news.

~~~

The indoor track was state of the art, built for the Washington elite by well-heeled lobbyists. The government of China had donated millions. The huge oval surrounded a park filled with cherry trees, dogwoods, azaleas, lilies and all manner of ornamentals and flowering plants, so joggers and walkers could take in a beautiful vista every time they came, regardless of season. Picnic tables dotted the manicured lawn and decorative wooden benches were placed along a series of ponds and waterfalls. There were several graceful, curved Japanese bridges built over the meandering waterway. All of which was encased in a giant, climate-controlled bubble so that sunshine was abundant, but heat was not.

Dr. Sullivan had suggested the outing and arranged for their admission as her guests. At first, Neave hadn't wanted to venture out but Will convinced her they needed a change of scenery. And she did want to see Kwan again. When she called to invite him, he said he'd bring his new best friend, Yong Li.

"They thought we were brothers," said Kwan, glancing at Yong as they walked around the track. "Can you believe that?"

Causing everyone to laugh.

They had started out on the track but the serious joggers quickly made it clear that people like them, moseying around the track four abreast, should stick to the sidewalks and the grass. So they strolled through the park, pausing to enjoy each pond and waterfall.

"So, Li, what's next for you?" she asked, as they made their way across a charming, curved footbridge.

He was wearing khakis and deck shoes but looked ill at ease in such casual attire.

"With the recommendation of Judge Mercado, the university has offered me a post in the Climatology Department as Adjunct Professor. It is beneficial to remain in America."

"And I offered my services," Kwan piped up, "as his graduate assistant." He draped his arm over Yong's shoulders. "I want to help Yong along."

"I thought his name was Yong Li," Will said.

Yong smiled appreciatively.

"I receive your joke," he said.

And they all laughed.

"You are kind to inquire about me," said Yong. "May I also ask about you?"

He nodded slightly at Neave, which said much more to her than his words did. It said he was concerned about his friend and that they'd been through a lot together. She had felt close to him during their frenzied trip to New Washington and throughout their ordeal trying to stop the treaty signing. And she now had a belated flash of intuition that he might have developed a fondness for her that went beyond mere friendship. Of course, now that she had Will back, Yong had returned to a more formal relationship.

She paused a moment to sit on a bench by a lovely pond stocked with orange and white Koi. Will sat down next to her and held her hand.

"I told Will I could never have made it without you. I'm not sure Kwan knows the whole story yet. But I want to thank you again, Li, for helping me."

"But I had ulterior motivations," he said. "When you revealed your wish to prevent the signing of the treaty between America and my country I desired to assist you because I shared your goal. It was logical that we combine forces."

"You're starting to sound way too much like Spock," said Kwan.

"Spock?" said Yong, raising his eyebrows.

"A character from the dawn of television," Kwan explained, and chuckled. "But you never answered his question, Neave. You got a plan?"

She looked at Will sitting to her left and squeezed his hand.

"I asked her to marry me," Will said, looking into her eyes. "And she said yes."

But there was a sad, distracted look about her that was obvious to everyone.

~~~

Peach walls. That's what she saw when she opened her eyes the next morning. Will was snuggled up behind her, his right arm draped over her, his hand gently cupping her breast through her nightgown. He kissed her softly behind the ear. She turned towards him and wrapped her arms around him.

"There's something I forgot to tell you," she said.

"Mm?"

"My grandfather wasn't really my grandfather."

"Yeah, I kind of figured that out."

"So... I'm glad."

"Me too," he said, pulling back so he could look in her eyes. He smiled but she looked down self-consciously.

"What is it?" he said.

She sighed and tried to compose her jumbled thoughts. She couldn't get over feeling dirty. She knew it was old-fashioned, but she'd saved herself for her true love only to have Nat ruin it. And she was angry. Angry at Nat and enraged at her father. Who the hell did he think he was, promising Nat he could marry her, like she was a family heirloom he could bequeath to a favorite nephew! And it made her sick to think of how he'd mistreated her mother and Rosa. He'd also been a horrible tyrant of a father, denying her the chance to direct her own life, denying her a loving home and friends. And worst of all – he ordered people murdered.

Lena, poor Lena, was dead because of him. And Dr. Osley. And Nat and Curt.

It grieved her to think about her mother. Her mother's whole life had been ruined by two men whose unslakable thirst for power and control sucked the life out of those unlucky enough to cross their paths. How did such people come to exist? Were they born? Or did something in their lives transform them into monsters?

Ironic, she thought, that people went around looking down their noses at clones, like they were subhuman – not good enough to be treated with respect – when, in her own experience, it was the so-called "real" people who did the horrible, unforgiveable things.

She closed her eyes and shook her head angrily.

"I'm so sorry," she said.

"For what?"

"For everything," she said, pulling away and sitting up in bed. "For dragging you into all…"

"You didn't drag me into…"

"But it was my fault that Nat sent Curt…"

"Your fault?"

"Yes, my…"

"No, it wasn't."

"All the sordid…"

"Neave, Neave. Okay, some bad things happened, but we'll get through it to the other side."

"But I…"

"You didn't cause any of that. And now it's in the past and we can look to the future."

"But I'm afraid I'm not good enough…"

"Neave, I love you. I want you. I need you. And now I've got you."

"But I'm ashamed…"

"You? You're the one who kept digging and digging until you found out the truth. You're the one who blew the whistle. You're the one who fought back. You have nothing to be ashamed of."

She heaved a tired sigh.

"Constant as the northern star," he said, smiling and leaning in close. "That's you."

She sighed again.

"Shakespeare's *Julius Caesar*," he explained.

Chapter 32

When their plane landed, the skies were overcast. She dreaded being questioned again but understood that Atlanta police needed to talk with them too. After checking into a hotel, Will talked her into dinner at Coffy's Café, within easy walking distance. The supper rush was over so they were able to get a spot by the window.

The café was a comfortable mishmash of retro and modern. Small round butcher block tables with padded blue plaid vinyl chairs. Large potted ferns gave it a patio touch. At the back of the shop, glass cabinets displayed a range of bagels, Danishes, doughnuts, sandwiches and salads. But the long walls running from front to back were view walls. If you wanted peace and beauty, all you had to do was aim your chair towards the wall on the left, which was filled with a never-ending series of scenic vistas slowly fading from one to the next: snow-capped mountains; gold and bronze leaves fluttering in a gentle breeze; ducks paddling across a picturesque pond; and on and on. To hear the sounds of nature accompanying each scene, you tuned your earbuds to that wall's signal. The other view wall was divided into six different webbio channels – two music video channels, two sports channels and two news channels. Again, to hear the broadcast, you just dialed into the corresponding signal on your iCom. Otherwise, soft instrumental music played in the background. Just enough to keep everyone from hearing each other's conversations.

Will pushed a bowl of vegetable soup towards her, and kept one for himself. It was a good evening for soup, she thought. Maybe it would help warm her soul.

Neither of them wanted to talk about recent events. So they ate in a companionable silence, watching people stroll by outside, occasionally looking into each other's eyes.

When their coffee cups were empty, Will jumped up to refill them. But when he didn't walk away, she looked up and found he was staring at a news channel on the view wall. A report was airing about her father. He set the mugs on the table and clicked on his iCom so he could hear it, motioning her to do the same. She pulled her iCom from her pocket and stared at it as she turned it over and over in her hands.

"Your father's attorney says Lena's secret messages shouldn't be allowed in court," he said, sitting back down in his chair.

She glanced toward the screen in time to see footage of her father in handcuffs, being escorted by police into the federal courthouse. Funny, she thought, one of the guards looked Chinese American. Then a prosecutor was speaking to a bank of cameras. She looked at her hands, absorbed in pushing her cuticles back.

"Prosecutors don't know which charges he'll be tried on first," Will said, "but they say there's important information in Lena's messages and they're sure those messages will be allowed."

She wished she could fast forward past the trial, the media coverage, the trips to New Washington to testify. But she knew it would drag out.

"Jeez, there's Rosa," he said.

She looked up to see a live picture of Rosa speaking to several reporters. So she clicked on her iCom and put an earbud in.

"...a sick man. My niece is dead because of him," Rosa said.

"What evidence do you have?" a reporter shouted.

"All I can say right now is that the truth will come out in court. Now, if you'll excuse me, I'm late for..."

Her words were lost as she moved past the microphones. Neave clicked off as a young reporter began recapping the story. She smiled weakly at Will.

"Oh, the coffee," he said, reaching for the mugs again. But his attention was drawn once again to the news broadcast. "There's your mother," he blurted.

Sure enough, on the other news channel, Dr. Sullivan was standing shoulder to shoulder with several people. Behind them was a sign reading "Clone-aid." Neave and Will snapped their iComs on in time to hear a young man introducing Dr. Sullivan.

"...a world renowned geneticist. Ironically, Clone-aid listed her for years as an enemy to the cause. And we were stunned to learn this week that Molly Sullivan, herself, is a clone. She is the most prominent clone to come out of the closet and we are thrilled she's agreed to become a member of the Clone-aid Board of Directors. Dr. Sullivan!"

He stepped away from the microphones, gesturing for her to take his place, front and center.

"Thank you, Akeem," Dr. Sullivan began, pausing for a few seconds. "Even as recently as a few days ago, I could not have imagined standing here today talking openly about being a clone. It's something I've hidden my entire life. I was always made to feel I had no right to happiness or self determination.

And I was afraid that my world would come crumbling down around me if people knew the truth. I didn't realize until this week that that's the best thing that could happen to me. And it was my daughter who showed me the way. She refused to be cowed. She refused to allow her father to dictate what she thought or what she did. She stood up for what was right, at great risk to herself. And it finally dawned on me that a large part of my world *needed* to crumble. Coming out of the closet, as Akeem calls it, freed me from the prison I've been living in all of my life." She swallowed and looked down for a moment. "And now… now, I can openly support the group I've watched from a distance. I very much appreciate how Clone-Aid supported me this week. And I look forward to fighting for the rights of clones here and abroad. I will do all I can to stop money-hungry scientists from creating multiple clones so rich couples can choose the best one to keep, discarding the others. I will also continue the research I've been involved with for nearly thirty years to perfect the regeneration of the human heart inside a patient's body so there will be no need or profit in creating clones to use for organ harvesting. This has been my goal and my passion since I first learned of this sickening practice."

"Dr. Sullivan!" several reporters shouted in unison.

But she waved her hand and smiled as she left the podium.

"Wow," Will said, clicking off his iCom. He was grinning broadly. "Did you know she was gonna do that?"

Neave shook her head. She was more surprised than anyone, as usual. It was so unlike the mother she'd known her whole life. It's like she'd been reborn. She was amazed by her mother's audacity. After living her life under the thumb of her father and then her husband, she was transforming herself into someone new – turning the page, starting a whole new chapter. And it was fascinating to learn that her mother had secretly been fighting to help clones for decades in her lab, using the skills forced on her by her father. It was inspiring. Her mother said it was Neave who inspired *her* to step forward. And now Neave realized that if her mother could leave the bad old days behind – and she certainly had had a lot of them – then Neave could get herself in gear and look forward to the future as well. And it was just possible that she, too, could use the skills forced on her by a domineering father. But she also realized the line her father fed her about the world needing more scientists was a lie. What the world really needed was leaders willing to act.

Will finally headed to the coffee urns to refill their mugs. She turned in her chair and watched him choose something from the sweets counter and pay for it, place everything on a small blue tray and make his way back to the table. She felt other eyes watching him too and was reminded of how good looking he was. She was so in love with him that she sometimes forgot what a strong first impression he'd made on her. Those dazzling sky blue eyes. The lopsided smile. The sexy dimple on his right cheek. He was grinning by the time he reached the table, watching her watching him. She knew she must be blushing.

He set the tray down and pulled his chair close beside hers. He slid into his seat and wrapped his arm around her waist, leaning in to kiss her earlobe.

She could feel people staring and imagined how they must look. Like a young couple very much in love. A sigh of contentment escaped. Looking into his eyes made her body vibrate like a tuning fork and she realized that true love did still exist and she had found it.

She leaned forward and kissed him on the mouth, a soft,

slow kiss. Her hands instinctively slid along his arms, up over his shoulders to his face, where she touched his cheeks. She realized how much she wanted him. And her desire might've overwhelmed any sense of propriety if they had not been startled by a huge boom that rattled the windows and caused them both to jump.

They looked out the window in alarm, but realized it was only thunder. They watched as a few large drops of rain splattered the dry sidewalk. The sky darkened and then the rain began in earnest.

"Let's go!" she said.

She laughed as she pulled him to the door. They stood for a moment, mesmerized by the downpour and the rivulets of water rushing along the street. She could see the rotating skyscrapers in the distance, their slowly changing contours bathed in green light. They reminded her now of lovers slow dancing in the night. She smiled at him, clasping his hand more tightly and together they walked through the door. They both turned their faces skyward, letting the rain wash over them and giggled like children as they trotted back to the hotel, full of anticipation.

The End

Review it

Please consider posting a customer review on Amazon, Barnes & Noble or Goodreads. Customer reviews help others decide whether they want to read the book. Thanks!

Read the sequel

Albedo Effect, Book 2 of The Shade Ring Trilogy

Threats from a power-hungry father. Rejection by the man she loves. An increasingly violent Mother Nature. And political upheaval over runaway global warming. Neave Alvarez faces danger on all fronts in *Albedo Effect, Book 2* of *The Shade Ring Trilogy*.

She's shocked that her father, the disgraced former Climate Secretary, has been extradited to China and won't face charges for two likely murders or fraud against his own country. And when it becomes obvious he'll stop at nothing to prevent her from marrying "a subhuman clone," she realizes she must fight back.

Set a hundred years in the future when sea levels have risen fifteen feet, *Albedo Effect* is about a gutsy young woman trying to navigate escalating political turmoil over a plan to shade the Earth from the sun. This, as she struggles to protect loved ones from her cold-blooded father.

Speculative Fiction, Climate Fiction, Romantic Suspense and Action/Adventure.

Book 3 coming 2017 - sign up to be notified on my website www.ConnieLacy.com

Contact

Email: con111elacy@connielacy.com

Sign up for occasional updates

Website: www.ConnieLacy.com

Follow

Facebook: www.Facebook.com/ConnieLacyBooks

Twitter: twitter.com/@cdlacy

Goodreads: www.Goodreads.com/ConnieLacy

Amazon: www.Amazon.com/author/connie.lacy

Pinterest: www.pinterest.com/cdlacy0736/

About

Connie writes science fiction and magical realism, all with a dollop of romance. She worked for many years in radio news as a reporter and news anchor. She's also the author of *Albedo Effect, Book 2 of The Shade Ring Trilogy, The Time Telephone* and *VisionSight: a Novel.* She lives in Atlanta.

Acknowledgements

Gratitude to Kip, Kyle and Doug for their encouragement. A ton of appreciation to my parents, Bobbie and Dorsey Dudley, for always believing in me. And special thanks to my first readers, Doug Lacy, Kyle Lacy and Jennifer Perry. ~ CL

Made in the USA
Charleston, SC
13 October 2016